# SINS OF TI

## By Kin

# CONTENTS

Copyright
Authors other works
Acknowledgement
Dedication
Quotes
Prologue
Chapter one
Chapter two
Chapter three
Chapter four
Chapter five
Chapter six
Chapter seven
Chapter eight
Chapter nine
Chapter ten
Chapter eleven
Chapter twelve
Chapter thirteen
Chapter fourteen
Chapter fifteen
Chapter sixteen
Chapter seventeen
Chapter eighteen
Chapter nineteen
Chapter twenty
Chapter twenty-one
Chapter twenty-two

Chapter twenty-three
Chapter twenty-four
Chapter twenty-five
Chapter twenty-six
Chapter twenty-seven
Chapter twenty-eight
Chapter twenty-nine
Chapter thirty
Epilogue

**Kim Hunter**

**Copyright © 2021 By Kim Hunter**

# OTHER WORKS BY KIM HUNTER

WHATEVER IT TAKES
EAST END HONOUR
TRAFFICKED
BELL LANE LONDON E1
EAST END LEGACY
EAST END A FAMILY OF STEEL
PHILLIMORE PLACE LONDON
EAST END LOTTERY
FAMILY BUSINESS
A DANGEROUS MIND
FAMILY FIRST
A SCORE TO SETTLE (BOOK ONE)
A SCORE SETTLED
A DANGEROUS MIND 2
BODILY HARM

**Web site** www.kimhunterauthor.com

# ACKNOWLEDGEMENT

KP, with thanks and much gratitude as always
xx

# DEDICATION

In Memory of Mary.  So wish I could have
known you longer xx

# QUOTES

Men are not punished for their sins, but by them.

Elbert Hubbard  (1856-1915)


If justice is denied, let the law of karma take the ride.
Nothing in this world is done without a price.

Author Unknown

# PROLOGUE

The flat on White Lion Street had been the family home for as many years as he could remember. Originally a council property, his father had, long before he was born, made full use of the right to buy scheme and now being owned outright, it had over the past couple of years undergone a few minor but visually impacting renovations, making it a desirable residence in a much sort after location. Purchased many years earlier, it would, if things went to plan, now command a sizeably high price and give them enough cash to relocate to somewhere far away from here. If on the other hand the dice didn't roll in his favour and his plan failed, then at least Steph wouldn't ever have to worry about money again.

Jamie Wilson, known to most as JJ, had been sitting at the kitchen table for over two hours. There was a Ray Charles hour on the radio and the legend was singing 'Georgia' but the sound was turned so low that the tune it emitted was almost inaudible. Jamie didn't care, with sleep having evading him for most of the night he had finally decided to get up at just before five and now as he watched the hands of the clock slowly move, each minute felt like a lifetime. Not due on shift until ten he knew that by the time he clocked in he would probably be asleep on his feet, which didn't bode well considering the line of work he was in. That was the least of his worries as today was the day, the day he would begin to finally seek justice for his dad not to mention his dear sweet mum. His father, known to everyone as Big Jimmy hadn't, through any fault of his own, been there through

Jamie's teens and formative years. Back then it hadn't really bothered Jamie but in the last few years it had begun to play on his mind and he was angry but then again, if he was being truly honest, this wasn't really about his father at all, it was down to the fact that on the day Big Jimmy had passed away JJ's mother Grace had also died, well at least the part of her that had made her a mother. The part of her that had loved him unconditionally and had been the reason she had so gently played with him and given him so much of her time. The part of her that had adored life and all that it offered in this shitty world, even if that life at times had consisted of living hand to mouth and always being dirt poor before she had met Big Jimmy. After she'd been informed that her man had been killed it was as if Grace was instantly covered in a fine, all consuming mist of despair, a mist that didn't lift until she took her last breath at the premature age of forty. In Jamie's eyes her life had been wasted and the pain she felt was at times so sad and so depressing that it had almost suffocated him.

This is all too rushed and I need to slow down and explain why times were so hard and why a very kind and special man was now about to do something so very wrong and which went against everything he believed in. It needs to start at the beginning and that beginning, for Jamie at least, would unknowingly arise from events in 1988 a year before he was even born. It had taken many questions to actually unearth the horrific events and reluctantly accept what had happened. Jamie now admitted to himself that deep down he had always known but had chosen, for selfish reasons he guessed, to push the truth to the back of his mind but with his mother on her deathbed they honestly and openly talked for the first time in his life. The events his mother described were vague and sketchy, maybe she couldn't remember or maybe she just didn't want to retrace the painful past in great detail. At times we all block out bad memories to protect ourselves and for some of us it's the only way we can survive. This story was told to me by a very special man, a man that didn't have a bad bone in his body but a man that was forced to change his way of thinking through love and the circumstances that had tragically been thrust upon him. I am still angry at the situation it has left me in and probably will be for the rest of my life but I am also immensely proud of him.

# CHAPTER ONE
## Summer 1987

Situated in the heart of Brick Lane and on the corner of Cheshire Street, the Carpenters Arms had long since been a pub of historical interest. Listed in 1871 as being on Hare Street until the street was renamed in 1940, it had served mainly Irish and Jewish immigrants but the place really earned its notoriety in the fifties and sixties as a Kray property. The twins had purchased the pub as a gift for their mother Violet and local legend states that the bar was made from an actual coffin lid, though that urban myth had never been proven as fact. After the twins' incarceration in the late sixties the pub continued trading under new ownership and became known for late night lock ins and license-flouting parties. By the mid-eighties it was being run by Sadie O'Connor but its true ownership lay in the hands of George Conway, a local face and someone you didn't dare cross unless you naively had a serious death wish. On Friday nights the large events room on the first floor was taken over as a disco for the local teenagers, all supposedly of legal drinking age of course and even though things often got out of hand, the takings were far too good for anyone to want to put a stop to the event.

Dark haired, handsome and weighing a little over twenty two stones, not to mention standing over six feet tall, James Kilham was simply known to all as Big Jimmy and was occasionally, actually more frequently that he would have liked, sent down to the Carpenters by his boss George Conway to get things back under control. Jimmy wasn't an overly vicious man and it was rare that he had to actually lay his hands on any of the youngsters as his mere arrival would normally curtail any trouble. That said, he wasn't against dishing out the odd slap should it be needed and being a large man, his sheer size alone would normally instil enough fear for the guilty parties to rapidly step back in line. Born in 1961 Big Jimmy had been a bit of a lost soul in his youth and had never really had much of an inclination regarding a career or his future. No job ever lasted more than a couple of years and his last, on a building site over Wembley way, had completed ten months earlier so he'd found himself once again unemployed. When on the off chance he was offered a job by George Conway he'd been more than happy to accept, that was until he found out what the man's business really entailed but by then it was too late to get out. From childhood memory he could still recall his mum's tales of the Krays and the terror they instilled and now aged twenty six it wasn't a life he really wanted for himself but he had a mortgage to pay so until another opportunity arose he was trapped. When he was regularly despatched down to the Carpenters on a Friday night, as much as the downright stupidity of the youngsters pissed him off, he was still relieved that for that night he wouldn't have to be involved in the seedier side of his boss' business.

One humid night in August of 1987 and totally out of the blue, the landlady of the Carpenters had called George in a state of sheer panic. The call had taken him by surprise, not in the fact that she had phoned for help as that was a normal occurrence. What had taken George by surprise was the obvious fear he could hear in her voice. Sadie O'Connor was nearly as round as she was tall and was also as tough as they came. Born and bred in the East End she knew how to take care of herself and if that had at times meant taking on the opposite sex, then so be it. Sadie could drink and fight like a navvy and had a punch so forceful that it could and had on occasions, decked disruptive blokes with a single hit. This night was different, different in the fact that she was scared shitless and George didn't want his staff to be frightened of anything. It wasn't good for business and should it ever get out, wouldn't reflect well in regards to his standing with other firms.

"What's up Sadie love?"

"Sorry to bother you Mr Conway but there's a couple of strangers upstairs. You know me, I ain't racial in anyway shape or form Mr Conway but these two are as black as the fuckin' ace of spades, not that it makes any difference but......"

"Sadie get to the point will you, I've got a lot on."

"Sorry Mr Conway. I ain't ever seen them before and I think they might be tooled up! Shannon my barmaid said she saw one of them carrying a blade. Now under normal circumstances you know I could handle things but these nutters are a new breed and even I don't want to take on some bastard coke head and risk getting stabbed with a one armed scissor."

"Leave it with me girl. Stay downstairs and I'll send over Big Jimmy to sort the fuckers out."

With that the line went dead and doing as she was told, Sadie nervously retreated back to the somewhat safety of the front bar and willed Jimmy Kilham to get here as soon as he possibly could. As usual, the regulars were well on the way to getting pissed, it was Friday night after all but even if they'd been sober she knew that they wouldn't get involved if the shit should hit the fan.

Upstairs in the events room the music was loud and pumping. Robert Palmer was belting out 'Simply Irresistible' and several young girls, complete with big heavy perms, wide shouldered jackets and large bead necklaces, were strutting their stuff and desperately attempting to do their best interpretation of city girls. Unaware that they were failing dismally, they re-enacted dance moves seen on their front room televisions, which they had then practiced over and over again in the privacy of their own bedrooms. Others stood around the room watching, girls who refused to succumb to the wannabes on the dancefloor. These were true East Enders who had little to no ambition save to be a replica of their mothers, pushing a pram and with a hoard of kids in tow. Sharon Stinton was one such girl, who being slightly overweight and bearing several scars from the remnants of her acne, was desperate to get up the duff. The only problem being, Sharon wasn't lucky in the looks department and even less on the man stakes. Not letting it bother her too much she had resigned herself to accepting the first bloke to show an interest. Dressed in a denim skirt and an oversized T-shirt, Sharon was well aware that if she offered a blow job and stopped just before the final moment she was liable to get her wish. A man about to cum

**4**

didn't like being stopped and if the only other alternative was to walk away with a hard on then he would rather shag any dirty slag in the place, even if she was a dog and her name was Sharon. When Leroy and Simo walked in dressed to the nines in parachute pants, leather bomber jackets and with their pearly white teeth gleaming she watched them intently for a while. Streetwise enough to know that they were out for trouble, she reasoned if she let them get a few drinks down their necks she could defuse the situation and get her wish all at the same time. Forty five minutes later and Sharon decided that she'd waited long enough and it was now time to go in for the kill. Sidling up to Leroy she smiled in the sweetest way she could and at the same time revealed her crocked decaying teeth that had long since evaded the dentist. Leaning over she whispered seductively into his ear.

"Not seen you here before pretty boy. Fancy a blowjob?"

Leroy Christian wasn't yet a member of any gang though it was his greatest wish and tonight he had high hopes of gaining his stripes as a hard man and then the enjoyment of seeing the invites come flooding in. That said, he wasn't about to turn down the easiest cock suck he had ever had so taking her hand he led Sharon down the stairs and out of the side door into the area loosely referred to as the beer garden. The concrete square, which on a good day could only actually pass and that was marginally, as a crate store, had one solitary pot plant pushed up against the boundary wall. In seconds she had lowered his trousers and was on her knees face to face with a penis that in her eyes, didn't exactly match her naïve dreams of shagging a black man. Still, beggars couldn't be choosers and it might have been on the small side but it was still definitely big enough to fill a pram. Greedily taking his manhood into her mouth she began to suck and lick and Leroy wore a massive grin of self-satisfaction as he continually clenched and released his fists in pure pleasure.

Meanwhile, Big Jimmy entered the pub and quickly made his way over to where Sadie was standing at the bar chatting to her barmaid Shannon.

"Still upstairs are they?"

"Thank the Lord you're here Jimmy. One is the others out the back with dirty Sharon."

Jimmy Kilham nodded his head and quietly exited through the door at the bottom of the stairs. Sharon and Leroy were far too engrossed in the act to hear him approach and when he flicked on the security light they were both highly illuminated. Stunned, they momentarily stopped to see what was happening.

"Fuck off you cunt! Can't you see me and the lady are busy?"

"Sharon ain't no lady sunshine!"

"Oi! You calling me a slapper!!!?"

"Shut it slag! Now I think it's about time you had it away on your fuckin' toes. We can do this the hard way or the easy way, choice is yours sunshine?"

Leroy forcibly shoved Sharon away from him and she landed heavily and with a thud onto the concrete ground. Quickly pulling up his trousers he proceeded to remove the blade he was carrying from his jacket pocket. Full of rage, his mouth wore a sneer of anger and taking a step forward Leroy lunged in Jimmy's direction.

"Silly fuckin' move sunshine!"

Jimmy grabbed the boy's wrist, twisted sharply and at the same time as the sound of bone snapping could be heard, the blade fell to the floor. Sharon scrambled to her feet and without looking back did a hasty retreat back into the pub. Running frantically up the stairs to the safety of her friends, she didn't look in Simo's direction or try to warn him as she knew what the consequences would be if she did. All Sharon was concerned about was getting out of harm's way and saving her own skin. Getting up the duff tonight was now out of the question but it was still better than what could have just happened outside. In the beer garden Leroy was lying on the concrete screaming in pain and while Jimmy knew that his action had hurt the boy, he also thought it was a slight exaggeration in regards to the amount of noise the pathetic youth was emitting.

"Shut the fuck up you baby before I do you some real harm. Now my advice would be to fuck off as fast as you can before I break the other one."

With no intention of doing as he'd been told Leroy was about to reach out and retrieve the knife but as he did so Jimmy's size tens stomped on the blade.

"I don't think so you little twat, now do one!!!!"

Leroy slowly hauled himself up with his good arm and staggered through the back gate and out onto the street. He'd stopped mouthing off, he knew better than to antagonise the bloke any further but he was hell bent on coming back when his wrist was healed and making the bastard pay for what he'd done.

7

Jimmy picked up the weapon and nonchalantly, like it was a daily occurrence, walked back into the bar and discreetly handed it to Sadie for disposal. It was now time to head upstairs and expel the second undesirable. He didn't have to ask about, as strangely Simo was the only black face in the room tonight and strolling over, Jimmy landed a single punch and the boy was out for the count and sliding down the wall. Feeling in the kids pocket Jimmy removed a second knife and shook his head as he did so. What the fuck was the world coming to when weapons like these were taken to a kids disco? Hauling Simo to his feet Jimmy slung one of the boy's arms over his shoulder and managed to somehow drag him downstairs. Opening the front door, he then threw him out onto the street and then for the second time that night entered the bar and handed over the knife to Sadie.

"Thanks love. Those little shits are getting worse and if this keeps up I'm sure Mr Conway will call a halt to the discos."

Jimmy Kilham smirked, was she really that stupid to think his boss would give up his profit when there was no risk to his own personal safety?

"We both know that ain't about to happen darlin' now don't we? Give us a shout if there's any more aggro alright?"

Big Jimmy did one last scan of the first floor room and confident that things were calm enough, he called it a night. Making his way back to his flat in Islington he went over all that had happened and realised that he really had to get another job or sooner or later one of those little scum bags would catch him off guard and he would end up getting wounded or

**8**

worse. As Jimmy placed his key in the lock and let himself into the small hallway that led to the stairs of his first floor flat, the smell of lavender air freshener filled his nostrils. Jimmy loved his little home and had lived here for the past six years. Even though it had previously been owned by the council, because it was situated in a Victorian terrace conversion you never would have known it. The décor was light and bright and he'd furnished it with the best items he could afford. The place was his own little sanctuary away from the seediness of London and the madness of the pubs and clubs he was forced to frequent. He never answered the door to strangers or ever invited anyone back to his sacred place and hopefully that was the way it would remain.

# CHAPTER TWO

After George Conway had ended the earlier call he'd
sat back in his gigantic leather armchair. He didn't
like being disturbed at home but as his staff were well
aware of that fact he knew that they wouldn't dare
bother him if it wasn't a real emergency. Good old
Sadie handled most things thrown at her and what she
couldn't Big Jimmy did, so things always turned out
well in the end but he was concerned that it was
happening more and more frequently of late. Flicking
through the channels on the massive, massive in those
days at least, television, George sighed heavily. He
had all the money and trapping you could wish for but
he was bored shitless. As far as he knew his men
were loyal, they did everything he ordered and did it
so well that the firm now ran like a well-oiled
machine but maybe it was time to get more involved
again. For some sick reason only known to him,
George had never felt better than when he was
planning a big job or knocking some twat senseless
and he missed those adrenalin rushes so much.
Thankfully he had recently made some plans that
would make him once again feel more alive and he
grinned knowingly at the thought.

Irina Ivanov entered the vast sitting room dressed in
high heels and a tight fitting lace basque. Her ample
breasts, paid for courtesy of George, didn't move an
inch as she smiled seductively running her tongue
over her top lip. Lately Irina had read the signs and
knew that George was getting bored with her and she

would do absolutely anything rather than be forced to return to Russia.

Born in Kapotnya, nineteen kilometres from the centre of Moscow, the district was classed as the bottom of the pile when it came down to the most disadvantaged. Hosting a huge oil processing plant, the area had no Metro station leaving the roads clogged and at times dangerous. The region's 27,000 people lived in brick low rise housing dating from the 1950s with few amenities bar basic water and sanitation. One of five children, Irina's upbringing had been horrendous and there was seldom enough food in the house. Both of her parents did manual work though her father had long absences of employment and his children would often go to bed hungry as a result. The one and only thing Irina had going for her was her figure and her looks so when at the age of twenty two she applied to be a mail order Russian bride she was under no illusion that the kind of man who would choose her wasn't going to be any kind of Hollywood lookalike, not that she'd ever actually seen an American movie, her only experience of those idols was gained through glimpsing the odd picture in a contraband magazine that has been somehow smuggled in from the West. Still under the Russian Soviet rule and four years away from the fall of communism, the practice was run by the Bratva (brotherhood) know to all in the west as the Russian Mafia. Leaving the country was banned so these women were shipped out illegally and under the cover of darkness. The Soviet Union would finally fall in 1991 but it would be a further fourteen years before the mail order trade in women would be officially recognised and looked upon as legitimate, so Irina thought of herself as a bit of a trailblazer and being such, the choice she made was fraught with danger. Thankfully Irina turned out to be one of the lucky ones, many others ended up in the Far East as sex slaves and far removed from their dreams of an affluent marriage.

The first time she set eyes on George she was over the moon, true he was a good ten years her senior and that was being somewhat generous but he was still handsome and his physique was toned and masculine. Irina wanted for nothing and the only downside was the fact that he wouldn't marry her and give her the security she so desperately craved.

"Hello baby, you want company, you want Irina to give massage?"

George knew exactly what her massages entailed and he loosened his bathrobe in anticipation. She could be a right dirty slut when it was needed and it was just the way he liked his women, that said he would never marry any of them and even though he'd kept this one in tow for a good three years now, as soon as she started to show any signs of wear he would send her back in exchange for a newer model. As the 'bridal arrangements' for want of a better phrase, were run illegally by Russian organised crime, as long as you stumped up the cash and in those days it was a lot of cash, you could have as many of these women as you desired. George didn't see that he was doing any harm, the girl had been dirt poor when she'd arrived and now she wore designer clothes, had all the usual beauty treatments at her disposal, she even had a credit card with a generous monthly allowance so there was, as far as he was concerned, little to complain about. All he asked of her was that she always looked good, catered to his every sexual desire and George even as he neared forty, had a massive sexual appetite that any twenty year old would be proud of. Of course he also expected her to accompany him to any event that other faces took their partners and longsuffering wives to, just so that he appeared to be the top dog, the stud amongst even the youngest of blokes.

Now on her knees Irina took him into her mouth, licking and sucking as if her life depended on it, actually her life did depend on it, well at least the life she had come to know. George lent over and reaching on the side table, grabbed a small packet of powder, a credit card (platinum of course) and a mirror plate that he kept for just such an occasion. Emptying out the contents he tapped away with the credit card and all the while Irina's head continued to bob up and down. Rolling up a fifty pound note he snorted up a line and then laid his head back against the headrest.

"That's so good baby!!!!"

Finally after George had climaxed and Irina had wiped the last traces of semen from the corner of her mouth, she stood up and made her way into the kitchen. After sex George always liked a glass of red wine and tottering back into the room she handed him the crystal glass.

"Thanks darlin', now you can get off to bed as you need your beauty sleep."

13

For a second she studied his face, was he saying that she was looking old? God she was only twenty five and in her country you weren't considered old until you were at least thirty. Well there was nothing for it, tomorrow she would have to start a strict diet and a detox. George entered his luxurious study and took a seat behind the antique desk. There were several high end jobs on the horizon and he needed to start planning in detail, something he'd learned early on in his career. In this game you had to stay one step ahead of the other players. Momentarily his mind drifted back to the beginning and he smiled to himself as the memories came flooding back.

For George Conway that career had begun back in the early seventies. Born in 1953 in Bethnal Green and the result of one of the area's sex workers accidently getting up the duff, George had no family. Raised by Mrs Cannon and her team of two staff in the small and little known Barnardo's home on Corfield Street, as an ignored resident, young George would soon be lost in the system until he reached the impressionable age of sixteen and it was time to depart the rat infested hovel that he'd had no alternative but to call home. At that time Barnardo's was widely known to most of the population and that would later include the colonisation scandal, when it was implicated in the Northern Ireland Historical Institutional Abuse Inquiry for sending British children to Australia where some were tortured, raped and enslaved and which didn't end until 1975.

George was so badly behaved that he was considered

unsuitable to move on anywhere least of all to a British colony. He refused to attend classes, was beaten regularly and by the age of thirteen would disappear for most of the day not returning until well after dark. In the summer of 1969 he closed the front door to the house on Corfield Street for the last time and headed towards the West End. He'd been told that it was full of wealthy people and ripe for dipping. Doing a detour, he never did reach his destination after meeting up with a man who went by the name of 'Liberty', obviously not his birth name but rather one he had chosen back in the heady days of the hippy movement in the mid-sixties. Now years later, 'Liberty' was lost in a world of drugs and alcohol but after a brief chat had for some reason taken an instant shine to young George and offered the boy free accommodation at a squat he was living in on Poland Street. The house was a large Georgian building situated in the middle of a rundown derelict terrace. On entering, the pungent aroma of weed filled George's nostrils, a drug he tried and rejected instantly but also one he got used to the smell of as the residents were rolling spliff's continually. George enjoyed his time at the squat, they fed him and made sure he was safe but even though he felt part of something, almost a family in some strange way, it wasn't the life he wanted for himself. He would go out daily on the rob and bring them all back treats while secretly stashing away a small hoard of cash that would one day enable him to move on and that move would happen abruptly one Sunday morning. Still asleep on his bed, well actually only a stained mattress on the filthy floor of a small box room but it

**15**

did allow him a modicum of privacy. Feeling the blanket being lifted he swiftly turned over coming face to face with the newcomer he'd met briefly the previous evening. Brandon Leeman had joined the group of squatters less than twenty four hours earlier and young George, for reasons he couldn't explain, had taken an instant dislike to him. Aged thirty one and rather well spoken, Brandon was a paedophile and had set his sights on young George the moment he'd clapped eyes on the boy. Suddenly Brandon pinned George down on the mattress and with his left hand clamped firmly over George's mouth, he felt the young boy's morning erection and began to violently masturbate him with his right hand. George instantly froze with fear which Brandon mistakenly took as a favourable response. Out of nowhere George somehow managed to move his head backwards and then landed a perfect head-butt onto his assailant's nose. Brandon screamed out in pain and with every ounce of strength he possessed, George fought and finally managed to wrestle himself off of the makeshift bed. Pulling on his trousers he frantically grabbed his few possession's that were permanently kept in a grubby rucksack and then bending down, he pulled his secret stash of cash out from under the mattress. At the same time he hawked as much phlegm as he could muster before spitting directly into Brandon's face. As he fled the room he could hear his attacker calling after him "Come on kid, I was only playing around for God's sake." Running along the street George couldn't help but sob uncontrollably, at sixteen he had experienced his first sexual attack and inexperienced not to mention uneducated, he thought that the man had been queer. From then on in he developed a deep hatred of homosexuals that would last a lifetime.

Mooching about with no place to live, it didn't take long for him to find the local bad boys and he began to run with them most days and nights. It was like a dream come true for George as he'd always hero worshipped the Krays and when they were finally locked up for the last time in the year George left Corfield Road, he had been devastated. For the next four years not much happened in George's quest to be a gangster, it was a closed business and difficult to get into as everyone was on their guard and scared of undercover Old Bill trying to infiltrate the firms. Sleeping rough for most of the time, his luck finally changed when he was arrested for dipping on Oxford Street along with David Trunch, also known as 'Shaky' due to his hand tremor and which was probably the reason he had been caught so many times. This time Shaky knew he would be going down and asked George to contact a man by the name of Smiler who drank over Spitalfields way in the Ten Bells. The message was simple, Shaky needed help as he was wanted inside because of a bloke named Terry Visor that Shaky had grassed on years earlier. The stranger pleaded with George to help him out, so after receiving a regulation caution as this was his first offence or at least the first time he'd had his collar felt, George set off for Spitalfields. The Ten Bells was dark and oppressive on the outside and even worse should you dare to enter. Men of all sizes and ages sat on long benches and all eyes were on the

**17**

young stranger as he stepped inside. Walking gingerly up to the bar George politely inquired if anyone called Smiler was here. The barman, who even standing behind the bar seemed to tower above the youngster, stared darkly in George's direction. "Who wants to know?"

"I do and I have a message for him."

Instantly George was tapped on the shoulder and turning, came face to face with a man who had a large crescent shaped scar running from one cheek, down under his nose and up to his other cheek. George quickly relayed the message but as he turned to leave was stopped, when totally out of the blue, Smiler asked if he wanted a job.

The rest so they say is history and by 1973 at the age of 20, George became a runner for Spencer (Spenny) Black. Spencer, wasn't actually that much higher up the food chain than George but was shown respect due to being known for his association with the Wembley Mob. George was soon introduced to the firm, a firm that specialised in armed robbery and was run by Mickey Green. Not that many years older than George, Green was a traditional gangster dealing in prostitution, long jobs and running a very lucrative protection racket but by the mid-seventies had decided to branch out into the rapidly expanding drug market. Business was massive and it wasn't too long before George rose through the ranks. Having earnt a reputation for being as hard as nails he was now working directly for Mickey as his right hand man. When Mickey Green suddenly announced and totally out of the blue, that he had decided to spend more time in Spain as things in England were getting too hot for him, he temporarily not to mention naively, put George in charge during his frequent absences. For Mickey this turned out to be a big mistake and towards the end of the seventies and still not thirty years old, George Conway had all but taken over the Wembley Firm. Initially there were heavies sent over from Spain to put him in his place but George's men were loyal, or at least more afraid of their new boss than they were of Mickey Green and as such had protected George to the hilt. Mickey soon got the message and as much as it went against the grain, he accepted the paltry monthly payment that was offered and decided to bow out gracefully. It turned out to be a wise move by Mickey and he soon ventured into much more lucrative areas of crime, operating in countries including the US, France and Morocco, even organising the running of cocaine from Columbia via Holland and Belgium. Now being fully accepted as the Boss, George bought up more pubs and clubs throughout London so that he could discreetly launder money and it didn't take too long for his wealth to rapidly grow beyond his wildest expectations. He soon became revered amongst the brotherhood of the London underworld and wherever he went, his notoriety preceded him.

# CHAPTER THREE
## Summer 1987

Centuries old Brick Lane is sadly now referred to as
Banglatown due to its many curry houses and vast
Bengali community. The area's façade is a bit ugly
and grubby but on the whole its residents gel along
quite happily, even if for some the living conditions
are cramped and leave a lot to be desired.

Daydreaming, Grace Wilson was swiftly brought
back to reality when she caught a whiff of the baked
beans as they began to burn on the bottom of the
saucepan. Quickly lifting the pan from the old gas
cooker she spooned out the meagre rations onto two
plates that each contained a single slice of toast.
"Danny! Marcus! Your tea's ready."
A couple of minutes later when there had been no
response, she raised her voice several octaves higher.
"Danny!!!! Marcus!!!! Get your arses in here now!!"
Her two younger brothers reluctantly made their way
into the kitchen and flopped down onto the hard
wooden chairs in a way that only young boys can do.
The table had an old sixties Formica top and had
come from a second hand shop years earlier. It was
rickety to say the least but not as much as the chairs
and every time you sat down they wobbled and
creaked. When the boys had taken their seats so
roughly, Grace winced in anticipation that they were
finally about to give up the ghost but once again they
somehow hung on. In disgust, Danny pushed the
beans off of his now soggy toast with the back of his
fork.

"Is this it!?"

"Don't be so fuckin' ungrateful and if the old man heard you you'd get a right belt."

The boys both bowed their heads and greedily tucked into the sorry excuse for a meal. Grace did her best but her father was a drunk and housekeeping was almost non-existent so she had to do whatever she could to feed the boys and it often meant going without herself. Today should have been special and a time for celebration as it was Grace's sixteenth birthday but sadly not one solitary person had congratulated her, there were no presents or cards save for the one her best and only friend Linda had given her which Grace would dearly treasure for the rest of her life.

Grace Wilson had lived on Brick Lane for the best part of fifteen years and it was the only real home that she had ever known. A rundown first floor two bedroom flat above 'The Bay of Bengal' Indian takeaway wasn't much to write home about but it was unfortunately all that they had. The boys shared a small box room and their father had the double bedroom so Grace was forced to sleep on the faded lumpy old sofa. I she was lucky, the urine stains left by her father after another drunken binge would be dry, if not then she covered the patch with a plastic bag but she didn't complain. Privately owned, the rent was extortionate but luckily it was paid for by the local borough and as her father loved the area and hadn't asked to be rehomed, just in case they were moved somewhere that wasn't within spitting distance of a pub, it was where they would ultimately remain. The noise and smells from downstairs filled the flat daily and the odour was so strong that everything reeked of curry, so much so that Grace's nickname at school had been 'The curry kid'. That was the least of her worries as since her mother had upped and left six years earlier she had been forced to take on the role of carer for her brothers. Danny was now twelve and Marcus ten and they were both always in some kind of trouble. If you could think of it then they were mixed up in it, everything from shoplifting to bullying for a few coppers. Their father Seamus O'Mara was a drunk and had beaten their mother mercilessly whenever he'd had a skinful, which was almost every minute of the day. Only having stayed with the man because she was pregnant, Sheila Wilson finally decided one day that enough was enough and with no thought for her children, had simply packed her bags and walked out of the door, never to be heard from again. Full of rage, that night Seamus had turned his violent temper in his daughter's direction but whereas he would beat his partner with no worries about the damage he caused, he knew with Grace he had to take a little more care or the authorities would get involved. Seamus had somehow wangled himself as being disabled due to a bad back but it didn't stop him working most days moving supplies about for the shops and stallholders in the area. Of course it was all cash in hand and every last penny was spent in 'The Pride of Spitalfields' pub on Henage Street. The weekly benefits Seamus received went on rent, gas and electricity but any spare was also spent down the pub. One night when she hadn't been able to feed the boys Grace had searched her father's overcoat for any spare change and she soon got into the habit of raiding his pockets every night when he'd passed out. Having sunk so much whiskey, when he woke the next morning he wasn't able to remember anything so couldn't recall if he'd had any money left or not. There was never much food but along with rummaging in the bin at the back of the shops for anything that had been thrown out and looked remotely edible, she was somehow able to get by. As Danny and Marcus grew this particular task was duly handed over to them. It was something they both hated and were so ashamed of doing that getting them both to go out and scavenge was a task in itself.

Grace was a kind young woman, the sort of girl anyone, sadly except for her own father, would be proud to call their daughter. She always wore a smile but because of the curry aromas that regularly wafted from her clothes she never had any friends, well not until she palled up with Linda Bird two years before they had both left school. Linda couldn't have been any different to Grace if she'd tried. Living in a small terraced house on Buxton Street and the only child of Mary and Stanley Bird, Linda didn't want for anything. Her father was a cabbie so money always seemed to be plentiful but from the start Mary Bird hadn't been happy about her daughter mixing with Grace, the girl stank and always had the look of being unwashed. The only problem Mary faced however, was the fact that her daughter also had no friends but for quite different reasons to Grace. She was spoilt, rude and at times could be cruel, so Mary, under protest, relented and let the Wilson girl come over to the house to visit. The first time she saw her new friend's home Grace had been totally awestruck, everything shone like a bright new pin and Linda's bedroom was like something out of a fairy tale. The walls, bedding and carpet were pink, with flowing drapes above the bed and there was even a small television just for Linda. Grace didn't mind her friend bragging and showing off all of the beautiful things she had and when Linda had given Grace a bag of her old clothes the almost destitute teenager was on cloud nine. A week before they officially left school they had hatched a plan to go to the disco at 'the Carpenters Arms' to celebrate Grace's birthday. Linda had turned sixteen a month earlier and they both now saw themselves as adults even if Grace had a another seven days to go before she could legally get a full time job.

As usual Seamus was in the pub and Grace knew he wouldn't be back until well after closing and only then if he hadn't pulled some rough old bit and gone back to hers for the night. Entering the tiny front room where her brothers were both engrossed in the old television set, she walked over, picked up the remote and switched off the box.
"Hey!! What did you do that for? Oh come on Gracie, we was watching that!"
"Because I want you both to listen to me. I'm going out tonight for a bit and I want you both to behave."
"Where you going Gracie?"
The question had been asked by her younger brother Marcus. Marcus, out of the two boys was the most

caring but would regularly step out of line after being urged on to do something wrong by his brother.

"Just to a disco for a couple of hours."

Danny grinned as he piped up and Grace felt like smacking him hard around the face.

"You'll be for it. When the old man finds out, there'll be fuckin' murders!"

"Mind your bleedin' language and he won't find out because if either of you two breathe a single word then I won't be feeding you for a week and that's a promise."

"Your cooking is shit anyway!"

"That might well be the case sunshine but it's all you get. Sometimes Danny, you can be a right horrible little bastard! It's my birthday today, not that either of you remembered, so don't you think I deserve to have a bit of freedom even if it is for only one night?"

Wide eyed they both stared at her and even Danny now felt a little guilty. Quickly leaving the room he returned a couple of minutes later and pressed a fifty pence coin into his sister's palm.

"Have a Coke on me Sis, I've been saving up for a second hand skateboard that old man Bentley's got for sale but I'd rather you have the money."

Grace smiled, rubbed her brother's head and at the same time pressed the coin back into his hand.

"That's very sweet Danny but Linda is paying for the drinks tonight as a treat so you keep the money and for fucks sake don't let the old man know you have spare cash or it will disappear in a flash. The boy smiled meekly and then placed a kiss onto his sister's check, she really was a diamond and at times he forgot just how lost he and Marcus would be without her.

As agreed, Linda was waiting for her friend just a few doors down as Grace didn't want to risk her father seeing them together. If he somehow caught a glimpse of his daughter, she would be able to come up with a plausible excuse for being out if she was alone. When the Carpenters Arms finally came into sight the girls got excited and as they neared the building Aswad's 'Don't Turn Around' could be heard escaping from one of the top room windows making Linda start to dance in the street.

"I hope that Graham from Grant's chippy is there, I really fancy him."

"Linda! He's eighteen and far too old for you!"

"No he ain't and I'll tell you something else! If he wanted to cop a feel I'd let him!"

"Linda! Your mum would go mad!"

As they nervously entered through the pub's front door Linda started to giggle.

"Well I wasn't planning on inviting her along Grace."

Grace started to laugh and when her eyes fell upon a pair of highly polished shoes, she looked up and came face to face with Jimmy Kilham. Abruptly she stopped laughing and she could feel her cheeks redden as his eyes seemed to bore into her very soul. Grace felt a shiver run down her spine, something she'd never experienced before. Upstairs the room was full to capacity with boys and girls all drinking and dancing. Sure enough, it wasn't long before Linda spotted Graham Talbot as he swaggered into the room. Always dressed in the most up to date fashion, it was only a matter of minutes before she caught his eye which had been helped along due to

the fact that she had been boldly staring at him and at
the same time willing him to see her.  By the time the
DJ announced the final song, Glenn Medeiros singing
'Nothings Gonna Change my Love For You', the
makeshift dance floor had filled up with new found
couples, all desperately hopeful of ending the night
together down some dark and secluded alleyway.
Grace frantically scanned the room for Linda but she
was nowhere to be seen.  Quickly coming to the
realisation that Graham Talbot was also missing, she
knew what had happened and just hoped that Linda
hadn't strayed too far and would be back in a minute
or so, so that they could walk home together.  Thirty
minutes later and with the room now rapidly
emptying Grace naturally began to panic, it was just
after eleven and the streets would be full of drunks.

Big Jimmy did his last check of the upstairs and was
about to lock the events room door when he spied a
forlorn Grace sitting alone in the corner.
"Sorry darlin' but I have to lock up now so you need
to shift your arse because......"
As he walked towards her Jimmy suddenly noticed
that the young girl was crying and always a soft touch
for a damsel in distress his tone instantly softened.
He was well used to young girls crying and
complaining about boys and fights with their
girlfriends but this one seemed different somehow, he
couldn't put his finger on why but it just did.
"Hey sweetheart, what's with the tears?"
Grace sniffed hard and readily accepted the tissue that
Jimmy dug out of his pocket.
"I came here with my friend and it's the first time

27

I've ever been out at night but she's disappeared and left me on me own and I'm too scared to walk home alone."

Jimmy sighed, this was all he needed at the end of a tiring and somewhat tedious shift.

"So, whereabouts' do you live darlin'?"

"Bottom of Brick Lane."

"What's another five minutes out of my life hey? Come on then. I'm now leaving off for the night so I'll walk you back."

Smiling, Grace mopped her tears and slowly inhaled with relief and when she looked into his eyes she once again felt the shiver of earlier as it tingled down her spine. True he was far too old for her but there was just something about him and she liked the warm feeling he instilled. Handing the keys over to Sadie, the woman winked knowingly when she spied the young girl he had in tow.

"Bit on the young side ain't she Jimmy?"

"Leave it out! I'm nearly old enough to be her father you soppy mare."

As it turned out Grace had been only too right to be scared. The Lane was full of drunks of all ages lurching about in search of a Friday night curry and when Jimmy offered her his hand for reassurance she gladly accepted. Living on the Lane and watching the late night shenanigans from the veritable safety of the flats upper front room window was one thing but to now actually be amongst all the noise and late night revellers was something completely different. When they reached her door Grace thanked the stranger and Jimmy Kilham smiled warmly as he turned to walk. He hadn't got more than a few steps when the door was flung open and Seamus O'Mara lurched out onto the pavement and grabbed his daughter by the hair, yanking it so hard that it made Grace scream out in pain.

"You dirty fuckin' slag, where the fuck have you been till this time?"

Jimmy spun around just in time to see Seamus raise his fist and swiftly moving her away, Jimmy grabbed the bastard before any damage could be done. At the same time he instantly smelled the bloke's rancid breath and knew that the poor little cow must be leading one hell of a life.

"Get ya feckin' hands off me!!!"

Grace was now leaning against the shopfront of the restaurant as she watched this kind stranger grapple with the monster she was unfortunately forced to call her father. Facing someone almost twice his size Seamus didn't really stand a chance and being a bit of a coward, as most bullies are, he soon retreated inside slamming the front door after him.

"Now what do I do?"

Jimmy sighed again for the second time that night and hoped against hope that the girl wasn't underage.

"I suppose you'd better stay at mine but it will have to be on the sofa?"

It was a two mile walk back to Islington and Jimmy really didn't feel like it now, much less having to try and make conversation with a teenager for the next twenty or so minutes. Pushing the boat out, he hailed a cab and the two set off towards Jimmy's flat. The cab driver made small talk but Grace didn't join in, she was starting to regret accepting his offer, after all she didn't know the first thing about him, he could be a serial killer or something for all she knew. The journey was over quickly but it was a journey that was about to change both of their lives forever.

# CHAPTER FOUR
## Early in 1988

One night turned into two and before long it felt as if
Grace was a permanent fixture in the little flat on
White Lion Street. Initially she had slept on the sofa
but one night after trying her best at cooking a nice
meal, opening a bottle of wine and even though she
still wasn't of official drinking age, things swiftly
moved up a level. Big Jimmy was over ten years
older than her and really should have known better
when she suddenly but innocently kissed him fully on
the lips. He wasn't a bad man but he was only human
and Christ she tasted so good. Grace, pretty, sweet
and innocent Grace had after all made the first move
and when she then began to kiss down the side of his
neck, in a deliberate and sensual way he just couldn't
contain himself. Lifting her small frame into his arms
Jimmy gently carried her through to the bedroom. As
he laid her down onto the bed her eyes followed him
in anticipation as he undressed and revealed a toned
muscular physic. Strangely, it wasn't awkward but
nor was it very exciting but it was what she wanted.
When Jimmy slowly but tenderly entered her, he
noticed the pained expression on her face and was
shocked at the realisation that she was still a virgin.
East End girls, well at least a lot of those that he'd
come into contact with, who derived from bad homes
with dysfunctional families, had a habit of giving it
away both early and easily, he'd seen enough of them
in his time. Clumsy fumbles around the back of the
pubs and clubs which more often than not ended up in

unwanted pregnancies. As he climaxed he suddenly stopped, they hadn't used any protection and she definitely wasn't on the pill as he hadn't seen any packets in the bathroom.

"Fuck!"

"What? What's wrong, wasn't I any good?"

Jimmy smiled gently at her and then kissed her tenderly on the forehead.

"Of course you were darlin', it's just that we didn't take any precautions and the last thing I need or want is a nipper in my life."

Grace wrapped her arms around his neck and meekly giggled.

"Silly! Everyone knows you can't get pregnant the first time."

Jimmy studied her elf like face, she really was that innocent and now he had robbed her of something so very precious that she should have saved for someone who really wanted her. He wasn't actually against her staying here, she looked after him and the flat and if he was honest, it was nice to come home to someone, come home to a hot meal every day and with his laundry all taken care of but he hoped that she realised it wasn't going to be forever. Luckily for Jimmy, in the short term at least, things would turn out okay but it made him take things more seriously and within the week Grace had been dispatched to the doctors and told she had to go on the pill.

Since moving to White Lion Street Grace had continually worried about her brothers but too fearful to face her father, Grace had only made her way back to Brick Lane once in the last six months. Knowing the boys hung out at a particular place over the weekend, Grace made her way to the Wandering Community Gardens. Set up by new age travellers left over from the sixties and now including aging punks still hanging onto the seventies, it helped or at least attempted to help local people come together to grow their own food and learn new skills. Sadly it also attracted drugs and the place was always buzzing on a weekend, so much so that it was hard to keep an eye on people, which allowed Danny to pinch whatever he could lay his thieving hands on. In the past, Sundays in the flat on Brick Lane had always been the best for cooking any fresh food that her brother had been able to steal the day before.

Mooching around the raised beds of vegetables she was about to give up on her hope of seeing her brothers, when unexpectedly she heard her name called. Out of nowhere a young boy flung his arms around her, his embrace so tight that it felt as if all the breath was being squeezed out of her.

"Oh Grace we've missed you so much."

Pushing him gently away, she momentarily held onto his shoulders as she looked him up and down for any signs that he was being mistreated.

"I've missed you too Marcus, where's Danny?"

"Dad makes him help with the loading now, says we both have to earn our keep since you fucked off."

"Marcus!!!"

"Sorry, but that's what he said. Anyway, I have to get what I can and if I go home empty handed I get a right belting. Oh Grace won't you come home? Please!!!"

Her heart went out to her little brother but she knew

to return would be dangerous and not only that, she actually liked her life now, liked being with Jimmy and for the first time in her miserable existence, liked feeling safe.

"Oh darlin' I can't and I think deep down you know that. Have you seen anything of Linda?"

"She came round the day after your birthday, you know when you'd been to the disco? Dad sent her away with a flea in her ear. I saw her a few weeks back and she ain't half got fat Gracie, big as a house she is."

Grace had a bad feeling that her friend wasn't actually fat but pregnant, still it would do no good to share her thoughts with her brother, so instead she took him over to the drinks stall and brought them both a freshly squeezed orange juice. Jimmy gave her twenty pounds a week, kind of like pocket money she supposed but she was grateful all the same. He hadn't asked her to get a job but she had still begun to look so that she could contribute more. Refreshed, the pair again made their way around the vegetable beds and when Grace spied a resident selling carrots and potatoes she purchased both and handed the tired looking carrier bag over to Marcus.

"What are they for?"

"So you don't have to nick anything for once and don't look at me like that, did you think I didn't know where the fresh stuff always came from."

Embarrassed, Marcus hung his head, he loved his sister and her words could still make him feel ashamed. Grace tenderly rubbed his head and at the same time could feel days of built up grease in his hair. To mention it would embarrass him further and there was no point because they probably had no hot water at home, Seamus had never been keen on paying his bills.

"I best be getting back sweetheart."

"Will I see you again Gracie?"

"Sure you will, I'll come back soon I promise."
Kissing his forehead she walked away and at the same time felt immense guilt at lying to her baby brother. There was no way she would be coming back here, it was a shithole that she would rather forget and in any case, Grace knew that if she bumped into her father there would be murders. Walking along she suddenly felt the now familiar churning in the pit of her stomach making her feel sick. It had been happening for the last couple of weeks and she really didn't know what was wrong with her. There was no way she could be pregnant as she'd been really good with the pills and had only missed taking a couple. She smiled when she thought of Jimmy, her Jimmy who she now loved with all of her heart. The age difference didn't bother Grace and if anything she had really started to grow up in the last few weeks. Keeping a home was nothing new to her but it was so much nicer when the house was clean and filled with lovely furniture. Suddenly she had an impulse to speak to Linda, so spying a phone box on the street corner she made her way inside and searched in her bag for some change. Tapping in the number Grace wrinkled her nose at the unpleasant smell, there was no doubt that someone had definitely been using the phone box as a toilet.

"Hello?"

"Hello Linda darlin', its Grace. How are you babe?"

There was silence for a few seconds more than was comfortable but finally her friend spoke.

"Good to hear your voice Grace, fancy coming round?  Mum and Dad have gone to Aunty Peggy's for the day so I'm home alone."

Grace looked at her watch, it would only take her five minutes to get over to Buxton Street and even if she had to catch a bus back to Islington she could afford to spend an hour with her friend and still be home by three which would leave her plenty of time to get Jimmy his dinner.  Just the thought of it made her smile, she really did love the man and couldn't have been any happier.  Knocking on the front door she waited for only a few seconds but she couldn't hide the look of shock on her face when Linda opened up.

"Oh my God!"

"Yeah I know, shit ain't it?"

Linda stood in the doorway with her vast stomach full of arms and legs and her face was one of total sadness and regret.

"You comin' in then or what?"

Grace allowed her friend to walk off in the direction of the kitchen first, there was no way she would ever have been able to pass the girl.  Five minutes later and the two were seated at the kitchen table with mugs of steaming hot tea.  For a few seconds nothing was said as they just stared at each other but Grace had to break the ice for both of their sakes.

"I take it that Graham Talbot is the father?"

"Yes he is, the scummy bastard!  As soon as I found out I was up the duff my dad went round to the chippy to confront him but he just laughed in dad's face.  My mum is inconsolable but at least they're

**36**

letting me bring the baby home after the birth, which I'm actually shitting myself about. Not coming back here, the birth I mean. I tell you something for nothing Grace, that bastard is going to pay for what he's done to me even if it is only from his wallet. So what's been happening with you? I came over Brick Lane but your dad called me everything from a pig to a dog. In the end I had to walk away as people were starting to stop and listen and it was fuckin' embarrassing. So come on, spill the beans. Where you living?"

Grace inhaled deeply and smiled.

"Islington, in a fantastic little flat with Jimmy."

"Jimmy! Jimmy who?"

"You know, the geezer from The Carpenters who was on door duty the night of the disco."

"The bouncer? But he's fuckin' ancient Grace!"

"He's in his late twenties and I certainly wouldn't call that ancient. Oh Linda, he's so kind to me and treats me so well."

"Yeah and I bet he's getting his leg over most nights?"

Her friends tone was cruel and sarcastic and Grace didn't much care for it and now really wished she hadn't bothered to visit. Linda always had a way of pissing on the matches and souring everything that was good.

"If you mean am I sleeping with him? Of course I am, actually Linda, I love the guy and you can be as spiteful as you want but at least I didn't give mine away to just anyone!"

It was the first time Grace had ever really stood up to her friend and Linda was speechless but it didn't last

**37**

for long.

"So are you up the duff yet?"

"No I am not!"

"Taking precautions?"

"Yes, well mostly but sometimes I miss the odd pill but I seem to get away with it."

Linda stood up and at the same time held her aching back, the kid inside of her was really taking its toll and she couldn't wait to get the little bastard out, no matter how painful that was going to be. Waddling over to the dresser she opened a drawer and pulled out a small cardboard box. Handing it to Grace she smirked in a nasty way that made Grace slowly shake her head.

"If you're so sure, do a test?"

"What?"

"If you're so cocksure that you won't get caught like I did, then do a test or are you too scared just in case you ain't no different to me?"

Grace snatched up the box and made her way up to the toilet. Her so-called friend was really starting to get on her nerves and Grace knew that after this visit she probably wouldn't bother coming back again but for one last time she would do as she was asked just to shut Linda up once and for all. Sitting on the pan she placed the wand in between her legs, peed on it and then laid it on the side of the sink. The leaflet said to wait for three minutes and by the time Grace had wiped herself and thoroughly washed her hands it was time to look. Picking it up she did a double take and then read and reread the leaflet before studying the wand for a final time. Grace placed the now offending item into her back pocket and slowly inhaling, took a deep breath before opening the door. When she emerged from the bathroom Linda was standing at the bottom of the stairs waiting.

"Well?"

"Negative, just as I knew it would be. Linda it feels as if you almost wanted me to be pregnant, wanted me to be as sad as you obviously are. I'm sorry to disappoint you but I'm not. Now I think it's about time I got off as I want to cook Jimmy a nice dinner before he goes out to work."

Collecting her bag, Grace lightly kissed her old friend on the cheek before leaving the house and setting off for home. When she was a safe enough distance away she stopped and out of the blue, burst into tears. How had this happened? How had she slipped up? There hadn't been any periods but that was because she'd been taking the pill consistently, well almost at least. This was awful, just awful and now she was worried, worried that Jimmy would make her go back to Brick Lane and a father who would beat not only the shit out of her but also the tiny defenceless baby growing inside of her.

# CHAPTER FIVE

The next few months passed by relatively smoothly even if the atmosphere in the flat was somewhat cold at times to say the least. Six months earlier when Grace had arrived home in floods of tears, Jimmy hadn't taken the news of the pregnancy at all well, in fact it was the first time Grace had ever seen him lose his temper with her but she had stood her ground. When she'd argued back that it took two to make a baby he had stormed over to her, his face red with rage and for the first time since they had met she felt scared.

"You are on the pill for God's sake!"

"I know and I'm sorry, I only forgot a couple Jimmy!"

"One is all that's needed and now because you're not fuckin' grown up enough to remember your contraception, I'm fuckin' saddled with a kid I don't need or want. There's only one thing for it Grace, get down the quack's tomorrow and get rid of it."

"I will not!"

"Oh yes you fuckin' well will!!!"

Of course that didn't happen and the subject thankfully was never again raised but Jimmy showed no interest in her when their child began to grow or if she told him it had moved or when it lay in a strange position and she couldn't get to sleep. Still Grace reasoned it was a small price to pay and maybe he would come around to things once baby Kilham entered the world.

A couple of weeks before her due date Jimmy came
home in a bad mood and seemed to find fault with
everything she did.

"What's for dinner?"

"Shepherd's pie and I've got some nice fresh veg."

"Veg! I ain't a fuckin' rabbit. I've been a work all
bleedin' day and I'm out again tonight and you feed
me fuckin' veg!?"

Grace's hormones were all over the place and when
she couldn't stand it any longer and began to cry, he
at last took her in his arms.

"I'm sorry darlin' I've had a shit day and to top it all
off we've been summoned to a dinner at some fancy
fuckin' restaurant just so George can show off his
latest bit of fuckin' stuff. It will cost me an arm and a
leg 'cause the tight sod won't pay for everyone but
there ain't much I can do about it."

"What about Irina, you said you liked her."

"Shipped back to Russia I presume, the new one is
from the Philippines or somewhere like that, at least I
think she is?"

"Does he buy them Jimmy?"

"I ain't sure but for fuck's sake don't ever say that
within his earshot or there will be fuckin' murders."

"Who else will be there?"

"Joe and Nancy, you met them a couple of months
back. Joe's a good mate actually and Nancy's okay
as it goes and that knob Dixie will be there with
whoever he's got on his arm at the moment. I'm sure
him and George are in fuckin' competition regarding
who has the best looking woman in tow, though none
of them can hold a bleedin' torch to you babe."

It was the first time Jimmy had ever said anything

even slightly romantic and for a short embarrassed moment they were both silent but it still made Grace feel all warm inside.

"Anyway, it's tomorrow night. So you need to get yourself something new to wear, something classy."

"What in my condition?"

With her index finger Grace pointed down to her ever expanding stomach which seemed to get bigger by the hour. Jimmy laughed as he pulled out a wad of twenty pound notes and reeling off several handed them to her.

The following day she went out shopping and after doing a double circuit of the shops and Chapel Street market and when her feet had swelled so much that she knew shoes for tonight were going to be a nightmare to get on, she settled on a plain black smock and a pair of flat pumps that were a size bigger than she normally took. By the time she got ready and had embellished the outfit with a chunky orange necklace and earrings, she had to admit that she looked good even for someone in the final stages of pregnancy. Her long blond hair was swept up into a French pleat and as she entered the room, Jimmy smiled and nodded his head in silent approval. A black cab pipped its horn from the road below and it was time to leave for the event that neither of them were remotely looking forward to in the least. Although she'd only met him a couple of times, Grace always felt inferior and somewhat dumb when it came to talking to George Conway and Jimmy, well by this point Jimmy had actually come to despise his boss.

As they entered 'Wiltons' on Jermyn Street, Jimmy leaned towards Grace and whispered in her ear. "And before you order the cheapest thing on the menu to keep the price down, it won't make a shits worth of difference as George always makes us split the bill equally. So tonight my little darlin', treat junior to a slap up meal and order whatever you like."

Originally opened as a shellfish mongers in seventeen forty two, it was now well respected and far more high end than Jimmy would have liked.
Shown over to a circular table which had four chairs on one half with the other seating being a semi-circular booth, Jimmy pulled out a chair knowing that Grace, in her condition would be constantly going to the toilet and would need a speedy exit. They hadn't been there more than five minutes when Joe and Nancy walked up swiftly followed by Dixie Milligan and a young woman who went by the name of Candice. Dixie had his own firm over in Croydon and he and George went back years. The two were constantly in completion with each other regarding which of them was doing better financially and even though Dixie's firm was a lot smaller than George's, he was a force to be reckoned with on the monetary front. Candice smiled at Grace and the look was almost one of pity as she sized the young girl up and down taking in the large belly and full breasts that looked like they could feed ten kids let alone the one she was carrying inside of her. The six began to chat away and the conversation was fun and light hearted but came to an abrupt halt when George sauntered over with a stunning looking woman on his arm and it

wasn't Irina Ivanov, who they had all come to know and actually quite liked.

"Well what a fucking motley crew and no mistake. Dalisay, I'd like you to me Joe, Nancy, Dixie and?"

"I'm Candice, please to meet you Mr Conway."

Dixie looked like he was chewing on a wasp at the stupid bitch's address.

"Please call me George darlin'. Fuck me Dixie, how'd you pull a stunner like her?"

George winked as he spoke, a trait he did a lot and which really got up Jimmy's nose. They had all laughed but Jimmy knew this wasn't going to bode well. Dixie would feel that he had been ridiculed and there was no way he would let the remark go without a comeback of some sort.

"This is Jimmy and sorry love, I've forgotten your name?"

Again he winked and when Jimmy gave a heavy sigh his boss looked at him with daggers. Grace stood up and held out her hand in the direction of Dalisay."

"Pleased to meet you, I'm Grace."

George's partner was stunning but had no manners and completely ignored the young woman's attempt at friendliness which went completely over George's head.

"Fuckin' hell Jimmy, kept that a bit quiet didn't you?"

Jimmy didn't reply but touching Grace's arm guided her back down to her seat. The Filipino woman had slighted Grace by not taking her hand and now Dixie wasn't the only one who was pissed off. The reason for this sudden inner anger was somehow strange to Jimmy and he now realised just how deeply he felt for

the little waif and stray that he had taken in several
months ago and who was now carrying his child.
Meanwhile George arrogantly clicked his fingers in
an unnecessarily rude manner in the waiter's direction
and a young lad of no more than twenty appeared to
glide across the floor.
"Look at this queer cunt!"
Everyone at the table, apart from George, desperately
attempted to look anywhere but at the poor waiter.
This behaviour was typical of the time and of the
Boss when someone showed the slightest bit of
effeminate behaviour.
"Good evening Sir, how may I help?"
"We're ready to order Doris."
"Excuse me?!"
Dalisay gently touched George on the arm, a silent
gesture that asked him not to cause a scene.
"Private joke kid."
The effeminate young man just pursed his lips and
turning to Grace, politely asked what she would like.
Doing as she'd been told by Jimmy, Grace ordered
enough to feed an army. Things seemed to have
calmed down but as the waiter headed in the direction
of the kitchen, George just had to have one last dig.
"I fuckin' hate queers!"
The waiter momentarily stopped in his tracks when he
heard the remark but he didn't react nor turn around
and Jimmy knew that he would probably, hopefully
do something disgusting to George's food. Twenty or
so minutes later and the plates began to arrive and
several of them were placed down in front of Grace.
French onion soup with artisan bread was followed by
oven baked lobster and pommes frites. Grace had

never tried shellfish before and didn't even know what a lobster looked like let alone tasted like. Side orders of onion rings and broccoli in lemon olive oil was then topped off with apple tarte Tatin and ice cream. An hour or so later and the others looked on in amazement when Grace had almost polished off every last morsel. With the very last mouthful swallowed, she sat back in her chair and puffed out her cheeks to the laughter of everyone else at the table which instantly then made her feel embarrassed.

"I think I need the loo Jimmy."

Standing up she was quick enough to see Dixie and George both nod their heads in their partner's direction. This was a signal that the men needed a few minutes alone and Joe whispered in Nancy's ear that perhaps she should also join the ladies. The toilet was as elaborate as the restaurant with highly polished wooden cubicles and a row of marble basins that each had top quality soap and an expensive fragrance to one side, although even in a high end establishment the latter was secured by a silver chain to stop any would-be thefts. Grace felt like she was peeing for England and when she eventually emerged, Nancy was the only one who smiled at her. Dalisay and Candice were reapplying lipstick, both in competition to try and look better than the other. When she'd finished, and in almost perfect English, Dalisay turned on Grace.

"So, when is your bastard due?"

"Excuse me!?"

"You heard me, I said when is the bastard due?"

As naive as she was Grace knew when someone was being rude and even though she shouldn't, she retaliated in the only way she knew how.

"I may not be married but my baby will have a mummy and a daddy who both love it. At least my Jimmy didn't buy me like a piece of meat on a supermarket shelf."

Dalisay stepped forward, raised her arm and was about to slap the little bitch in front of her but was stopped when Nancy grabbed her wrist.

"I don't know what you do in your fuckin' part of the world sweetheart but we do not raise a hand to a pregnant woman in this country so I suggest you wind your fuckin' neck in and learn that if you dish it out you have to be able to fuckin' take it!"

Back in the restaurant the four men had moved seats and were now in a compact huddle. A robbery at Boswell's Security was planned to take place in three weeks' time and Big Jimmy was to lead the men. George wanted all the loose ends tied up in readiness but as usual neither he nor Dixie would be in attendance. They were strictly planners and didn't take any risks themselves though they were more than happy for the other to do so. Dixie informed his old friend that he would be contributing a couple of bodies so manpower wise with Jimmy and Joe it would be a team of four plus the driver, who had yet to be agreed upon. As the ladies made their way back from the toilets, ever the gentleman George stood up but one look at Dalisay's face told him she wasn't a happy bunny.

"What's up babe?"

Dalisay turned to look at him and her face was full of rage. She then pointed a finely manicured finger so close to Grace's face that she almost made contact with the young woman's skin.

"She!!! Had the cheek to ask if you paid for me." George's face turned scarlet with anger and standing up he walked around to where Jimmy was sitting. Without warning he slapped Jimmy's face so hard that his head actually lopped over to one side.

"Keep that little bitch under control you cunt or you will pay the price for her fuckin' big mouth!"

Grace couldn't believe what she was seeing but worse than that, she couldn't understand why Jimmy hadn't reacted. He stood over a foot taller than his employer and was twice as broad but he just meekly sat there and took the slap and abuse without uttering a single word. The rest of the night was a total disaster, Joe was mortified for Jimmy and even Dixie thought it was well out of order. George Conway continually stared menacingly at Jimmy and it was unnerving for them all. By just after ten the party dispersed and after settling the bill the evening had not only been disastrous but including drinks, had set Jimmy back just over three hundred quid. Hailing a cab, the couple rode in total silence but once they closed the front door there was all hell to pay.

"What the fuck did you say that for? I told you before we fuckin' went out never to mention it but could you keep your fuckin' trap shut? Oh no, you just had to bring it up and not with George but you said it to the woman herself! Fuck me Grace, I will be paying for your big fuckin' mouth for weeks now!"

Grace stood and took the verbal assault but when she didn't argue back Jimmy suddenly stopped and looked at her. Grace had pools of tears in her eyes and as hard as he was he couldn't stop his heart from melting.

"Please don't cry babe, but you really have to learn to be more tactful and…"

Jimmy didn't get to finish his sentence because what she said next made him see red.

"Dalisay asked in front of everyone when my bastard was due."

"What!!!?"

"She looked me up and down like I was dirt, shit on her shoes and then in front of the others called my baby a bastard. I retaliated, I'm sorry but I couldn't help myself and then she went to hit me."

"She did what!!!!?"

"If Nancy hadn't have grabbed her wrist then she would have Jimmy, in my condition she would have hit me."

Now he felt like a complete and utter twat. He'd acted before knowing the full facts, something he didn't usually do and for that he was truly sorry.

"Why didn't you stand up to him Jimmy? Why did you let him slap you and not punch his fuckin' lights out?"

Jimmy took her hand and led Grace over to the sofa.

"Men like George Conway are nutter's darlin' and they didn't get where they are by being nice. George would put a bullet in your brain and not think twice about it. Now as much as I wasn't happy about the baby in the beginning, I still want to be around to watch the poor little sod grow up."

"Well why don't you just leave and get another job so you don't have to put up with him?"

"Because my sweet innocent love, I know too much.
You don't leave a firm once you've worked for them,
at least not without repercussions and I have too
much to lose now."
"So we're trapped then?"
Jimmy pulled her to him and placed his arm around
her shoulder.
"Seems like it babe, at least until I can find a way of
making enough dough so that the three of us can just
disappear. I've also been thinking about when the
nipper gets here."
Grace nuzzled her head into the chest of this huge
gentle giant that she'd quickly come to love and
adore.
"What have you been thinking Jimmy?"
"I don't want him to have my surname, I want him to
have yours."
"You mean register him or her as 'father unknown'?
I don't think so! No child of mine will be known as a
bastard for the rest of its life. My old man might have
been a complete arsehole when it came down to mine
and my brothers' upbringing and we were known by
all the locals as Seamus's bastards but no child of
mine will go through that! So whether you like it or
not my baby will have the surname of Kilham and
that's an end to it!"
Jimmy pulled himself away and taking her firmly by
the elbows stared deeply into Grace's eyes.
"It has nothing whatsoever to do with that, I am proud
beyond belief but I don't want him, or her come to
that, to be associated with me when they grow up.
This shitty life is hard enough as it is without every
fuckin' scumbag wanting to take a pop at you because

**50**

your old man is Big Jimmy Kilham and he'd slighted
you for whatever reason years earlier. This ain't up
for discussion Grace, my mind is made up."
Grace didn't bother arguing, there was plenty of time
left to work on him and if it turned out that he
wouldn't budge on the matter, then if only for the
loving reason he had just given, it wouldn't really be
the end of the world.

# CHAPTER SIX
## 1988

The robbery at Boswell's had gone well and even though the pay-out had been vast, as expected and purely because of Grace's remark, George had still tried to make Jimmy's life unbearable for the ensuing couple of weeks. Strangely and maybe for the first time ever he didn't let George's actions get to him, there was someone far more important on his mind and it made Jimmy realise that absolutely nothing in the world mattered to him as much as she did. Grace was now ten days over her due date and the poor little cow was so big that she was having trouble getting around the flat, let alone venturing outside. Grace was booked in to be induced the following day and it hadn't helped matters when feeling stir-crazy she decided to go out, it didn't matter where but she was starting to feel as if the walls were rapidly closing in on her. In the past the market always cheered her up with its colourful array of stall holders calling out their wares and the locals, many of who shopped there daily, and who would always say 'hello' if you smiled in their direction.

Out of the blue and for the first time since she'd discovered she was pregnant, Grace bumped into her old friend down Chapel Street. Linda Bird was shopping for bits for her new Georgian basement flat that the council had given her on Platt Street in Somers town. It sounded far grander than it actually was, in reality it was dark, damp and not at all suitable for a young mother and her baby. After spending just over a week decorating and with the help of several hired portable heaters to dry the place out, her dad had given her a couple of grand to help towards furnishing it. Old Stan Bird was getting fed up with the noise of a crying baby and as much as he loved his only daughter, she had been a big disappointment to him and his wife and now they just wanted her out of the house as quickly as possible. Linda was lazy and not really interested in being a mother, so much so that she had left everything down to her mum and Stan could see that Mary was worn out looking after a baby at her age. Taking his daughter up the council offices he had been blunt in his turn of phrase and Linda could only stare at her father in disbelief.

"I need you to give my daughter a house and give it to her now, or come the weekend the lazy little mare will be out on the bleedin' street! I pay my taxes and we ain't moving until you find her somethin'!"

The housing officer tried to explain that there was very little available but Stan Bird was insistent and stood his ground. Back then council housing wasn't that difficult to come by for locals and by the end of the day, a basement flat had miraculously become available. Linda had wanted to inspect it first but Stan had already accepted on her behalf and now here she was shopping away to her heart's content all courtesy of her parents.

"Grace? Grace is that you?"

Grace turned around as quickly as she could and when she saw her old friend's face staring back at her she immediately began to cry.

"So you were up the duff after all! Don't start crying,

whatever's the matter with you, you soppy mare?"

"Oh I don't know Linda, my hormones are all over the place and I'm so tired. So, what did you have?" Grace sniffed loudly before peering into the high end pram come pushchair that looked more like some luxury toy than an actual baby carriage.

"A fuckin' boy! The little bastard screams from morning till night and every time I look at him all I can see is the face of that wanker Graham Talbot staring back at me. I called him Zachary but usually refer to him as Zach the cack on account of how many shitty nappies he turns out a day."

"Linda!!!"

Grace reached into the expensive contraption and gently lifted out the crying infant. Instantly she could smell that his nappy was soiled and pulling a tissue from her pocket she tenderly wiped away the snot from around his nose. Staring into her face Zachary momentarily stopped crying and began to smile and gurgle at her.

"You wait till it's your turn, feels like your guts are being ripped out. I was twenty three hours like that and then they had to cut my fanny to make it wider! There was blood everywhere and the pain? Never felt pain like it my life. I tell you Grace, rather you than me 'cause I ain't going through that again for all the bleedin' tea in China."

For a second or two Grace could only stare at her friend in stunned silence. Linda could be tactless at times but not now, now she was just being her usual spiteful bitchy self. Grace placed the baby back into the pram and he instantly began to cry again.

"Well thanks for that snippet of information Linda

you've made me feel a whole lot better."

"What you on about?"

Grace began to walk away but as she did, she called back over her shoulder.

"Just because your life is shit you want to spoil everyone else's and yes, giving birth might hurt a lot but at the end of it me and Jimmy will hopefully have a beautiful baby who we will love and cherish. I feel really sorry for Zachary, having you as his mum."

There was absolutely no comeback as Linda couldn't really reply to that statement and Grace continued on her way but when she arrived back at the flat she was in floods of tears. Jimmy had gotten home thirty minutes earlier and finding the flat empty he was a nervous wreck and was about to start phoning around the hospitals.

"Where on earth have you been? I've been going out of my bleedin' mind imaginin' all sorts had happened!"

"I just had to get out of this place Jimmy, honestly it felt as if the walls were closing in on me and then I bumped into Linda and….."

The tears had now turned into sobs and once again taking her in his arms he gently rubbed her back as he tried to sooth her. Jimmy was supposed to be with George, Dixie and Joe in less than half an hour but when Grace's water then broke he knew he wouldn't be making the appointment. There was no time to phone his boss as he had to focus on keeping Grace calm and within twenty minutes they were speeding towards Charing Cross Hospital. As it turned out Linda was wrong, Grace's labour was fast and in less than three hours she was sitting up in bed holding her son. Jimmy couldn't believe how he was feeling. Up until now he hadn't experienced too much love in his own life but what he now felt for this tiny bundle of arms and legs was indescribable.

"So what do you want to call him Grace?"

"James of course, after you but JJ for short."

Jimmy could feel himself begin to well up and walking over to the window he attempted to discreetly wipe his eyes without her seeing. He was unsuccessful but Grace saved him the embarrassment and didn't mention his show of emotion.

"Sweetheart, I have to shoot off for a bit. I was supposed to be at a meeting with George and the others hours ago. I'm in deep shit as it is so I have to at least show my face. As soon as we've finished I'll come straight back, anything you need from home?"

Grace smiled lovingly and at the same time shook her head. As Jimmy left the hospital he was grinning from ear to ear. He had a son, actually had a baby and one thing was for sure, he was going to make damn sure that his boy didn't end up working for someone like George Conway.

The ancient borough of Stepney goes back hundreds of years. Severely damaged in the Second World War it was then subject to slum clearance in the sixties with many properties demolished to make way for tower blocks and so-called modern housing. Of late George Conway, with the assistance of Dixie Milligan and much to the distaste of his other men, had started to use the services of local gangs from the Mile End Road to do menial but often dangerous tasks. In their late teens, most would be classed as just kids really and Jimmy found them arrogant, cocky and disrespectful and although he didn't voice his views, knew it was only a matter of time before something went wrong and the shit would hit the fan in the most spectacular way. Jimmy was still grinning from ear to ear as he walked into the now defunct bar area of The Kit Kat on Aylward Street. The pub still contained all of the fixtures and fittings but nowadays was used as a kind of waiting area for firm employees or anyone wishing to do business with George. The real hub however was upstairs and save for a small kitchen area, most of the first floor had been knocked into one, making a vast office space for sole use by the revered Mr Conway, a term of address George insisted was used by all except Dixie. Joe was pacing the floor when his partner in crime finally entered and his face was ashen.

"Where the fuck have you been? The guv's doin' his bleedin' nut up there, called you everything from a pig to a fuckin' dog!"

"I'm a dad Joe! Grace had a beautiful bouncing baby boy, born just over an hour ago!"

Joe Boswell took a step forwards and held out his hand.

"Really!? Well congratulations mate I'm made up for you big style. Nancy and me are tryin', have been for a while now but nothin's happened as yet. We're thinkin' of……"

"Is that cunt here yet!!!!?"

The two men were silenced by the sound of George's voice as it bellowed down the staircase. Joe looked into his friend's eyes with a sad expression.

"You best get your arse up there Jimmy and face the

**57**

music.  Remember, whatever he says or does, won't change the fact that you're a dad, a real dad, something that cunt will never be even if he has fathered gawd knows how many fuckin' mini Conway bastards over the years."

With a heavy heart Jimmy nervously began the slow laborious climb to the upper floor and his legs felt like lead weights with every step he took.  The office door was already open but nonetheless he knocked on the frame before entering.

"Mr Conway."

"Don't fuckin' Mr Conway me you cunt!  You were due here fuckin' hours ago so where the fuck do you get off just not turnin' up for a meeting?"

"I know and I'm sorry but……"

"Shut your fuckin' trap, when I give you an order you do as you're fuckin' told!"

"Cut me a bit of slack Mr Conway, my son was born this today."

"So fuckin' what!  I don't care if that kid you're shacked up with produced a sprog every fuckin' day do you hear me?  You work for me and I come before anyone else, so when I say be here at a certain time you will be here or face the fuckin' consequences!"

Meanwhile, Joe stood at the bottom of the staircase and cringing, did the finger across his throat gesture when he'd heard Jimmy stupidly dare to answer back.  No one ever answered back if they knew what was good for them and Jimmy had been in the firm long enough now to know that.  Joe liked Jimmy, they went back a long way and he also knew his old pal hated working for George.  If Joe was truthful, he was of the same mind set but like his friend he was only

**58**

too aware that there was no way out for either of them. George walked to the other side of his desk and stopped directly in front of Jimmy. Looking beyond his employee in the direction of the supposedly empty doorway, he gave his familiar wink and as he nodded his head, two thickset henchmen seemed to appear from nowhere. Frank and Steve Abbot were recent additions to the firm and Jimmy thought that as blokes they were okay but as new recruits he was also only too aware that they were eager to please. Jimmy turned instinctively and on seeing the pair momentarily panicked that his time might finally be up, that he wouldn't get to see Grace and the baby again and all because he'd been late for a bloody appointment!

"Please Mr Conway, I'm really sorry and I'll make it up to you I promise."

"Too fuckin' right you will sunshine but I still need to be seen to make you pay! If I don't the rest of my firm would see me as weak and we can't be havin' that Jimmy, now can we?"

In a flash George brought his knee up sharply and made contact with Jimmy's balls. Screaming in pain he instantly dropped to his knees and at the same time George grabbed a heavy crystal ashtray from the top of the desk and smashed it into Jimmy's nose. Blood splattered in all directions and with one hand still clasping his crown jewels Jimmy reactively placed the other over his nose in a desperate attempt to stop the flow of blood. Size-wise, George Conway in no way came close to the height or stature of his employee and in all honesty would be no match for the man if it came to a physical fight but he was confident that Big Jimmy wouldn't dare to retaliate. If, he strangely and miraculously grew some balls and did decide to take a pop, then he would be forced to immediately flee the Capital in desperate fear for his and his family's lives. A bully is a bully and you can't dress it up to be anything other than that and unfortunately George Conway was definitely at the top of the pile when it came to intimidation and cruelty to others.

"Take that as a warning, 'cause if you ever let me down again Jimmy you won't fuckin' live to tell the tale. Now get the fuck out, I'm sick of lookin' at your pathetic fuckin' face!"

George nodded in the direction of the two men and as they stepped forward in unison, they each grabbed one of Jimmy's arms to help him up. Jimmy slowly got to his feet, his balls were throbbing beyond belief and the blood from his nose was still flowing and had run down onto the front of his shirt and formed a large crimson patch. When his friend finally staggered down the stairs Joe could only frown and shake his head slowly in knowing disbelief.

"Well I suppose it could have been a hell of a lot worse pal. Come on, I'll drive you back home so you can get cleaned up, don't want young Grace seeing you in this fuckin' mess."

When he arrived at the hospital a couple of hours later and Grace saw the state he was in, even though his appearance was vastly improved, she instantly clasped her hand over her mouth in a gesture of shock.

"Oh my God Jimmy, whatever happened?"

"I fell down the stairs but I'm fine babe, now where's the fruit of my loins?"

Grace didn't know whether to believe him but by the look on Jimmy's face, she knew better than to quiz him any further, he only ever told her what he wanted her to know so even if there was more to it she wouldn't find out anyway.

"He's with the nurse, just doing a few tests. They are so pleased with him and say we can go home in a couple of days."

Just then the door opened and a young nurse walked in carrying a bundle and then tenderly placed Jamie into his father's arms. He didn't cry or make a fuss and was content to just be in these huge arms that were radiating more love than any baby could possibly ever wish for.

# CHAPTER SEVEN

When the baby was only a few months old and the couple had just about settled into the manic and unfamiliar routine that all new parents find themselves thrown into, an unexpected visitor came calling. Big Jimmy was out running errands for his boss which unusually he was glad of. Little Jamie had been awake with colic for what felt like the entire night and Jimmy was totally exhausted. His head ached from the constant noise of crying and as big and tough as he was, Jimmy felt utterly useless. Grace had just put the baby down in his cot and with the flat now finally silent, she decided to lie on the settee in the vain hope of getting at least a few minutes shuteye. In seconds a wonderful deep sleep engulfed her but it was to last no more than a few minutes. The intercom going off saw her fly up and run to answer so that the loud buzzing noise wouldn't wake JJ. Generally he was as good as gold but now that he was starting to teethe he was clingy, grumpy and once disturbed there was absolutely no settling him. Grace almost whispered into the device, desperate to maintain the peace that had taken her hours to achieve.

"Hello?"

"Open this fuckin' door ya dirty little whore!!!!!?"

For a brief moment Grace was stunned into shocked silence. She recognised the voice immediately and could feel her legs begin to instinctively shake. Her father had always been able to instil the most horrific fear with just the mere sound of his voice and even though it had been well over a year since she'd last seen him, nothing had changed. A few weeks ago Grace had been down the market and had bumped into Hasin, one of the waiters from the Bay of Bengal, who'd informed her that Seamus had unfortunately suffered a stroke. Grace hadn't been upset but now, well it must have been a very mild stroke, that or Hasin had been over exaggerating. Either way she was now about to find out and she was dreading seeing her brute of a father again. Grace was jolted back to reality when the buzzer went again only this time her father didn't remove his finger. It felt as it the whole flat was filled with the annoying, droning white noise and then just as she pressed the door release to let him in, Jamie began to cry out. Torn between opening the upper door to the flat and allow him entry or going to her desperately unhappy baby, she chose the former and suddenly coming face to face with her estranged dad she could feel herself begin to tremble.

"Get outta my way ya filthy slut!!!"

Seamus stormed into the front room and as he pushed passed her Grace could smell the stale alcohol on his rancid breath. His clothes were filthy and she guessed he hadn't been home in a few days let alone used any soap and water.

"I have to see to the baby, sit down and don't touch anything!"

"Who the feck do ya think your talkin' to!?"

As she frantically disappeared down the hallway she heard the sneering tone in his voice as he called after her.

"Ya cheeky little bitch, you'll get back here now if ya

know what's good for ya."

Ignoring him, she entered JJ's nursery and tenderly picked up her now sobbing son. His cheeks were a bright red colour and as she nestled him into her neck she could feel the heat from his skin.

"Bless your little heart, there must be another tooth about to poke through."

Reaching onto the bedside table she expertly removed the lid from the tube of teething gel and with one hand, managed to squirt a little of the contents onto her index finger. Gently lifting Jamie's head she rubbed the gel onto his gums and his crying slowly subsided. Thankfully a couple of minutes later he had fallen asleep in her arms and after tenderly laying him down Grace quietly closed the bedroom door. Re-entering the front room she saw that her father had also fallen asleep but if she had her way he wasn't about to stay that way for much longer.

"Dad! Dad!!! Wake up!"

Seamus's slightly opened one eye and for a fleeting moment, just stared blankly at her as he tried to remember where he actually was.

"Ya dirty fuckin' whore, I heard you'd got ya skinny arse up the duff. So where is it?"

"Where is what?"

"The little bastard who's brought shame onto me feckin' family!"

His words infuriated Grace and she almost screamed out her reply.

"You are the only one who has brought shame on this family and if you're referring to my son then he's asleep and he's no bastard. The only bastard in this house is you and now I'd like you to sod off before

**64**

Jimmy gets back. If he finds you here there'll be hell to pay and I can assure you of one thing dad, you will come off far worse!"

"Ya feckin' bitch!!!!"

Seamus struggled to get to his feet and as Grace watched in horror, the anticipation of the beating to come saw her start to shake uncontrollably.

Outside Jimmy was about to put his key in the lock when the adjoining door to the ground floor flat opened. Old Billy Preston had lived in the area for his entire life and while he'd always got on fine with Jimmy, he was also well aware of what his neighbour did for a living, knew of his reputation and more so that of George Conway's, so Billy was always careful when he spoke.

"Morning Billy, sorry if the baby kept you awake last night. Poor little sod is teething."

"Not a problem son, we were all babies once upon a time…... Jimmy?"

"Yeah, what's up mate?"

"I hope everything's okay, only some old drunk was bangin' on your street door loud enough to wake the bleedin' dead!"

"When?"

"Only about ten minutes or so ago and Gracie must have let him in as I heard the door slam shut and then it all went silent. I hope you don't think I'm poking my nose in, only I feel a little responsible for your Gracie and the baby when you're not about?"

"Not in the least Billy and I'm thankful that you're around, now I best get up there and find out what the fuck's happening."

Up in the flat, both Grace and Seamus heard the ground floor door slam shut and then heavy footsteps as someone marched purposefully up the stairs. Their neighbour's well intentioned words had been enough to put Jimmy in a foul mood and now he suddenly stopped dead in his tracks as his eyes darted from Grace to her father then back to Grace again.

"What the fuck's goin' on here girl?"

"I'm sorry but I had to let him in Jimmy, he wouldn't stop pressing the buzzer and I'd only just managed to get Jamie off to sleep."

Seamus began to sway from side to side. Unexpectedly he then lunged in Jimmy's direction but he was so drunk that his arms appeared to be flailing in all directions. It would have been comical if it wasn't so sad and with clenched fists he pathetically attempted to land a punch on Jimmy's chin but missed on all counts.

"Leave it out old man for fuck's sake! Now I don't want to hurt you but you really are startin' to piss me off and pushing all the wrong fuckin' buttons mate!"

"Ya fuckin' kiddie fiddler, she's only a girl! I'll get the Old Bill onto you, ya dirty filthy bastard!"

As much as he loved her, Jimmy had long since felt guilt about the age difference not to mention robbing Grace of her virginity. Exhausted from the sheer lack of sleep, her father's words were like the proverbial red rag to a bull.

"Get the fuck out of my house before I do you some real fuckin' damage!"

The advice fell on deaf ears and Seamus again lunged in Jimmy's direction. Now well and truly losing his rag, Jimmy grabbed hold of Seamus by the collar and

**66**

roughly hauled him in the direction of the front door.
Without a second thought he then proceeded to throw
Seamus out. Missing his footing, the drunk tumbled
down the stairs and both Grace and Jimmy heard the
dull thud as he hit the floor at the bottom of the stairs.
There was now only silence and the pair could only
stare at one another in complete shock at what had
just occurred. For a fleeting second Grace was
surprised at her total and utter lack of any emotion, he
was her father after all but as hard as she tried she felt
absolutely nothing.

"Oh Jimmy, whatever have you done. What if he's
dead?"

"I very much doubt that and in any case, the old cunt
was so pissed it wouldn't be seen as anything more
than an accident."

As much as Grace detested her father, at that moment
she saw a side to her partner that she didn't much like
but her thoughts were interrupted when Jamie once
again began to cry.

"Go and see to the kid and I'll sort your old man out."
Grace dutifully did as she was told but not before she
glanced at the formerly pristine sofa to see a large wet
patch where Seamus had relieved himself during his
short nap. Jimmy was so particular and Grace knew
this was really going to anger him. Maybe once she'd
settled JJ she could scrub it clean but there would still
be ructions when Jimmy noticed it. Jimmy hadn't let
on but as he was about to descend the stairs he was
more than a little concerned about what was waiting
to greet him at the bottom. He didn't care if the bloke
was dead or not, after all Seamus was a complete
wanker and Jimmy had seen enough dead bodies to

last him a lifetime. What he did care about however was the fact that it had occurred in his home and it was an unwritten rule that you should never shit on your own doorstep, especially in his line of work. To put it mildly, if he brought the Old Bill into his home it wouldn't go down too well if George Conway ever found out. Luckily when he reached the bottom he found Seamus bloody but snoring softly. Opening the street door, he hauled the pathetic excuse for a human being outside and propped him up against the wall. Unable to stand, Seamus O'Mara slowly slid down onto the pavement. As the stench of faeces invaded his nostrils, Jimmy realised that the drunken mess of a man had actually shat and pissed himself. Suddenly the adjoining front door opened and as if by magic, Billy Preston once more appeared.

"Everything alright Jimmy? Phew what a bleedin' stink!"

Billy was harmless enough but loneliness had turned him into a gossip who loved a bit of bother and having heard the commotion, he was now standing in his open doorway.

"Do us a favour Bill, call an ambulance for me. Tell them a drunk is causing aggro outside your gaff and you think he's hurt."

"Will do!"

Billy smiled in his neighbour's direction before disappearing back inside. Jimmy hated involving anyone else but at least this way he would be able to keep out of things and besides, Billy wasn't a fool and knew it would be in his best interest to keep his trap well and truly shut. Upstairs Grace had thankfully managed to settle the baby again and now stood at the kitchen sink furiously scrubbing the sofa cushion. She was fearful of what Jimmy had done to her dad and even more fearful of what he was going to do to her for letting Seamus into the flat in the first place. It was silly as he'd never so much as laid a finger on her but something about the way he'd acted and spoke had now made her feel unsure. He was somehow instilling a fear that she'd never felt before and didn't much like. Hearing him enter the kitchen she hung her head ready for the onslaught.

"Why the fuck did you let him in?"

"The baby was crying."

"Leave it out Grace, the kid has cried for the entire night!"

"I know and I'd just managed to get him to sleep but my dad wouldn't stop ringing that bloody bell and then Jamie woke up again and oh I don't know I just wanted all the noise to stop!"

He wasn't shouting, in fact he wasn't doing anything but asking a simple question but he could see that something in his demeanour was scaring her and in his line of work, Jimmy had seen that look a thousand times before. He was actually paid well to get the same response but now it was coming from his own partner, it made him feel really bad, not to mention ashamed that he could get this reaction from the woman he loved so much. Moving forward he gently took Grace into his strong arms and held her close.

"I'm sorry if I'm frightening you babe but you know I can't afford to have the Old Bill sniffing around and if George ever got wind he would do his fuckin' nut."
Gently lifting her chin until she was staring into his eyes, Jimmy tenderly kissed her on the lips.

"Please don't ever be frightened of me, I would rather die that hurt you in any way. It might be what I do to earn a living but my work never comes home with me. Here I'm just a dad and your partner and you both mean the absolute world to me. Where you're concerned my bark is worse than my bite but Grace, you have my word that I will never let either of you down."

Grace smiled lovingly, she adored this big hulk of a man with all of her being and now felt guilty for ever doubting him.

"Have you seen the sofa?"

Jimmy glanced over and sighed angrily.

"The dirty old bastard!"

Something in his tone made Grace start to giggle and then out of the blue Jimmy joined in.

"Fancy going back to bed?"

"Why Mr Kilham, I do believe you are randy."

"Not a chance babe, I'm knackered and only want to sleep."

"We'll see about that!"

Fortunately they didn't hear anything more from Seamus and a few weeks later Jamie finally got his last tooth. Things quickly settled down into a routine again and once more, for the time being at least, the family were one happy little unit.

# CHAPTER EIGHT
## 1998

The next few years had passed by without much event and the family were both happy and content. Jamie didn't see a lot of his dad as by the time he came home from school Big Jimmy was getting ready to go out to work. Even at such a young age Jamie knew that his father's line of work wasn't strictly legal but it never bothered him and he didn't ask any questions. He studied hard knowing it made his old dad proud and Jamie would do anything to please him. Grace loved her little family and would have liked to have added to her brood but as much as she tried there would never be any more additions to the clan.

Saturdays were always the best part of the week as far as Jamie was concerned and sometimes he was allowed to go to work with his dad for a couple of hours or so. Once a week Big Jimmy had the use of a vehicle as he did a weekly run to collect takings from the pubs and clubs after busy Friday nights and even though Jamie was mostly told to stay in the car, sometimes he was allowed inside one of the smelly places where his dad worked. The landlord or landlady always made a fuss of him and a Coke and a packet of crisps were mostly the order of the day. Occasionally father and son would meet up with Joe Boswell for a swift pint at lunchtime and it made Jamie feel like a real grown up. As he sipped his Coke or if he was really lucky a can of Vimto, he would listen intently to the men's conversation but knew better than to ever interrupt or comment. Jamie liked Uncle Joe, he was kind and always had time to ask the small boy how he was and how he was doing in school which went a long way in Jamie's innocent estimation.

A very large and lucrative job was on the horizon for the Conway firm but it had been kept strictly on a need to know basis. Now it was time to reveal all and a meeting had been planned for Saturday morning at the Kit Kat. Jimmy really didn't want to take Jamie along but Grace had made plans to visit Brick Lane in the hope of seeing her brothers and to check they were alright. Her father had recently suffered another alcohol induced stroke but this time it had been severe, so the boys now lived alone in the flat and even though they were both young adults, she worried terribly that they weren't looking after themselves. There was no way that Jimmy would ask her to change her plans so he'd reluctantly offered to take the youngster with him. A few seconds before they entered the building on Aylward Street he stopped and bending down looked deeply into his son's eyes. "Now you shouldn't really be here JJ and I know you are a good boy and always keep your trap shut but today of all days please don't break that rule. My Boss will be in there and he really ain't a nice man. Uncle Joe will be there as well and if you sit quietly in the corner he'll get you a Coke for being a good boy. You got your Walkman and headphones?" Jamie nodded his head eagerly.
"Well pop them on then."
Jamie placed the little foam discs onto his ears, and frowned. They itched his ears but he never

complained as his dad had bought them for him and he didn't want to upset him. As Jimmy pushed on the door he could feel Jamie grip his hand and realised that the little boy was frightened. He hated knowing that he'd caused that feeling but he really didn't want to get off on the wrong foot with George should JJ decide to speak up. Dixie Milligan and Joe Boswell were already in attendance and out of the corner of his eye Jamie spied a man that he assumed was Mr Conway at the far end of the room.

"Well, well, well, look what the fuckin' cat's dragged in and he's got his sprog in tow. Startin' him off young ain't you Big Jim?"

Joe was standing at the bar with his back to the others as Jimmy walked in and hearing George's comment, prayed that today wouldn't be the day that Jimmy had finally had enough. Out of the blue the door abruptly opened again and when a stranger poked his head inside and smiled in George's direction, it instantly defused what could have turned into a volatile situation.

"Hello sweet cheeks, I'm looking for Malcom. Malcom Watson? Said he lived around here. Do you know him perchance?"

George ran forwards while screaming at the top of his voice 'fuck off out of here you queer cunt!!!'

Not needing to be told twice, the stranger beat a hasty retreat and the door slammed shut. Jamie was wide eyed at what he'd just seen but as odd as the situation was, he giggled when George Conway looked directly at him.

"Dirty bastards them Queers, I fuckin' hate 'em. Be on your guard at all time's kid."

Then, as if nothing had happened, George nonchalantly walked over to Jamie, stooped down so that his face was almost level with the boy's and then winked, before reaching out and nipping his cheek. "Chip off the old block kid and no mistake. Right let's get down to business!"

Instantly Jamie stopped giggling as he rubbed at his face which had turned a bright shade of red. There and then, he decided that he didn't much like his dad's boss after all. The men headed towards a table in the middle of the bar area and Jamie did just as he'd been told and took a seat in the corner. He was still rubbing his face when Uncle Joe came over with his drink a few minutes later.

"You okay kid?"

Sliding the bolt across the front door, he had his back to Jamie as he spoke but when he'd finished and turned to face the child he could see tears in the little boy's eyes. Joe smiled and at the same time rubbed the hair on Jamie's head. He was a good kid and really shouldn't be in a place like this but it was up to Jimmy how he raised his own son so Joe didn't feel it was his place to voice an opinion.

"Won't be long sunshine, then you and your old dad will be out of here."

Things didn't go exactly to plan and it wasn't long before voices were raised. George had it on good authority that Union Haulage over in Stoke Newington was taking delivery of gold bullion in readiness for transportation on Monday morning. The company was nondescript and usually transported items of low value which was probably the reason the bullion company had chosen them, little risk of anyone bothering to rob them. The area would be quiet and the gateman was on board, so it should be as sweet as a nut but Jimmy wasn't happy with the timing and location, not to mention that it was out of their territory and by going ahead they would be stepping on the toes of Harry Day and his firm. George's cocaine consumption was increasing by the week and he was now experiencing deep paranoia which had seen his acts of violence increase. Jimmy now foolishly dared to voice his views, much to the annoyance of George who within seconds was out of his seat and grabbing a large handful of Big Jimmy's hair, yanked his head forcefully backwards.

"The tail don't wag the fuckin' dog you cunt! This is my job, my firm and you toerag, will do exactly what I fuckin' tell you to do, understood!!!?"

"Easy there Mr Conway, Jimmy was only offering his opinion, surely you can't have a go at him for using his brain?"

"And you can shut your fuckin' trap Joe, or do you want some as well?"

Instantly Joe hung his head, he hated the cunt as much as Jimmy but he hated it even more when George picked on his pal. There wasn't a lot Joe could do about it as the only person who was physically capable of tackling the situation was sitting meekly at the table with his boss hovering threateningly over him. Joe prayed that the day would never come when Big Jimmy finally lost the plot because it would be total carnage, a fucking blood bath, ending with George badly hurt or worse and Jimmy having a large price on his head.

"Right, let's get back to business. As I was saying

before I was so rudely fuckin' interrupted, we go tomorrow night. Dixie will be in charge of storage once the work is done. Jimmy you'll drive getaway, Joe will be going in with a couple of lads who are helping out as a one off. Pick them up on the corner of Aberavon Road at seven sharp."

Joe glanced in his friend's direction and they both knew that the lads in question would be gang members from the Mile End Road, full of attitude and not a clue what they were doing. George at last dismissed the meeting and making his way over to his son, Jimmy could see that there'd been a slight accident. Jamie was staring wide eyed down at his trousers which were now soaking and had turned several shades darker. Realising that it had occurred because of what his boy had seen and heard, even though he shouldn't have been listening, Jimmy smiled and took his son by the hand. He could see that the kid was mortified and embarrassed so he didn't mention the state of his son's clothing.

"Come on kid, let's get you home. Don't forget your Walkman!"

Jamie grabbed the small silver box and was out of his seat in a flash. Grabbing his father's hand as tightly as he could, he didn't even bother saying goodbye to Uncle Joe as he pulled Jimmy towards the door.

At a little after ten on Sunday morning, Grace glanced up at the wall clock and frowned with a look of concern on her face.

"Strange that the boy isn't up yet, usually nothing keeps him in bed, well not unless he's sick. Was he okay yesterday Jimmy?"

Jimmy guiltily nodded his head and then walked through to find out if his son was alright. The reason Jamie hadn't got out of bed was because he'd unfortunately had another accident in the night and was too embarrassed to say anything to his mum and dad. Jimmy poked his head into the bedroom and on seeing Jamie awake but with the covers pulled up tightly around his neck he entered and took a seat on the side of the bed.

"You okay JJ?"

Jamie timidly nodded his head but his eyes spoke volumes and Jimmy could see that something was troubling the boy. Pulling back the bedclothes he saw the large yellow wet patch.

"Come on you, let's get you washed. It's nothing to get upset about JJ, we all slip up now and again. Go and get in the shower while I strip this lot."

Jimmy knew the real cause of this sudden onset of bed wetting but didn't want to mention it to his boy and least of all to Grace as she would hit the roof, so the sheets were placed in the laundry basket and the bed left open to dry out. Jimmy would pull Grace to one side when he got the chance and let her know what had occurred but he wasn't looking forward to it. He didn't have to wait too long as she could smell the offending bedding as soon as she walked into the bathroom.

"You did what!!!? You took our boy to where that monster was? No wonder he was so scared that he wet himself, how could you Jimmy!!!?"

"I'm sorry but I couldn't get out of it and you had plans and I didn't want to spoil things for you. Please Gracie, I'm sorry and it won't happen again I promise. Let me make it up to you both and take you out for a treat?"

Grace sighed heavily but as much as she was angry, she knew that Jimmy loved their boy and would never intentionally put him in harm's way. Smiling, she rolled her eyes upwards and shook her head in mock surrender.

The day was spent at the park and then as an extra special treat, Grace had allowed them to stop off at Mac's burger van for tea. She was always careful to make sure her little family ate healthily but after Jimmy had told her all that had happened she knew that her son needed to feel safe, secure and above all else loved. To the amazement of his parents, Jamie had wolfed down his hotdog and fries but by the time they got home at just after six he was looking decidedly green around the gills.

"You feeling alright Jamie?"

Jamie shook his head and as his throat started to fill he ran to the bathroom to throw up. This continued for several hours but with the added addition of diarrhoea. Finally at just before ten and when he hadn't reappeared for over twenty minutes Grace went to look for him. Seconds later her screaming had Jimmy in the bathroom in an instant. Jamie was lying on the floor, evidence of vomit was still in the pan and now his eyes had begun to roll as he started to fit.

"Call an ambulance!!!"

Twenty minutes later and the three were speeding through the streets en route to Whittington Heath General. Jamie was already hooked up to a drip and

Grace's face was ashen. Jamie's seizures were now happening every couple of minutes and the look of concern on the paramedic's face as the ambulance sped through the capital was clear for all to see. Jimmy could feel his heart racing with fear, he was worried sick about his boy but he was also due at the Kit Kat in less than an hour. There was no way he was going to make it and George would hit the roof so the least he could do was let them all know. As soon as they arrived at the hospital he headed for a pay phone as he knew it was risky to use his mobile and after fishing about in his pocket for change, he tapped in Joe Boswell's number.

"Joe its Jimmy, I ain't gonna make the job tonight. I'm up the hospital with Gracie and the boy."

"What's happened?"

"Dodgy grub I think, they said something about food poisoning and now the poor little sod is having fits. Can you explain to George for me?"

"Oh fuck!!!! I'll try pal but you know what a cunt he is, this ain't goin' to go down well mate."

Joe heard Jimmy sigh heavily on the other end of the line and then there was a few seconds silence before Jimmy spoke again.

"I know what this means Joe but what the fuck can I do about it? My boy is in there fightin' for his fuckin' life!"

"I know mate, leave it with me and I'll try and calm the waters. When I've sorted it I'll give you a ring but it might be late?"

"That's fine Joe, good luck for tonight and now I best get back inside as Grace is in a right old state."

The line went dead and Joe Boswell could only shake

**79**

his head in disbelief, this wasn't good, wasn't good at all. Back inside the hospital Jimmy could only hold Grace as they waited for any news, news that wouldn't come for over two hours. Finally they were approached by a young doctor with a kindly face.

"Mr and Mrs Wilson?"

Neither corrected the mistake regarding being married though Grace had previously mentioned that she and her son were Wilsons but that her partner was Mr Kilham.

"Would you both be more comfortable going somewhere private?"

Grace and Jimmy shook their heads in unison, desperate to hear any news relating to their child's condition.

"No doctor here is fine, how is my little boy?"

"Jamie has severe salmonella food poisoning and you did the right thing in getting him here so fast or it could have been an entirely different outcome. The seizures were caused by dehydration due to the vomiting and diarrhoea but I'm happy to say that we now have this under control and have a saline drip in place so there is no reason why he shouldn't make a complete recovery. Purely for observation I would like him to remain here overnight but I would imagine he will be able to return home tomorrow. I must warn you however that for a short period of time he may be able to pass the bacteria onto anyone he has physical contact with and though it doesn't happen that often, strict hygiene rules need to be adhered to back in the home. For now there's nothing more either of you can do. I suggest you both go home and get some much needed rest as the next few days will be very tiring for you both. Would you like to say goodnight to him before you leave?"

Both Grace and Jimmy had made their way to the door before the doctor had finished talking and after being shown inside they were each standing at the side of the bed in seconds. Mindful of the doctor's advice, Grace bent over and tenderly kissed her son on the top of his head. Jamie was sleeping soundly and the colour had thankfully returned to his cheeks which made his mother feel a bit better at least.

"Poor little mite, he must be exhausted Jim. Come on, let's get off so we don't wake him."

Expecting her man to instantly walk in the direction of the door, she was surprised when he hovered for a few seconds longer and then bending over their son, also tenderly kissed Jamie's head. Grace's eyes filled with tears, she had never felt more love for her man than she did right at this moment.

# CHAPTER NINE

Joe Boswell had gone along to the Kit Kat with something of a heavy heart. He knew George only too well and there was absolutely no way he was ever going to let this drop, Joe just hoped that the punishment would fit the crime and not be over the top and too severe. Everyone was due to meet in half an hour to receive their final orders and run over things one last time and luckily no one else had arrived yet. Pushing nervously on the door Joe entered and saw his boss sitting at the same table where the meeting had been held the previous day.

"A bit fuckin' keen ain't you?"

Joe didn't reply and one look at his face told George something was amiss.

"What's up?"

"I've just had a call from Big Jimmy, he ain't gonna make it tonight on account of having to rush his kid into hospital. The poor little sod is fitting and I think......."

George was out of his seat in an instant and as he paced up and down began to rage with anger.

"That cunt! That fuckin' low life cunt!!!!"

"Mr Conway he wouldn't have cancelled lightly! Apparently poor little Jamie could be at death's door."

"Fuckin' death's door? Jimmy will be at fuckin' death's door when I get my fuckin' hands on him."

The raging instantly stopped when the door opened and Dixie Milligan strode in. He could immediately tell something was going down by the look on the

Men's faces but it could be personal so he knew better than to poke his nose in.

"George, Joe."

George walked over to his long-time friend who was also at times his adversary. After sucking in his cheeks and blowing out heavily in frustration, he slowly began to speak.

"We need another driver."

"Why?"

"Never mind about that now but if we don't find someone within the next hour this job will be fucked."

Dixie thought for a few seconds. He was aware of several blokes who would be more than willing to step in at short notice but he also knew that if it went tits up for some reason then the blame would be laid firmly at his own door. Whilst he'd always viewed himself as an equal to George Conway, at least when it came down to business, there was no way that Dixie wanted to go head to head with him when it came to a violent outburst but Dixie also knew he had to step up to the plate to save some sort of face.

"Let me make a couple of calls."

Within the hour Laney Watson had turned up. Laney was a freelancer and mainly worked out in Essex. Good at his job, he had an excellent reputation as a getaway driver having only had his collar felt once in the whole of his twenty plus years career. The only problem was, it would cost the firm double what Jimmy would have been paid but at least the job could still go ahead but it certainly added fuel to the fire as far as George Conway was concerned. The young recruits from the Mile End Road area didn't know exactly who they were working for and would be picked up en route, so with everyone else in attendance they were about to leave when George called Joe back over to the table.

"When you're done, call that cunt and tell him to be here at noon tomorrow, dead kid or no dead kid!"

"But Jamie might still be……….."

"Did you not hear what I just said or are you goin' a bit fuckin' soft in the head?"

"Yes Mr Conway."


As usual the drive to the impending robbery was taken in anxious silence. Even though they were all experienced, including the two gang boys who had done heists for other faces in the past, they were still nervous in the knowledge that if it went tits up and they got caught, then they would be facing lengthy sentences. Keith Dobson, having got the job as gateman at Union Haulage under false pretences as he'd previously served time inside, had been coached by Dixie Milligan to take the wrap if it went wrong. He would be paid well for his silence and was informed to lay the blame solely at the door of the Mile End lads and no one else's name was to be mentioned. Thankfully everything went smoothly enough and just before two am, when the bullion had been stashed in a secret destination that only Dixie and George were privy to, Joe drove a safe enough distance away from the Kat, parked up and then removing his phone, made the call. On purpose Jimmy had worn his dressing gown to bed and had placed his mobile into the pocket. The device was on vibrate only so as not to wake Grace and unable to sleep, as soon as he felt it move, Jimmy was out of the bed like a shot and making his way to the bathroom.

"Job go okay?"

"Sweet as a nut thanks. How's the nipper?"

"Still up the hospital but he's gonna be okay thank God, coming home this morning as it goes. So how was the guv'nor?"

On hearing the instructions Jimmy's heart sank.

"Not good pal. You've been ordered to the Kat at noon so be ready for a kicking when you turn up."

"Already am, you gonna be there?"

"You want me to be?"

"Safety in numbers and all that, though I don't expect you to step in or anything but it's always nice to have a friendly face on hand when you're getting the shit kicked out of you."

Joe laughed at the joke but it was a hollow laugh which didn't go unnoticed by Jimmy.

The next day Grace and Jimmy had taken a cab to collect their son and after the doctor's rounds, Jamie was discharged from hospital at eleven that morning. He was very subdued and his mother could see that it had been a traumatic experience for the poor little sod. Back at the flat he was tucked up in bed and when Grace returned to the front room Jimmy was putting on his jacket.

"Where you off to?"

"I have to pop and see George babe, shouldn't be more than an hour or so. Put your feet up while his nibs is kipping, you look done in."

Jimmy kissed Grace tenderly, stared into her eyes a

**85**

moment longer than usual and then left the flat. The second cab of the day was hailed, it was expensive but time was ticking by fast and Jimmy couldn't take the risk of being late and facing even more of his boss's wrath. By the skin of his teeth he made it in time and entered The Kit Kat at a minute to midday. Joe stood at the bar and turning instantly when he heard the door open, wore a look of fear on his face. "Alright?"

"Hi Jim, guv's upstairs and said to tell you to go up. For fuck's sake just take whatever he dishes out pal and then we can all get back to normal."

Jimmy nodded but as he uneasily climbed the stairs he could feel his heart begin to race. This was ridiculous, it really was, he towered head and shoulders above George Conway but like all bullies, George had such a way of intimidating a person that it wouldn't have mattered if he'd only stood four feet tall. The door was open wide as Jimmy approached the office but nonetheless, he still tapped on the frame.
"Enter."
Stepping inside he could see that a chair had been placed in front of George's desk and when instructed Jimmy stepped forward and took a seat.
"Hear your kid is sick?"
"Yes Mr Conway and it was touch and go for a bit but he's on the mend now."
"Shame that, must be a constant worry when you've got a nipper?"
Jimmy was growing increasingly nervous at George's show of emotion, as he generally only ever cared

about himself and this was so out of character. Pulling a bottle of scotch and two tumblers out of his desk drawer, George poured them both a drink and then passed one to his employee.

"Now, as much as you let me down and contrary to what people think, I ain't got a heart of fuckin' stone. That said Jimmy….."

Within a split second George was suddenly standing beside his employee and with one swift movement had Jimmy in a head lock and began to bellow in his ear.

"This is the second time I've warned you and there won't be a fuckin' third! You let me down again cunt and little Grace won't need to cook anymore dinners for you sunshine! Understood?"

As difficult as it was, somehow Big Jimmy managed to nod his head several times in quick succession. Then suddenly and as swiftly as he had appeared George was once again on the other side of the desk, smiling and sipping his drink as if nothing at all had happened. Jimmy knew that the serious amount of coke his boss had been consuming was slowly sending him crazy and it was only a matter of time before he did someone a serious injury. Jimmy Kilham just silently prayed to himself that he wouldn't be the one on the receiving end. George was staring him out and Jimmy was getting more nervous by the second but luck was on his side when a few seconds later George's mobile suddenly began to ring. Not being given the signal to leave Jimmy could only wait as his boss took the call.

"Are you having a fuckin' laugh Dixie? Well we need to move the bloody stash. I'm well aware that we are the only two who know the location but I would just feel better that's all. Well you'll just have to fuckin' trust me won't you? Don't contact me for a few weeks 'cause once they've pulled you in and even though they won't be able to link you, the Old Bill will be watching you like a fuckin' hawk." George ended the conversation and then threw his phone onto the desk.

"Joe!!! Get your arse up here!"

Joe Boswell sprinted up the stairs and inwardly breathed in a huge sigh of relief when he saw his pal was unharmed.

"Get the car, we need to move the gold. Seems that cunt of a gateman has only had his fuckin' collar felt. Dixie didn't do his homework 'cause the bastard's done time for robbery in the past so it didn't take the plods long to run his name through the fuckin' system and bingo!"

"We okay boss?"

"Yeah, those two niggers are being blamed and they can't give any clues as they don't know who the main man is. Dixie squared then both up with a monkey each before they got out of the van. If they manage to name Dixie he might get a pull but he'll deny anything and his alibi is watertight. It might get a bit hot for a while but I'm pretty confident that we're all in the fuckin' clear."

This newest problem, at least for the time being, had taken the heat off of Jimmy and for that he was eternally grateful but he still wondered just how long it would be until his boss' next outburst.

Just after Jamie's tenth birthday, another ghost from

the past manifested itself. Grace had been shopping
down Chapel Street market and laden down with bags
was just about to put her key in the street door when
she heard her name shouted out. She swiftly turned
to see her brother Danny standing on the opposite
side of the street. He was so grown up that for a
second Grace didn't recognise him, it had been years
and when she tried to recall exactly how long,
realised that she hadn't set eyes on her brother since
before Jamie had been born. He'd changed so much
but strangely, at the same time it was almost like
looking at a mirror image of her father in his younger
days. She smiled unconvincingly and at the same
time recalled Seamus' last visit, why whenever a
member of her family turned up did it have to be a
bad experience? Grace longed for a family like so
many others had, a family that would happily come
on Sundays to visit JJ and want nothing more than to
be a part of something. Her brother was tall, thick
set, with a mass of jet black hair and Grace had to
admit he was as handsome as a film star.
"Hello Danny love, whatever you doing here?"
"Well that's a warm bleedin' welcome I must say."
Straightaway she realised that she'd been rude and
placing the bags down onto the floor, hugged her little
brother.
"I'm sorry, that didn't come out right, it's just a shock
to see you that's all. There's nothing wrong is
there?"
"You gonna stick that kettle on and we can have a
good old catch up."
He hadn't answered her question and now Grace
could feel a tightening in the pit of her stomach.

**89**

Danny picked up her bags and then followed her up the stairs to the flat. Luckily Jamie was having a sleepover at one of his school friends because Grace didn't feel at all like having to explain why she'd never mentioned the fact that he had uncles or a grandad.

"Nice gaff!"

"Thanks. Jimmy works hard and me and Jamie don't go without anything."

"Oh yeah, fat Linda told me you'd got a kid."

"Fat?"

"Big as a fuckin' house, they took her kid away you know?"

"No, I didn't know that but the last time I saw her I got the feeling she wasn't cut out for motherhood, mind you that was years ago."

"You can say that again, the poor little fucker was neglected beyond belief. The social was involved after he kept turning up to school with bruises. She lost her pad and moved back in with her mum and dad. It was her old man who finally reported her as it goes but the hard hearted bastard didn't want to take the kid on though, so he's in a home somewhere."

"Oh no, the poor little mite! And Linda?"

"Last I heard she's on the game."

"You are joking!!!?"

"No seems she's fond of the old pork sausage, her old man tried dragging her home a few times but gave up in the end. Anyway, you gonna put that kettle on or what?"

Grace walked through to the kitchen and Danny moved around the room picking up ornaments and inspecting them. Everything was good quality and it seemed like she'd landed on her feet.

"Here you go."

Grace placed two mugs down onto the coffee table and then took a seat on the sofa.

"So how are things over on Brick Lane?"

"The old man's still in a home, it's three fuckin' strokes now and the old cunt is still somehow alive! Apparently they let him out a few years back just to see how he would cope but instead of going back to the flat, the silly old fucker was straight down the pub with his Zimmer frame."

Grace couldn't hold back her smile, it wasn't that she was being mean spirited but the image of her dad walking with an old people's frame was just so funny.

"He got so paralytic that he fell badly and banged his bonce again. It resulted in another bleed on the brain, so its irreversible brain damage. Bad news for him they said, fuckin' lucky break for us I say!"

For a fleeting moment Grace was suddenly silent as that fateful day back when Jamie was a tiny baby invaded her thoughts. What if Jimmy had caused the damage, what if all this was inadvertently her fault? He may have been a drunk and a very nasty one at that but did he deserve this? Then again there hadn't been any mention or sight of a Zimmer so maybe, hopefully, it was another occasion that had caused the second stroke.

"Sis?"

"Sorry! And Marcus?"

"A smackhead, ain't got a clue where he is though, the last I heard he was selling his arse on Leicester Square but he could be back on the lane by now I suppose."

"Oh no!!! Don't say things like that Danny."

"It's the truth I swear! Barry Carson was takin' his missus to a show up the West End and as bold as brass and touting for business, he saw Marcus approached by some queer and the two walked off somewhere together, arm in fuckin' arm no less!"

Sheepishly Danny looked at his sister and could see the tears that now streamed down her face. Placing his cup onto the coffee table he awkwardly put his arm around her shoulder and pulled her to him.

"You silly cow, what you crying for? None of this is your fault, you did what you had to do and thank fuck you did or it could have been you who ended up on the game instead of fat Linda and our Marcus."

That image brought a smile to her face and Danny chuckled.

"See, things are never as bad as they seem."

Hearing the door they both looked up just as Jimmy walked in. His eyes narrowed when he saw this handsome bloke with his arm around HIS Grace. She instantly recognised that look but thankfully, was able to defuse the situation immediately.

"Jimmy, this is my brother Danny."

The two men eyed each other cautiously, Jimmy didn't like strangers in his house and Danny was only too aware of the reputation Jimmy Kilham held. Grace held her breath when Jimmy slowly stepped forward but breathed a huge sigh of relief when he held out his hand.

"Pleased to meet you Danny."

"Likewise. Now, as much as I wanted to catch up with my sis', it's actually you I came to see. I've been doin' a bit of runnin' for Sainty Andrews over in

**92**

Hoxton. Nothing too heavy I might add, it's just the odd bag of coke and makin' a few payoffs. To be honest its crap, Sainty don't wanna pay and it's like pullin' fuckin' teeth trying to get your wedge at the end of the week. So, as things on the work front are crap, well at least they are for me, I wondered if you might be able to help me out. I heard on the grapevine that you worked for George Conway and wondered if there's any chance of an introduction seein' as we're family, well almost?"

Grace stood up so that Jimmy could take her seat and she had a gut feeling this wasn't going to turn out well.

"I'll get you some tea darlin'."

Jimmy reluctantly sat down, this was all he bloody needed after a hard day's graft but he would be polite if only for Graces' sake. He took a moment to mull over the request. George didn't like strangers and having something of a tie to Jimmy wouldn't count for much. That said, his boss wasn't averse to using the Mile End Road crews and an extra body might come in handy and possibly score Jimmy some brownie points he supposed.

"If you really fancy it I can try and arrange a meet but you'll regret it. The bloke is a complete cunt of the highest calibre and once you're in you never get out, apart from in a wooden box. Is that really what you want?' I'm tellin' you now kid, if I had my time over again I wouldn't have gone anywhere near the geezer."

"You're still working for him then?"

"Like I said, you never get out. So are you sure about this? If he takes you on and then you have a change of heart, there'll be fuck all I can do to help you?"

"Yeah but I don't care about getting out, it's getting in I'm interested in."

Danny stood up and then handed Jimmy a folded piece of paper which contained his phone number.

"Thanks Jimmy, thanks a lot."

"Hold off on the thanks sunshine, you ain't in yet and if it does happen, you just might end up regretting it."

When she heard the street door close Grace was a little put out that he hadn't even bothered to say goodbye to her. Gingerly she walked into the front room and as she took a seat next to him, Jimmy saw the look of concern on her a face and knew she would now start with the questions.

"Are you sure about this Jimmy? I mean, I know how much you hate George."

"That ain't got anythin' to do with it sweetheart! Your brother is a big boy now and makes his own decisions. I would rather not get involved but I've got a sneakin' suspicion that if I don't then your Danny will only seek Conway out on his own and then how would that make me look? It aint an ideal situation and to be truthful I wish he hadn't come here today but he did so I just have to deal with it. Now stop worryin' and go fix me some grub."

# CHAPTER TEN
## 1999

Unfortunately, by the end of the year, George Conway's consumption of cocaine had reached an all-time high. He still somehow just about managed to function well enough to run his corrupt empire but his paranoia was now beyond belief. His entire firm were living on their nerves, never knowing when or where he would kick off and for no apparent reason. It wasn't only in the work place that his behaviour was becoming increasingly erratic and at times he was so paranoid that even Dalisay had to be on her guard. The first woman to ever get under his skin, George absolutely adored her and had, even in his wired state, considered popping the question. Of late he had begun to watch her like a hawk, his mistrust was in constant overdrive wondering what she was up to when he wasn't at home and the constant questioning had really begun to stifle her. George didn't need to worry, the amount of cash he threw her way was too much to ever put their relationship at risk, at least it was until the day Danny Wilson was sent to collect her and take her to lunch at a restaurant George had been carrying out a spot of business in.

Several months earlier and very reluctantly, Big Jimmy had plucked up the courage and approached his boss about a possible position for Danny. He hoped that the answer would be a swift 'no' but that didn't turn out to be the case. On introducing the two it was clear to Jimmy that they were going to get along well and straight away it unnerved him.

His brother-in-law, albeit not in law, was sneaky and Jimmy wouldn't put it past him to repeat anything he heard in the flat and report it back to the boss. As Danny was kipping on the sofa until he found a place Jimmy was permanently on tenterhooks. Luckily within a few weeks of his new employment Danny was given a large deposit by George so that he was able to get his own gaff over on Walter Terrace. Only a couple of streets away from the Kit Kat, it meant that the new recruit would be at George's' beck and call at any time of the night or day, so in reality the deposit really had nothing whatsoever to do with helping out the new recruit. Danny wasn't stupid and knew exactly what his employer's game was but as unsurprisingly he was also a user, he would take whatever he could, whenever he could. The flat above a dry cleaners, had recently been renovated and was contemporary and up to the minute in décor. For as long as he worked for George Conway, Danny knew that the owners would never even contemplate asking him to leave, so in effect, he had a home for life.

Glenilla Road in Belsize Park was and still is a very affluent area and George had moved to the address some five years earlier. A large house spanning three storeys it was magnificent in every detail but the couple only inhabited the first and second floor. Knowing that he was at his most vulnerable when at home, George had turned the entire ground floor into a state of the art fortress. Internal steel doors, showing no locks or hinges, were accessed by an electronic pad which had to have a code entered before the door in question would open. Only George and Dalisay were privy to the code and due to his increasing paranoia, it was regularly changed at whim. The garden to the rear was landscaped in a traditional stately home style but much to Dalisay's disappointment, was only ever admired from the upper windows. Under strict instructions that she must never leave the confines of the house unless he sent someone to both collect and escort her, she was to all intent and purposes a prisoner in her own home but nonetheless, a prisoner that lived in the lap of absolute luxury.

Seeing Dalisay for the first time as she exited the main door of the house, Danny's eyes were instantly out on stalks. Admittedly she was several years older than him but he couldn't take his eyes off of her figure. The expensive dress clung onto every curve and he couldn't be off noticing her braless erect nipples as they gently brushed against the sheer fabric. Once inside the car he eagerly but failing dismally at any attempt of discretion, repeatedly glanced at her through the rear view mirror, so much so that eventually she finally noticed. Dalisay studied the young guy, yes he definitely had a good physique and she couldn't deny that he was handsome in a rugged, naughty boy sort of way. Highly sexed and with George now shoving so much Colombian marching powder up his nose that fucking was the last thing on his mind, she wondered if it was maybe time to have a little discreet adult fun. How could it hurt as long as George never found out? By the time Danny dropped her at the restaurant she had his number and he was now well aware that it wouldn't be much longer before the stunning woman was in his bed. That realisation came sooner than he expected and the following day when he wasn't due at the Kat for several hours and was enjoying an all too rare lie in, his Nokia suddenly burst into life. Hearing her voice Danny waited for her to ask him something but no question came, merely an order to collect her in thirty minutes.

On White Lion Street, Grace slammed the door to the flat and struggled into the front room carrying several bags of groceries. In a second Jimmy was out of the armchair and relieving her of the weighty bags.
"Feeding an army are we babe?"
"No, some of this is for Danny. I said I'd do a bit of a shop for him, I'm sure he isn't looking after himself properly. You wouldn't do me a favour and drop it round to his flat when you go out would you, I have a key?"
"Gracie he's a grown man for gawd's sake!"
"To me he will always be my baby brother. So will you?"
Reluctantly Jimmy agreed, recently he'd come to hate her bloody brother but when Grace asked him to do something Jimmy never seemed able to refuse. A little before two he set off as he was due to be at a meeting with George, Dixie and Joe at just after three. Letting himself in through the street door he carried the bags up the stairs and into the kitchen. That was as far as his act of charity was going to go, the lazy twat could unload his own shopping. About to open the front door to leave, Jimmy stopped when he heard

a giggle. Making his way back up the stairs and after creeping along the small landing he peered through the open door and his jaw suddenly dropped when his eyes reached the bed. Both of its occupants were heavily engaged in giving and receiving oral sex and Dalisay was underneath so her face could clearly be seen. Jimmy made a very swift exit and tiptoeing down the stairs, he let himself out onto the street. The pair had been so engrossed in their desire that they hadn't even heard him but what Jimmy Kilham had witnessed, would undoubtedly be the end of them both. Now Jimmy had a dilemma, keep schtum and say nothing or grass Danny up in the knowledge that the stupid twat wouldn't live to see another day? As much as he loathed Grace's brother, Jimmy wasn't a bad man but there was just one problem, in keeping quiet, should George ever find out that he was aware of the affair and hadn't said anything, then the boss might well take his vengeance out on Jimmy. Who was he kidding? Of course he bloody would and then what would happen to Grace and Jamie? There was also the chance that he would be made to suffer just for introducing Danny in the first place but Jimmy would just have to take a gamble on that one. When it came down to the brass tacks, there really was only one option left open to him, get in first!

Entering the Kit Kat with an obvious heavy heart, he nodded in the direction of Mac and Frank. The two were on security duty for the day and Jimmy had an intense dislike of them both. They were out and out bullies, with black hearts and cared little for anyone except themselves. Hesitantly heading up the stairs to his boss's office Jimmy was still fighting the demons within, he knew he had to come clean but signing someone's death warrant didn't sit well. Luckily none of the others had arrived yet and tapping on the frame of the open door Jimmy coughed nervously.

"Can I have a word Guv?"

George briefly lifted his head from the desk and beckoned Jimmy in. A rolled up fifty pound note was in his hand and the residue of white powder was smeared around his left nostril.

"What's up?"

"You ain't gonna like it Mr Conway and believe you me I had nothing to do with it, that's why when I found out I came straight here to tell you but well......."

"For fucks sake spit it out you soppy twat!"

"Grace asked me to drop off some groceries over at Danny's on my way here and well..........."

"Jimmy! You are really starting to fuckin' piss me off now!"

"I let myself in and heard a noise comin' from the bedroom and, well they were at it."

"Who was?"

"Now please whatever you do, don't kick off Mr Conway but it was Danny and your Dalisay. For all I know they're still there?"

As the bearer of bad news he reactively studied George's face, praying desperately that it wasn't going to end badly for him, then suddenly George Conway's eyes narrowed, which was never a good sign.

"Go and get the car and pick me up out the front."

Doing as he was told Jimmy didn't dare ask for a

destination but he already had a good idea where they were heading. A few minutes later he parked the car up a few doors down from Danny's flat on the opposite side of the road. They waited in silence for what seemed like an age until George had wound himself up to such a degree that he couldn't wait any longer. Pulling out his phone, he tapped in Danny's number but when he began to speak it sounded like everything in the world was rosie.

"Danny, I've got a bit of a problem over at the office that I need you to sort out as soon as possible?"

"Give me fifteen Mr Conway and I'll be with you."

Quickly pulling on some clothes, Danny threw a twenty down onto the bed and told Dalisay to get a cab, it didn't go down too well as he made her feel like some cheap whore but when he explained who'd been on the phone her face went as white as a sheet. The couple, in a desperate panic as they exited the flat as fast as they could, didn't notice the parked up Jag and at the same time Jimmy studied his boss for a reaction in the rear view mirror. George's face gave nothing away but his eyes just stared coldly ahead, telling Jimmy that all his fears for Danny were about to come to fruition.

"Take me back and put your fuckin' foot down!"

With one of her family back in the fold, Grace had planned on paying a visit to Brick Lane in the hope of finding her younger brother Marcus. She'd recently got word that he was hanging about down the community gardens again and even though it would be like looking for a needle in a haystack, Grace had to give it a try. If luck was on her side and she somehow did manage to find him she was also very aware that helping him get clean was a dream that in reality was probably never going to come true but it would ease her conscience if she could just make sure that he at least had food to eat. After collecting Jamie from school, Grace realised that it wouldn't be a good idea to take her son along. Even if she could find him she didn't have a clue what state Marcus would be in and she really didn't want Jamie experiencing the sight of drug use at such an early age. Knowing that Jimmy was over at the Kat, she couldn't see any harm in dropping their son off there. It wasn't as if he hadn't been to the place before and even though her Jimmy might not be too happy about it, she was willing to take the risk and worry about the consequences later.

"Go on inside son, tell your dad I sent you and that I'll explain everything later."

Innocently doing as he was told the little boy pushed on the front door and came face to face with Frank Garrow.

"Hello sunshine! Whatever are you doin' here?"

"My mum sent me, said I had to wait for me dad."

"Well take a seat in the corner and if you're quiet I'll bring you over a bag of crisps, alright?"

Jamie grinned from ear to ear, since the wetting incident Mr Conway hadn't been here on any of his Saturday morning visits and so long as he didn't have to see his dad's boss then Jamie liked coming to the Kat. He suddenly remembered that this wasn't a Saturday it was a school day and he just hoped that Mr Conway wouldn't be here because Mr Conway was a bully and his parents told him that bullying was wrong no matter who was dishing it out. Several minutes passed and when the crisps still hadn't arrived, Jamie decided to see where everyone was. Hesitantly climbing the stairs, he stopped on the third tread from the top when he heard voices and timidly he stared through the bannisters into the open office. Jamie could see his dad, Mr Conway, Frank and Mac, oh and there was Uncle Danny. But why did Uncle Danny have a wire around his neck and why was Mr Conway pulling it tight, so tight that Uncle Danny's neck was beginning to bleed and ………….. Jamie turned and ran down the stairs not caring who heard his pounding footsteps.

"What was that?"

Frank Garrow walked swiftly out onto the landing, looked around and then shrugged his shoulders before, shit! He suddenly remembering the kid downstairs. He took a moment to think about the situation and quickly came to the decision that maybe in this instance silence was the best policy. After all, Jimmy's boy was a good lad and to grass would not end well if the kid's dad ever found out. Going back into the office it had now conveniently slipped his mind that Jamie had ever been in the building.

"Nothing Boss! Wind must have caught the front doors I expect."

Racing along the street, not caring where he was going but knowing that he had to get as far away from that horrible place and all that was happening inside, Jamie didn't stop for what to his small legs, felt like miles. Within a few minutes he made it to Stepney Green Park and stopping he took a seat on one of the ornate Victorian benches. Suddenly and without warning Jamie burst into tears, he cried for what he had seen, cried with the knowledge that his own dad was somehow involved and then he cried again when he looked down and saw the huge wet patch that had now changed his light grey trousers to a dark shade of charcoal.

With the grisly deed done and as Frank and Mac were in the process of disposing of the body Jimmy just stared intently in the direction of his boss, waiting nervously to find out if he was next but what George then said shocked him to the core.

"Thanks for that Jimmy. It must have taken a lot of balls to shop your own brother in law?"

Jimmy could only nod his head, he felt deep shame and horrendous guilt like he'd never felt before. How the hell was he going to face Grace and lie as if his life depended on it? He really didn't have a clue, let alone know if he could even pull it off! True he really wasn't a fan of Danny but the bastard was still Grace's brother but what choice did he have? In this game it was dog eat dog and when George finally found out, which he undoubtedly would have, well Jimmy was under no illusion whatsoever that he would have definitely been next if he'd turned a blind eye and kept his trap shut.

"I have some business at home to take care of so you get off. You've shown loyalty today Jimmy and you know that goes a long way with me."

Once again Jimmy obediently nodded but as he stepped out onto the street he felt like the lowest of the low. Needing to gather his thoughts and calm down he made his way to the park and did a double

take when he spied his son sitting all alone on the
bench looking totally forlorn. Jamie had his head in
his hands and as Jimmy approached he could see that
there had once again been an embarrassing accident.
"You okay kid?"
Reluctantly lifting his head and seeing his father
standing in front of him made Jamie recoil in fear.
His son's reaction instantly told Jimmy that the wind
hadn't caught the pub doors at all and that his boy had
been an unwilling witness to everything. Taking a
seat beside Jamie, Jimmy gently placed his arm
around his son and he felt Jamie relax slightly. Now
with his face buried deeply in his father's chest he
began to sob uncontrollably so Jimmy patiently
waited for it to subside before he gently spoke.
"I know what you saw and I wish with all of my heart
that you hadn't. Now I'm going to explain everything
to you and it's then up to you to decide what you
want to do about it, okay?"
Jamie meekly nodded his head but he didn't utter a
word.
"Mr Conway is not a nice man. Uncle Danny did
something very bad and Mr Conway just lost his
temper. We all lose our rag from time to time son,
even you! Now it was wrong but there's nothing we
can do about it now. Jamie, if I go to the police then
me, you and mum would never be safe, do you
understand?"
Again the little boy nodded.
"So what do you want to do son?"
Feeling utterly lost and confused, Jamie stared up into
the face of the only man he truly adored and with
tears in his eyes and a snot filled nose, he slightly

**105**

stuttered when he began to speak, his words coming out in almost a whisper.

"K, k, keep m, me trap shut like you always taught m, m, me."

"Good boy, now let's get you home and not a word to your mum about any of this, she's a woman and would never understand like us men do."

Jimmy absolutely hated putting so much pressure onto his young son's shoulders but he really hadn't a clue what else he could do. Today's little accident could easily be explained but from now on the boy would wet the bed every single night and sooner or later he would undoubtedly break, of that Big Jimmy Kilham was sure.

# CHAPTER ELEVEN
## The day the sky fell in!

A little under six months later and just as Jimmy had thought would happen, Jamie finally broke his silence. It just came out one morning when he was sitting at the table eating breakfast with his mum. Grace casually mentioned Danny's disappearance which was nothing new as she had spoken about her brother on numerous occasions but today a strange feeling inside Jamie made him feel an overwhelming sense of guilt and pressure and he just knew he had to finally come clean and tell all that he knew.

"Mr Conway hurt Uncle Danny and daddy was there. Why didn't he help Uncle Danny mum?"

For a moment Grace just couldn't speak and could only stare at her son in complete and utter shock. Jamie placed his spoon down onto the table and then the tears came thick and fast. Grace was desperate to quiz her boy further but not wanting to upset him anymore than was necessary, nor take the risk of Jimmy hearing, knowing he could get out of bed at any minute, she passed Jamie a tissue and at the same time lovingly ruffled his hair.

"Don't worry about it, now blow your nose and eat your breakfast darlin', we'll have a chat about it on the way to school, okay?"

Jamie nodded and reluctantly tried to force the cereal down but his normal early morning appetite had completely disappeared. Thirty minutes earlier than their usual leaving time Grace closed the front door and then she and Jamie took a leisurely stroll towards Saint Andrew's primary school via Barnard Park.

"Come on son, let's take a seat and watch the ducks for a bit."

Jamie studied his mother with a quizzical look, they only ever stopped at places after school.

"Now, about what you told me this morning? I don't want you to get upset as you've done nothing wrong. You're actually a good boy for telling me the truth, even if it did take you more than a month of Sundays to do it. Start at the beginning Jamie, take your time my love and try to remember everything."

It wasn't difficult, since that fateful day Jamie hadn't been able to think of anything else. He began from the moment his mother had dropped him off at the Kit Kat and even though he went into every single minute detail regarding Frank and the crisps that never appeared, Grace didn't interrupt. When Jamie got to the part about George Conway garrotting Danny, though he didn't know the correct term and said a wire around Uncle Danny's neck, Grace thought she was about to explode although her face somehow remained calm and she wore a slight smile so as to keep her son calm.

"I ran then, ran and ran until I couldn't breathe mum and then dad came and found me and….."

He began to cry and Grace could feel her heart break, no child should ever witness anything so horrific and what made matters even worse was the fact that her poor boy's own father was involved.

After dropping Jamie off at school and assuring him that everything was fine, Grace told him to enjoy his day and then she made her way over to the Kit Kat. Knocking frantically on the front door several times

**108**

she waited impatiently to be let inside.

"Hello Grace love, what brings you here?"

Without even saying 'hello', Grace barged straight past Joe and marched towards the stairs.

"You can't go up there babe."

"Either I go up there, or I start shouting my mouth off to anyone who cares to listen about how that bastard George Conway murdered my brother!"

George was already in his office and when he heard the commotion, swiftly made his way downstairs.

"Well if it isn't Big Jimmy's little girl come to pay me a visit, what can I do for you sweetheart?"

"I know what you did you bastard!!!!"

George looked in Joe's direction, pursed his lips and at the same time rolled his eyes upwards.

"What the fuck is the silly cow on about?"

"You murdered my brother, in cold fuckin' blood you put a wire around his neck and choked the fuckin' life out of him!"

Before she knew what was happening Grace was suddenly slammed up against the wall and George had his hand wrapped tightly around her throat. With the other he pointed his index finger so close that it almost made contact with her right eye. As George squeezed even tighter she could feel the breath leaving her body and as her eyes bulged and filled with water she started to pass out.

"Easy there Boss!"

"And you can shut the fuck up Joe or you'll be fuckin' next."

Joe Boswell really didn't know what the hell to do but the one thing he did know, was that if Jimmy ever found out about this there would be murders and the first victim would end up being George Conway.

"Get upstairs, use my phone and call that cunt Kilham, tell him to get his fuckin' arse over here pronto!"

Reluctantly Joe did as he was told and as he dialled he could feel his heart pounding, this was going to be so, so bad.

"Hi boss, what's up?"

"Jimmy, its Joe and you need to get over here fast! Your Grace has come in all guns blazing, she knows Jimmy, she fuckin' knows!"

Within twenty minutes Jimmy burst through the pub doors to find Grace cowering nervously in the corner. He rushed over to her and after making sure she was okay, told her to go back to the flat and stay there. Scared beyond words she didn't dare argue and after he kissed her quickly on the forehead she headed home, visibly shaken but glad to still be alive.

"Where is the cunt!!!!?"

Joe had been dreading this moment, he'd been told to keep Grace on the premises but in all honesty she was so scared that he hadn't had to utter a single word to her. This was all so wrong, Jimmy was his mate and Joe and Nancy had shared many nights out together with the couple. Now here he stood guarding a woman that he looked upon as a family friend and waiting to find out if his boss would kill her. The shit was about to hit the fan in the most spectacular way and he was fearful for all concerned. There was only one way this was all going to end but who would come out the victor he wasn't entirely sure.

"Upstairs but fuck me Jimmy, what a mess!"

"What happened?"

"Your Gracie marched in here all guns blazing and shouting her mouth off. Jimmy, she knows about Danny! Why didn't you keep your bleedin' trap shut mate?"

Jimmy knew that to mention Jamie to anyone, possibly even Joe, would mean a certain death sentence for his boy so instead he took the full blame. "Oh I don't fuckin' know, it just came out in the heat of the moment one night. I never thought in a million years that she'd do anything like this but I suppose, when it comes down to it blood really is thicker than water, though what the fuck she hoped to achieve I really don't know."

After slowly making his way up the stairs he spied George sitting behind his desk but this time he didn't wait to be invited inside. Marching across the room he suddenly stopped in surprised when his boss looked up and began to speak in a calm and relaxed manner.

"Jimmy, glad you could get here so fast. We need to have a chat pal, take a seat and we'll try to sort this fuckin' mess out."

Jimmy did as he was told. Admittedly he wanted to knock seven bells out of the bastard but he knew that wasn't the way to go, he had his family to think about and if it meant grovelling to make things right, then grovel he would do.

"I'm sorry about Grace coming here Mr Conway, it was bang out of order but I suppose where family is concerned people do strange things."

"That's not what's bothering me Jimmy, what's bothering me is the fuckin' fact that she has knowledge of my business and what's gone on. You

**111**

must realise that it puts me in a very difficult position?"

George slowly stood up and after staring intensely at Jimmy, began to walk around the desk.

"Drink?"

Jimmy nodded, this really wasn't going how he thought it would. Maybe, just maybe there might be a way out of this without too much damage. George walked over to a filing cabinet that was situated next to the open doorway. Standing at the foot of the stairs Joe was all ears and to him things sounded, under the circumstances at least, as if they were going okay which all things considered, was a result. Opening a drawer, George discreetly removed a handgun and as he casually walked towards Jimmy, continued to talk in a friendly manner. A split second later and Jimmy felt the cold metal as it was rammed against the back of his skull. He instantly knew his time was up and in a nanosecond his past life flashed before his eyes. He saw the countless women he had slept with and then cruelly discarded regardless of their feelings. He saw the many victims he'd inflicted so much pain upon on the say so of another, people he would never get the opportunity to apologise to. Then he saw his Grace, beautiful sweet Gracie who had never asked more of him than to be loved. The woman had given him a son that he adored, a son that he would never see grow up or get married nor see the children that Jamie would father. The last realisation hit him like a hammer and as he felt the solitary tear drop from his eye he would have done anything to change this situation. Total sadness now enveloped him but it wasn't for himself but for Gracie and his boy.

**112**

"You've fucked me over for the last time, you cunt!"
The single shot was deafening when it rang out and
Joe raced up the stairs to see what the hell had
happened. The sight which greeted him made Joe
double over and vomit up the entire contents of his
stomach. George was still standing behind Jimmy,
his eyes were wide and staring crazily as he focused
on what was left of Jimmy's head. The rest was
splattered all over the room and down George
Conway's previously pristine white shirt.
About to go forward and remove the gun from his
boss's hand Joe suddenly changed his mind and
turning, walked briskly out of the office, ran down the
stairs and out into the street. This was all totally
insane, George was a lunatic and had finally lost the
plot. From now on none of them would be safe and
besides, he owed it to his friend to get justice.
Running down the street he stopped at one of the few
remaining phone boxes that had yet to be vandalised
and dialled the emergency services. Anonymously he
reported the shooting before hanging up and making
himself very scarce. He hadn't got much further
down the road when he heard the sirens of two police
cars. With blue lights flashing they roared down the
street and then came to a screeching halt outside the
now defunct pub. Joe knew his career in the city's
underworld was now well and truly over, he also
reasoned that he had several hours before him and
Nancy had to disappear forever or stay and wait to be
hunted down, which he was under no illusion, would
definitely happen. Jumping into the back of a black
cab he gave the driver his address and instructed the
cabbie to take him home. As the taxi drove past the

**113**

police cars Joe discreetly ducked down in his seat. "Wonder what's occurred in there? I tell you, this fuckin' place is a nightmare, ain't safe to let your old mum go out on her own these days."

Joe didn't reply and for the rest of the short journey, didn't bother to engage in any conversation no matter how much the cabbie talked. Reaching his address, Joe simply threw a twenty in the driver's direction before disappearing inside. Nancy was in the middle of hoovering when he walked in and pulling the plug from the wall, he made her jump in shock.

"What the ….. Oh, hello love, didn't expect you back so soon. Cuppa?"

Joe shook his head and something about the look on his face told her that there was trouble in store.

"What? What's happened Joe, whatever! is the matter?"

"I want you to listen to me Nancy. I don't want any questions and what I tell you to do, I want done without complaint. Pack as much of our stuff as you can, the rest I'll have sent over to your mum's for safe keeping. The furniture will just have to be left I'm afraid."

He waited for the shouting to start but it didn't come. Nancy Carter knew her man only too well and when Joe said 'listen', you listened. Whatever had caused this must be serious and she wasn't about to risk their lives or love by asking a barrage of stupid questions.

"I'll be back in an hour, so be ready to go."

Joe kissed her tenderly and then promptly disappeared outside where he flagged down his second taxi of the day and asked the driver to take him over to White Lion Street in Islington. In the past he'd always loved visiting the little flat, Grace kept a nice tidy home and was always so welcoming but today he knew that wouldn't be the case at all.

Taking Jamie out of school early on the ruse of a dental appointment, Grace returned to the flat and in no uncertain terms told her son to go to his room and not to come out again until she said he could. She was still sitting on the sofa nervously biting her finger nails when the intercom sounded, Grace had in fact been there ever since her return and now her nerves were in shreds as she wondered what was happening to her man. At the same time as pressing the door release button, she peered into the newly installed, small but very effective screen and only relaxed a little when she saw the face of her partner's friend. "Oh hello Joe, come on up."
Surprised at being taken out of school early and when he had been told by his mum to go to his room and stay there, Jamie was scared as this was so unlike her. Instantly he'd fallen asleep. All of the upset, added to the relief he'd felt at unburdening his secret had made him tired beyond belief. The sound of the bell woke him and now feeling much better he got out of bed and opened the door slightly so he could look through the crack.
Ascending the staircase, every step Joe took felt like a lead weight and he was dreading what he was about to say to one of the sweetest, most innocent young women, he had ever had the privilege to know. The upper front door was now on the latch and stepping inside he gently closed it behind him and walked into the front room. Grace stood at the window and was

**115**

trembling in fear at the thought of what she might be told.

"Where's Jimmy?"

For a few moments Joe didn't answer, he felt sick to the stomach and the words seemed to get stuck in his throat as he tried to summon up the sentence that he knew would rip out this young girl's heart.

Something about the look on her visitor's face made Grace furrow her brow and she tilted her head slightly to one side in a questioning manner. Guiding her by the elbow, Joe slowly led her over to the sofa and when he took her hands in his she could see tears as they began to well up in his eyes.

"What is it Joe?"

When he didn't reply the panic she was feeling made her voice come out in an almost whisper.

"Joe? You're starting to scare me now!"

"Somethings happened, something really, really bad babe. Jimmy's been shot."

"Shot!!!!?"

"You pissed George off big style and the nutter took a fuckin' shooter and....... He ain't comin' home again sweetheart."

In his bedroom Jamie heard a noise so terrifying and so painful, like the sound he'd heard on the telly when an animal had been injured. Opening the door he quietly crept along the landing and peered into the front room. His mother was now on her knees with her arms wrapped around her body, sobbing uncontrollably and rocking back and forth. Uncle Joe just sat on the settee and he was crying too, so Jamie ran forward and innocently tried to comfort his mother but Grace roughly pushed him away.

**116**

Joe stood up and taking the boy's hand, led him back to the bedroom and all the while Jamie could hear his mother screeching out the words 'I want my Jimmy, I want my Jimmy!' over and over again.

Closing the door Joe took a seat on the bed and then patted the space next to him. As Jamie sat down he had also begun to cry though he didn't really know why, maybe it was just seeing his mum in so much pain.

"I've just had to give your mum some bad news son and things ain't ever goin' to be the same around here again. I need you to be a big boy and be strong when I tell you what's happened. Your old dad was so proud of you JJ and I know you will hold it together, just like he knew you would."

Jamie slowly nodded his head, his eyes were as wide as saucers and he was scared about what he was going to hear.

"Jamie, your dad died today."

"Was it that nasty man Mr Conway?"

For a split second Jamie's words stunned Joe, the boy had been privy to too much and now it would create an even bigger problem if they weren't careful.

"No son, I'm sure it wasn't but you must never mention that thought to anyone again, do you understand me? Your mum will need to be looked after and that will be your job from now on, okay?"

"Okay Uncle Joe."

"Promise?"

"I promise, cross my heart and hope to die."

Joe kissed Jamie tenderly on the forehead and then went back into the front room. Getting off the bed Jamie crept over to the door and as quietly as he

**117**

could he opened it just enough so that he could hear the grown-ups voices. They were whispering and he couldn't really make out what was being said until his mother got angry and started to shout. Jamie wished he knew what was going on, there was never shouting in this house, his dad wouldn't allow it but then his dad wasn't here was he and once again the poor little boy began to cry. Shortly after, Uncle Joe left the flat and Jamie never got to see him again, it was almost as if he and Nancy had disappeared from the face of the earth or at least that's what his mother would tell him whenever he asked about them over the ensuing months……..

# CHAPTER TWELVE

It was noted in the Evening Standard that when the armed police arrived at the pub on Aylward Street, George Conway was still holding the gun. He was covered from head to foot in blood and brain tissue and the police report stated that his eyes were wild and staring, almost demonic was actually the description given by the first officer on the scene. George had been so out of it after ingesting several lines of snow that he was now actually crashing down from the cocaine and feeling immense fatigue and depression. Strangely he didn't resist arrest and the fun and games wouldn't start until later during his police interview. Kelvin Armstrong from Armstrong and Savage Law Firm had represented George for the past twenty odd years but this was one case Kelvin knew he wasn't going to win. Hearing the overwhelming evidence he had advised George to plead guilty and that's when the shit had really hit the fan. George had jumped out of his seat and attacked his brief without mercy and it had taken four officers to pull him off of his victim. Kelvin immediately walked away from the case as did the next three solicitors who were instructed. Finally a call was made to Terry Fitzroy of Fitzroy Patience and Long. The firm of solicitors were based on Limeburner Lane and just a stone's throw away from the Old Bailey. Terry was instructed and straightaway he informed George in no uncertain terms that there was absolutely no chance whatsoever of getting him off. However, there was a slim possibility that he could get the charges reduced to manslaughter on account of temporary insanity. On hearing the word 'insanity', George had hit the roof. When Terry went on to explain that it could be linked to George's drug dependency and classed as a mental disorder. As such if the plea was accepted, the jail time would be far less, George suddenly began to come around to the idea. At the end of the day it was all they had so basically there was Hobson's choice in the matter.

George finally saw the light after a visit from Dixie Milligan. With his head now clear from drugs, for a short time at least, he took in all that his old friend said to him. The pair had an in depth conversation regarding everything that had happened but Dixie's last sentence really hit home.

"You ain't walking away from this one George old boy, you have to go with your brief's suggestion. You do know that, right?"

George looked at his long-time friend and Dixie could have sworn that George had tears in his eyes, something Dixie had never seen before and would never see again.

"Yeah I know, what a fuckin' mess Dixie. I should have topped that cunt years ago but I didn't, so now I have to pay the price. Who called the Old Bill on me, any ideas?"

"Not really, I asked about but there seems to be a wall of silence. I went round the Kat but it's locked up with police tape across the doors. I did go round to Joe Boswell's gaff on the off chance of learning something but seems he's upped sticks and gone, so maybe that's where the answer lies.

We also seriously need to talk about your businesses George or what will be left of them if we don't act fast. The vultures are already circling so if you don't nominate someone pretty damn quick, then the other firms will carve it up pal."

The two eventually came to some sort of an agreement, George would hold his hands up and not try to fight the charge and Dixie would take over all of George's company dealings but should George ever get released, then the ownership would instantly revert back. It wasn't ideal but George had no other option and at least this way his firm wouldn't fold, though how easy it would be to get it back if the situation ever arose was another matter altogether. Just before the visit finished, George told Dixie to contact Dalisay and get her to visit pronto, he hadn't heard a single word from her and was beginning to get paranoid. Two days later she dutifully did as she'd been asked and when she confidently walked into the visiting room all eyes were on the sexy Asian looking woman. After Danny's demise and when George hadn't punished her in any way, she had naively believed she had gotten away with the fling. Nothing was further from the truth but he loved her and to have mentioned her treachery would undoubtedly have led to her leaving so George had remained silent. As she approached he stood up to embrace her but Dalisay immediately sat straight down and George narrowed his eyes suspiciously.
"What's up?"
"Nothing! I just don't like being told what to do."
Now he was angry and his voice was full of venom when he spoke.

"Told what to do!!? You're fuckin' living in my gaff rent free! Not to mention the fact that you're probably spending as much of my fuckin' money as you can get your greedy little hands on. Now listen! I'm gonna be in here a long time and I want the place looked after. I don't want to know what you're up to 'cause it'll only send me round the fuckin' bend but when I do eventually get out I expect us to pick up where we left off. Dixie will sort you out a monthly allowance so you won't want for anythin'. So, what do you say?"

His words were like music to her ears, she could now take as many lovers as she liked and get paid for the privilege at the same time. Leaning over the table Dalisay took his hand in hers.

"Thank you Georgie, thank you so much and when you do come home, I promise I will be waiting."

It was several weeks before a funeral could be held for Jimmy Kilham and on that fateful day Grace was so sedated that it felt to Jamie as if his mother wasn't really there, at least not mentally. At the four o'clock service very few people were in attendance. They didn't want to appear to be taking sides but the no show of Joe Boswell and Nancy was the most hurtful. In total there were only five mourners, Grace, Jamie, Old Billy Preston from the flat downstairs, Dixie Milligan, who now knowing that he would be stepping into George's shoes, wanted to make sure that nothing more was going to raise its ugly head and cause him unwanted aggro and some scruffy looking geezer who said his name was Marcus and who weirdly introduced himself as Jamie's uncle. With

the cremation over, Jamie, his mum and the scruffy
stranger returned to the flat on White Lion Street
where Grace quickly disappeared into the bedroom
slamming the door as she went, a signal to them both
that she wanted to be left alone.
"So, how old are you kid?"
Jamie, for reasons unknown to even him, had taken
an instant dislike to the stranger and now oddly didn't
feel safe around him.  He may have only been ten but
even at such a tender young age, Jamie had always
been able to tell the goodies from the baddies.
"I'm ten and a half and I don't think my dad would
want you here, so can you please go now?"
Marcus quietly laughed in a mocking, kind of
condescending way and switching on the television,
dropped down heavily onto the settee.
"Your dad keep any booze in the house?"
Jamie just shook his head, even if his dad did have a
few beers stashed away Jamie had no intention of
giving them to this weirdo.  He took a seat at the table
and staring intently, watched the unwanted guest
closely.  It didn't take long before Marcus became
really agitated and began to nervously scratch at his
skin whilst glaring at the television screen and it
seemed to Jamie as if the man didn't even know he
was doing it.  Jamie also noticed the dirty fingernails
and how greasy this Marcus's hair was.  When he
stood up and began to pace up and down Jamie
became afraid and retreating to the safety of his
bedroom, placed a chair firmly under the door handle.
Taking a seat on the bed he'd had no intention of
falling asleep but there was little choice in the matter
as he was totally exhausted.

**123**

Woken by the sunlight streaming through the open curtains he glanced bleary eyed at the bedside clock and saw that it was ten past seven, he'd been asleep for just over twelve hours! The Batman clock had been a gift from Uncle Joe on his ninth birthday and was a treasured possession. Instantly Jamie began to cry, oh how he wished Uncle Joe was here now to sort everything out, he would have seen the newcomer off with a flea in his ear of that he was certain.

Still dressed in his funeral clothes Jamie quietly opened the door and crept along the hallway. The front door was wide open and he closed it before entering the front room. Glancing nervously towards the sofa he let out a huge sigh of relief when he realised that the stranger had left but on scanning the entire room and seeing that the television was missing, along with the mantle clock that his dad had brought his mum last Christmas, his heart lurched. It was silver with a cream dial and had tiny butterflies on the sides. Jamie thought back to that day and he remembered the sheer smile of joy on his mum's face, remembered her saying that she would treasure it always. With his shoulders slumped in defeat he quietly turned the handle on his mum's bedroom door and walked over to the bed. Grace was awake but her eyes were unmoving and fixed on the ceiling above.

"You okay mum?"

Grace didn't utter a word and Jamie once again began to cry. Only a child, he didn't know what to do, didn't know who to ask for help.

"Please speak to me mum, mum? Please!!!!"

"Get out and leave me alone, don't you understand I

**124**

don't want to be here…… I only want to be with my Jimmy!"

"But dad's dead mum."

"Exactly!"

"Oh please don't say that mum, I couldn't bear to lose you as well and that horrible bloke has stolen the telly and your clock."

The mere mention of the clock got a very sudden and instant reaction as Grace swiftly turned to face her son."

"What!?"

Jamie could only nod his head and at the same time he watched as his mother shot out of the bed and ran to the front room as fast as she could. Straightaway the howling began and when Jamie ran into the room he saw her dropped to her knees and sobbing uncontrollably. He lovingly tried to comfort her in his childlike way but once again she shoved him away, only this time it was violently and he ended up in a heap on the floor. She seemed so angry and fine spittle escaped from her mouth as she almost hissed her words through tightly pursed lips.

"Why didn't you stop him, how could you let him take it!!!!?"

To Jamie it felt that everything was always his fault, the telly and clock going, telling his mum about Uncle Danny and knowing that his dad probably died because of it, no matter what Uncle Joe had told him.

Unfortunately the next few days passed very much the same, Grace stayed in bed and Jamie tried to amuse himself as best he could. The proper food had quickly run out and there were only so many things you could put on toast. Finally, when dear old Billy from the ground floor flat buzzed the intercom, Jamie ran to glance at the entry screen. Spying a familiar friendly face Jamie couldn't let the old man in fast. Billy was in his mid-seventies and it seemed like it had taken him an age to climb the single flight of stairs. When he at last reached the top he was bent over and breathless.

"Give us a minute son, my old lungs ain't what they used to be."

When he'd at last sufficiently composed himself, Billy stumbled slowly into the flat and was shocked at the utter mess of the place. Empty crisp packets and biscuit wrappers littered the floor, the curtains were only half open, though not the windows and there was an obvious sour smell about the place.

"What's been going on here then sonny, where's your mum?"

"She's in bed, mostly been there since the funeral."

"So who's been looking after you?"

"I've been looking after myself Billy, I am ten and a half now you know!?"

"Ten and a half! Really? Well bless my soul, you're almost a man."

Billy smiled knowingly and rubbed Jamie's hair. He could feel the grease and looking at the state of the place, knew that the kid probably hadn't had a wash since the day of the funeral.

"My dad always told me I was his little man, so that must make me a grown-up mustn't it?"

"Of course you are son, of course you are. Now I need to go and have a word with your old mum, you just wait here until I've finished okay?"

Jamie could only nod his head innocently and seconds later Billy had sternly knocked on the door and without waiting to be invited inside, barged in regardless. This room also smelt sour, absolutely stank in fact and Billy wrinkled his nose at the pungent odour.

"Grace, we need to have a little chat about that boy of yours."

"What's he done now?"

"Sweetheart he ain't done a thing but the poor little sod is living like a street urchin. When was the last time he had a proper meal?"

"I can't Billy, I just can't. I need to grieve for my Jimmy and JJ is a constant reminder that if I hadn't gone and…….."

Grace suddenly stopped herself before she said too much but Billy wasn't stupid, he knew who Jimmy had worked for and what that cruel bastard had been and was still capable of doing.

"Ain't there anyone who can help you out, family?"

"I've got a brother who's a drug addict, maybe I should give him a call? I need to be on my own Billy, didn't you when your Betty died or is it a case of being a man you were far stronger than me?"

The sarcasm didn't go unnoticed but Billy Preston wasn't going to give up that easily.

"I know you do sweetheart but if you carry on like this that kid is gonna be taken into care and there's no way on this earth that Jimmy would have wanted that to happen. Now I have a suggestion?"

Grace didn't reply, she wasn't at all interested in what the old boy had to say but she was however, beginning to feel bad about what he'd said regarding

**127**

her Jimmy.

"Let Jamie come and stay with me, that way I can at least make sure he's clean and fed and goes to school. We can both keep an eye on you and you'll be able to have all the grieving time you need. So what do you say girl?"

Mulling over what he'd said, Grace slowly and reluctantly nodded but then then rolling over, quickly pulled the covers over her head to shut out the world. To begin with Jamie hadn't been too pleased when told what was going to happen. In his mind he was more than capable of looking after himself and apart from having no telly, liked spending his time alone in the flat but he knew that he had to do as he was told. Reluctantly he threw a few of his things into a carrier bag and begrudgingly followed old Billy down the stairs. Entering the ground floor flat felt like stepping back in time just like in the films he's seen at school. The décor hadn't changed since the sixties and there was a strange smell, almost the smell of old age and decay and it was now his turn to wrinkle his nose. It really wasn't as bad as he'd imagined and a few minutes later, when he'd got used to it, even the smell became liveable. The small single bedroom at the rear was a mirror image of his own, albeit it only in size but the bed was so high and when he eventually managed to sit on it he sank into the most comfortable mattress he'd ever known.

"Nice ain't it? It's feather and belonged to my old mum, never had the heart to get rid and to be honest you wouldn't be able to buy one these days."

The next six months or so passed almost without

event and Billy kept an eye out for Grace. Apart from a couple of occasions she never left the flat so daily he would take her a plate of food, much of which went untouched. Jamie barely bothered and almost had to be forced to go and see his mum but the visits never lasted for more than a few minutes. He had come to love living at Billy's, there was always an old fashioned hot cooked meal on the table when he got in from school and evenings were spent talking about when Billy was a boy. Jamie marvelled at what life was like in the thirties and he couldn't believe there were no televisions or Sega games. Billy entertained him with childhood stories about growing up in the East End and then he covered the war years often laughing when he noticed that Jamie was listening so intently that he had his mouth wide open. "You'll catch a fly in a minute kid!"

They would both regularly laugh out loud and Jamie gradually came to realise that this was the safest and most loved he'd felt since before his dad had died. It wasn't all one sided though, Billy had been lonely for years, in fact ever since his Betty had passed away and having no children of his own it felt like Jamie was a kind of substitute grandson. The day that Jamie innocently referred to him as grandad had brought a tear to the old man's eye. They had been down at the greengrocers one Saturday morning and Billy had been picking out some veg for a roast the next day when suddenly from further down the aisle he'd heard a familiar voice.

"Grandad, shall we get a few strawberries for our pudding?"

Billy was so choked up that he had only been able to

manage a gentle nod of his head but from that moment on it became his given name and he couldn't have been happier. As with everything in life, all good things must come to an end and for Jamie Wilson that end would tragically come in the most awful way imaginable!

# CHAPTER THIRTEEN

A bleary-eyed Grace lay on the top of the bed waiting to hear the lunchtime news, it was about as much as she could concentrate on these days. At least today she had at last managed to get dressed and brush her greasy hair, it was only one small step but all the same it was a step in the right direction. Her heart still ached for Jimmy and she was no nearer wanting Jamie home but at least her mind was at ease knowing Billy was taking good care of the boy. When the hands on her watched moved to one o'clock she turned up the volume on the bedroom television. Grace wasn't at all expecting to hear what she did and suddenly her mind went into frantic overdrive.

'Killer George Conway was today sentenced to a thirty year prison term for the gangland murder of James Patrick Kilham. The case was deemed to be so important that His Honour Lord chief justice Michael St Halverson resided. A minimum twenty year term was also levied before parole would be considered. Conway, known to the Police for his underworld connections, had for some time been deemed high on the list of people of interest. David Furness, reporting for the BBC today, said Court One at the Old Bailey was packed to capacity and that the verdict was a move in the ……"

Grace didn't hear the rest of the report as her extreme wailing and sobbing drowned out any other noise. It was almost as if this sound was coming from somewhere or someone else and she was desperate for it to stop but she didn't know. The room began to swim and it felt as if the carpet was rising slowly from the floor and coming up to greet her. The walls appeared to be moving and she could feel a rushing sound, a kind of nondescript white noise as it invaded her ears and moved painfully through her head at lightning speed. Images of Jimmy began to rapidly flash before her eyes and the pain and anxiety of the last few months seemed to pale into insignificance when compared to what she was feeling now. Her body then began to move but she had no control of her legs as she glided through the doorway and into the front room. Then the frantic search for her beloved clock began as she ripped opened cupboard doors and pulled off the seating pads, all in a desperate attempt to find her most treasured possession. Any rational reasoning had left her and the fact that she already knew deep down that Marcus had taken it didn't seem to make any difference.

In the ground floor flat Billy had also been tuned into the news and when the commotion began upstairs it wasn't rocket science to put the two together and realise what was now going on. Leaving the comfort of his own home and with the aid of Jamie's key, he let himself into Jimmy's place and slowly climbed the stairs. Grace was still in the front room hysterically pacing up and down and when Billy gently spoke to her she didn't hear him, instead she continued to pace all the time emitting this awful wounded sound, the likes of which Billy had never heard before. Walking over to the young woman he tenderly touched her shoulder in an attempt to break the trance-like state but it didn't work. Grace just barged past him and as he almost stumbled backwards she didn't bat an eyelid. Billy was scared for her and when he realised that it was totally useless trying to break down an invisible, unbreakable barrier, he retreated back to his flat to call an ambulance. He knew the score, knew that by saying he was frightened that she was going to harm herself it would bring help quickly and sure enough, just less than thirty minutes later, a rapid response vehicle screeched to a halt outside with an ambulance arriving a few minutes after.

Billy was out of his front door and quickly explaining what had happened regarding the state that he'd found her in before the paramedic raced upstairs. Caine Long had been in the job for several years and there wasn't much he hadn't come into contact with. Mental health was on the increase in a huge way and Grace was showing the classic signs of a complete mental breakdown. He desperately tried to calm her but it was utterly futile, she didn't acknowledge him when he spoke and her face wore a totally blank expression as if there wasn't anything going on inside of her head, no thoughts, no emotions, nothing. When Cain was joined a few minutes later by two colleagues, he went downstairs to find out as much as he could about the patient and her situation and even though Billy felt exhausted and very anxious, he still did his best to explain. He revealed all about Jimmy's murder and how Grace had totally lost the plot after the funeral. He told about the unexpected shock of hearing the trial outcome on the radio earlier that day and realising that Grace must have been listening too. Finally, a slight smile formed at the corners of his mouth when he began to speak about

**133**

Jamie and all that the boy had been forced to endure. The mention of him and the fact that the child had been staying in the ground floor flat of an old man made alarm bells start to ring and by the time Grace Wilson was being stretchered outside, a social worker was already on the scene. Justine Gamble had worked for Islington Social Services for close on five years and in that time she had been witness to so many horrendous atrocities, that at times the horrific details had made her wake in a cold sweat. The depraved depths that a human being will sink to never ceased to amaze Justine and she began to ask some very personal questions, questions that shocked Billy to the core but also ones he didn't feel comfortable about. It felt to him as if he was somehow being accused of something sinister and he didn't like it one bit.

"I'm sorry Mr?"

"Preston, Billy Preston."

"I'm sorry Mr Preston but there's no way that the boy can remain here with you, at least until we have done checks into your background. We have a duty of care to the child."

"So do I!!!!"

"That might well be the case but should any harm come to him then…."

"Any harm!!!? What on earth are you talkin' about girl?"

"I'm sure I don't need to elaborate Mr Preston, you read the news like everyone else."

"So you think I'm some kind of paedo?"

"I didn't say that. They are your words not mine but it has happened before and therefore I am not

**134**

prepared to take any chances. Everything you have told me might well be true but don't you imagine that all situations like this have been described in the same way and would you like to hazard a guess at how many were far from the idyllic settings that they were portrayed to be? I'm sorry but this is out of my hands and if you wish to apply to Social Services as a foster carer, we can possibly look into Jamie coming to stay with you at a later date but I must warn you, it takes a considerable amount of time and I shouldn't really mention this fact but your age will almost certainly go against you. Now I need to return to the office to open this case formally and I'll come back when the boy gets home from school. Please don't get any silly ideas of trying to forewarn Jamie as the outcome will be the same no matter what and all you will achieve is upsetting the boy further."

Billy really couldn't believe what he was hearing, Jamie and him had been getting along so well and for the first time in years Billy hadn't felt alone. Now everything was suddenly ending and he knew he wasn't the only one who was going to suffer.

By the time Jamie returned from school, to him the street remained the epitome of normality and it wasn't until he stepped inside the front door that he heard the voice of a stranger.

"So you see Mr Preston, after talking it over with my supervisor, we have come to the decision that there is no other alternative but to admit James into care for his own safety. I know it's not what you wanted to hear but we have to put James's wellbeing at the foremost of this whole sorry situation."

Jamie barged into the front room, marched over to Billy and wrapped his arms tightly around the man's waist. Lovingly looking up into Billy's face Jamie could see the pools of tears in the old man's eyes.

"What's goin' on grandad?"

"Grandad!?"

"He calls me that on account of the fact that at the moment he doesn't feel as if he's got any other family. Why, is that a problem? Does him calling me grandad mean that I've been touching him or something?"

"Now you're being ridiculous!"

"Not half as ridiculous as you lot barging in here and upsetting what was a perfectly happy little arrangement that was working well for all concerned!"

Justine took a seat on the ancient sofa and could feel the nineteen fifties fabric as it prickled the skin on her legs. She politely asked Jamie to join her but he didn't move a muscle until Billy smiled and nodded his head. Sitting as far away from the strange woman as he possibly could, made it obvious to all in the room that this wasn't going to be an easy situation to deal with. As soon as Jamie was told what was going to happen he instantly ran back over to Billy and clung onto the old man as if his entire life depended on it.

"I ain't goin' lady, do you hear me, I ain't goin' and you can't make me!"

"I'm afraid you don't have any say in the matter young man, in the eyes of the law you are a minor and as such the borough has a duty of care to make sure that you are protected.

**136**

"Fuck the borough!"

"Jamie! Just calm down will you? Look son, there ain't anything that we can do about it at the moment. Your mum's gone to hospital and you have to be a man just like your old dad would have wanted. I'll come see you as soon as I can, I promise."

Billy knew that the mere mention of Jamie's father would do the trick and he now looked in Justine's direction for some kind of confirmation that a visit would be allowed.

"I'm sure we can arrange something Mr Preston, once young James here has settled in and you have passed all the relevant checks."

There really was very little left to say and after Jamie hurriedly placed a few things into a wicker basket Billy had given to him, he was led outside to Justine's car. Billy stood numbly on the doorstep and watched but just as he was about to get into the back seat, Jamie turned and running back to the front door, flung his arms around Billy. His voice was pleading and just the tone brought a lump to the old man's throat.

"Please grandad don't make me go, please!!!!!!"

Billy slowly pushed Jamie away and at arm's length stared deeply into the boy's eyes.

"Son, sometimes in this life we have to do things we don't want to, have to let go of things and people we love but that don't mean we don't love them. I will do all that I can to get you back here but for now you just have to toe the line. Will you do that for me Jamie?"

With tears streaming down his face, Jamie sniffed loudly and then nodded his head. Billy continued to watch until the car disappeared out of sight and after wiping his eyes, with a heavy heart he finally closed the front door on a cold and unfeeling world.

Grace was taken over to Cayman Secure Mental Hospital in Beckton. Built in nineteen ninety six it was still relatively new and as such was very bright and airy but as far as Grace's mental state was concerned it might as well have been the bowels of hell, she was so out of it on sedation that she didn't see anyone or anything as she was stretchered inside. Moved onto a bed in one of the secure single rooms, she was left to sleep off the sedation but was religiously checked every fifteen minutes.

As of yet there had been no fatalities at Caymen and that was how the staff wanted it to stay. There were eight trained therapy staff working at the sixteen bed unit, so the treatment would be intense and carried out daily. It was a new trial that had been put into place by the current Health Secretary in the hope that with more one to one care, patients would rapidly recover and therefore be able to hopefully re-join society quicker. As such it would release beds for a continuing stream of women in need but it wasn't long before the system disappeared and the minimal mental health care of today would quickly become the norm.

In Grace's case it was going to be a long drawn out episode. She was resistant to any kind of help on offer and though no longer manic, would just lie and stare blankly at the ceiling for hours on end, just as she had back at the flat on White Lion Street. It took several weeks before staff members were able to break down the barriers in even the smallest of ways and her stay would eventually last for well over eighteen months.  Not once did she ask after her son, not even to inquire if he was at least alright and after background checks were tirelessly carried out and learning just how close the two previously were, both doctors and staff were totally baffled.  With the backup of a social worker Grace was finally released from the hospital just before Jamie's thirteenth birthday but blissfully unaware of that fact, he would be closer to fourteen before the subject of him re-joining his mother was even mentioned.

# CHAPTER FOURTEEN

A few hours after Grace's admission to hospital, Justine Gamble's white Vauxhall Astra had pulled into the carpark of New Start Care Home over in Maidstone, Kent. The building was a large detached Victorian house that had been converted in the seventies as temporary foster care when no other places were available, or when the children sent there had been so badly behaved or had such horrific psychological problems, that no other foster family could, nor would deal with them. Jamie however didn't fall into either of the latter two categories, he'd just been unlucky in the fact that everywhere else which was even remotely suitable, was full to capacity. New Start had ten bedrooms in all and that included sleeping accommodation for the manager. Seven of the rooms were single occupancy and two had been designed to take a maximum of three beds, unfortunately Jamie drew the short straw. Justine went to take his hand but he shrugged her away.

"There's no point in being awkward James, it won't change anything and you will just make things difficult for yourself."

"My name is Jamie not James. Are you deaf you stupid bitch!?"

Justine ignored the boy, she'd heard far worse in her time but what she didn't realise was the fact that the outburst was really so unlike Jamie. His mother had always instilled manners, morals and treating others how you would wish to be treated yourself. Jamie was just lashing out and was trying to control a situation that was way over his head. Knocking on the door they waited for the high bolt and key to be turned before coming face to face with Steve Moore. To Jamie it felt as if he was entering a prison and to all intent and purpose that's exactly what it was, at least as far as the authorities knew.

"Hi there Justine and who do we have here then?" Justine Gamble giggled in a girlish kind of way which made Jamie roll his eyes upwards.

"This is James Wilson."

"I told you it's Jamie!!!"

Neither the man nor the woman took any notice whatsoever of his protest and stepping inside Jamie apprehensively glanced all around. The place was so dated with old fashioned wallpaper and furniture that had seen it best days long since pass. He wrinkled his nose in disgust at the distinct whiff of over boiled cabbage that seemed to be permeating the air. As far as he was concerned this was a living nightmare and as soon as he had figured out a plan, he was getting out of here even if he had to break his way out

"Come with me sonny and I'll show you where you'll be sleeping. We're a bit tight for space at the moment so you'll be bunking in with Delbert if that's alright?" The question was rhetorical and as Steve began to climb the stairs, he didn't wait for a reply. Instantly Jamie's guard went up, he hadn't planned on sharing a room with anyone least of all someone called Delbert! The room was large but that was where anything good about it ended. Wallpaper with trains covered the walls and was probably the remnant left from some occupant long before Jamie was born. The furniture, which Jamie would learn years later

**141**

was ex-military of defence, was scratched and bore the names of many sad predecessors. As it happened his roommate was okay and after a short initial period of silence the two sat down on the bed and eventually began to chat. Delbert Grant was three years older than Jamie and had been resident at New Start for almost the last five years.

"So what's your name kid?"

"Jamie but me mum calls me JJ."

"I'm Delbert."

Jamie let out a slight giggle that made Delbert sigh, he'd had the same response for as long as he could remember and he was pretty fed up with it.

"I know, shit name ain't it but it's the only one I've got so you'd better get used to it. They say I'm uncontrollable."

"And are you?"

"Nah not really but they kept placing me with old people who gave me shit food and make me turn in at ten. It's better here though, you get left alone, foods not so bad and you go to bed when you like. Here, have a look at this."

Delbert walked over to the window and sliding up the sash, pointed to a heavy cast iron down pipe.

"It's in pretty good nick for its age and it takes my weight easily."

"Why would you want to climb a drainpipe?"

"To get out of this shithole that's why! I go out most nights, once Steve's turned in for the night which is usually about eleven. He's got a bit of stuff who works at the kebab shop, she comes round all the time when they think we're all asleep. You should hear them going at it, like a couple of fuckin' rabbits."

Jamie wasn't quite sure he understood the terminology but he laughed all the same.

"So where do you go to?"

"Just over Vinters Park, it's shit really but at least it's somewhere to go."

Again Jamie giggled, Delbert seemed to use the word shit in almost every sentence.

"What's so funny?"

"Nothing, I've just got the giggles today that's all."

"Where was I? Oh yeah, there's this guy Nick who hangs out with us and gives us bottles of cider, we have to pay him of course. He used to be a resident here a few years back, moved away for a bit but something keeps him coming back to this shit area. I suppose we're the only family he's got, come to that we're the only family any of us have got."

"I've got family!"

"Really?"

Delbert's reply sounded a bit sarcastic and Jamie didn't like it, sure his mum was sick and he couldn't stay at Billy's anymore but he still had family, still had people that cared about him, he was sure of that.

"Anyway, let's not worry about any of that now. As I was saying, Nick will be there and then Steph and Helen will turn up, I think Nick wants to get in the girl's kickers but he's on a hiding to nothing where that's concerned, those two ain't gonna let just anyone pop their cherries but we have a right old laugh all the same. I'll warn you, you have to go easy on the old White Lightning if you ain't had it before or you'll end up with a shit head the next morning. You up for it later?"

Jamie didn't have a clue what a girl's cherry was or

**143**

White Lightening come to that but nodded his head all the same as he didn't want to be seen as wet behind the ears. This all seemed exciting but then his mind drifted to thoughts of Billy all alone in his flat and he began to miss the old man desperately.

"So what's your story?"

Jamie was still on his guard and knew it was probably best not to trust anyone for the time being. He explained that his dad was dead but didn't go into too much detail and he said that his mum was in the looney bin after having some kind of breakdown. He then explained about living with Billy Preston.

"Did he feel you up or make you do stuff to him?"

"No! Of course he didn't, Billy is like my grandad only we ain't related if that makes any sense."

"Fair play, I was just askin'. You get some dirty old cunts hanging about outside this place because they know who lives here. Steve chases them off but they always come back, like fuckin' vultures they are. If you ever have a problem with them just shout out paedo as loud as you can and they run a mile, shit themselves they do!"

Delbert began to laugh and it was so infectious that Jamie soon joined in. When they finally composed themselves Jamie had some questions he wanted to ask.

"So what time do we go to school and are the other children who live here nice?"

"School!? You are a right muppet Jamie, we don't go to school or not much anyway. No one really gives a shit about us but you get used to it after a while. The others? Well most of the bods you'll get along with though a couple of the girls are right cunts but you'll find that out for yourself soon enough. Give them a wide birth is my advice."

Jamie placed his hand over his mouth in shock. It wasn't that he hadn't heard the C word used before, he'd heard it on occasion when one of the market traders was getting irate with a fussy customer but for Delbert to use it?

"What's up with you?"

"Nothing!"

Later that night and just as he'd said, Delbert checked that Steve's door was closed and the light was out before sliding up the window and crawling out onto the sill. Glancing back into the bedroom he grinned.

"You comin' Jamie?"

Jamie nervously glanced around the room at nothing in particular and then rapidly nodded his head. Climbing down the drainpipe was nerve wracking and when he eventually made it to the ground he wiped the perspiration from his brow. The park Delbert had mentioned earlier was only a short walk away but still far enough that the laughter coming from the group couldn't be heard by anyone at the home. Delbert introduced the others to Jamie and in less than an hour he felt as if he'd know the little group for the whole of his life. He was strangely drawn to Step, she was much quieter than Helen and kind of pretty for a girl he supposed. It turned out that Stephanie Barton's story was far more heart breaking than Jamie's. She lived close by in a flat on Wheeler Street. After suffering years of horrific sexual abuse at the hands of her own father and when her mother had flatly refused to believe her and had actually beaten Steph badly for telling lies, Steph had run away and after dropping off the radar had somehow ended up in Maidstone. Helen had befriended her one Saturday afternoon when the two had been hanging out on the High Street. Helen Granger was the daughter of a brass and as such was allowed to do pretty much whatever she wanted so long as she kept out of her mother's way and didn't draw any attention from the Old Bill. Taking Steph home hadn't been an issue for Helen's mum and two years later the pair were still sharing a room together. The two girls were as different as chalk and cheese, Helen was daring, loud and crazy, the stereotypical wild child really, whereas Steph was quiet and reserved to the point of rudeness at times but there was something about her, something that at such a tender age Jamie felt was special.

The motley crew all came from different backgrounds, had different, sometimes very harrowing stories to tell but the little group never seemed to judge the residents of New Start, well except for when it came down to a certain Deborah Oldham and Jamie couldn't believe what he heard on his second visit to the park. All laughter stopped when a young girl of around fourteen walked by on the other side of the road to the park.

"There she goes the dirty slag! Slag, slag, dirty rotten whore!"

"Delbert!"

"What? You ain't got a clue Jamie, that piece of shit is what gives us home kids a bad name."

Debbie continued to walk by and with her head held high, ignored the shouting and disgusting names that

were directly aimed at her. Dressed to the nines she had business to attend to, unlike the reprobates that she unfortunately had to share a home with and who had nothing better to do with their time than hang around on a filthy old piece of waste ground that someone had for reasons she had never been able to fathom, deemed to name a park.
"Whore, slut, hope you catch Aids!"

Deborah Oldham came from the borough of Lewisham, Deptford to be precise. An only child, her father had upped and left one night when Debbie was just a baby. There began the age old struggle for her mother Sandra to raise Debbie as a single parent and the constant reminders by her mother, father and sister, that she had married beneath her. Sandra's parents Bob and Julie Riches owned a small private hire company and had done very well for themselves financially, even though Bob Riches was somewhat reluctant to share the wealth with his wife and daughters. Sandra's sister Lisa was two years younger than Sandra and had married well. As such she was able to give her own daughter everything that the child asked for. It didn't bother Sandra and she constantly reminded her own little girl that there was far more to life than how much a person's clothes cost or how much gold they could fit around their wrists. Debbie had tried hard to understand but when every Christmas or at family birthday gatherings the money and gifts were rammed down her throat by her mean spirited cousin Simone, Debbie grew resentful. Her grandparents had little time for her preferring to shower their love and attention on Simone and it was

**147**

openly carried out for all to see when they continually asked her why she couldn't be more like Simone. Her Nan would ridicule her for her weight and tell her she had the slovenly traits of her bloody father, "He was no good and you'll turn out just like him. Our Sandra would have been much better off if she'd never married him let alone had you! All you've done is drag her down!" If the material things and the cruel words weren't enough to make her envious and resentful, then the fact that Simone was only a few months younger than her cousin and whereas Debbie was plump with lank mousy hair, her cousin was a blue eyed blonde and slim, did! Simone's physical perfection made Debbie's jealousy regularly reach boiling point. By the time the two became teenagers and Simone was always dressed in the latest fashion, clothes that Sandra just simply couldn't afford for her daughter, the family bond had widened even further. It fell apart completely when Sandra was rushed into hospital and Debbie was brought to New Start, not one member of her family, not her grandparents or even her aunt, came forward with an offer to take her in. To the young girl it was yet another slap in the face and total proof that no one cared about her, cared if she lived or died and she quickly became angry. Not only angry with her family but with the whole wide world in general and naively she decided that somehow she would earn her own money and in doing so make her cousin and the rest of the family envious of her for a change.

Discovering, after a quick fumble that resulted in losing her virginity around the back of the old coal shed with a tradesman old enough to be her father, that she really liked sex, it didn't take Debbie long to work out that she could charge the curb crawlers who loitered in the street outside, way over the odds. They were more than willing to pay whatever she asked to fuck an underage girl who hadn't been around the block like most other brasses. As such she was soon able to afford all the luxuries she'd only dreamed of for the last few years, luxuries that had been paraded in front of her by her spiteful spoilt cousin. There was just one problem, Debbie soon turned into a person just like her cousin only she couldn't see it. Like so many before her, she didn't confide in anyone or share her background so her story went unheard and as usual in life, people came to their own conclusions and that included the boys and girls at New Start.

Now even Steph was joining in which totally surprised Jamie. When she saw the look of horror on his face she marched over to where he was standing and pulling him to one side, began to set him straight as to why they were all behaving in such a cruel way. "Please don't look at me like that Jamie because you don't know the facts. We, on the other hand know all about her sort, or at least Delbert does. Before her mum got sick that bitch had a good life and unlike me she wasn't abused in anyway. So when Delbert learned that when the time came she'd refused to go back home, he made it his mission to find out why. In the beginning when he'd seen her get into a stranger's car he had thought that she was being groomed and he wanted to help her but it soon came to light she had put herself on the game, she is still only fourteen for Christ's sake! Now Delbert didn't see that as too much of a problem in itself, each to his own and all that, what he did have an issue with was when she returned with bag after bag of flashy goods and proceeded to flaunt her spoils in front of the others at the home. Debbie took particular fun in winding up a girl named Kelly Cosgrove, a very vulnerable, damaged kid who though Delbert wasn't exactly sure, he guessed she was around eleven years old. Anyway, it didn't take long for Debbie to groom this gullible young girl and within a month Kelly was out every night working the streets to line Debbie's pocket. The poor little cow was so awestruck that she hung on that bitch's every word and never complained when Debbie took almost every penny Kelly earned. New Start was a safe home and it has allowed them to work without any interference so long as they sneak out after dark. Delbert was desperate to save the younger of the two but there was nothing he could do. He tried talking to Kelly, tried to warn her that she was being used but she only laughed in his face. She was eleven Jamie, just eleven years old and on the fuckin' game! Delbert considered speaking to Steve Moore but only for a second because deep down he knew it was taboo to grass anyone, even if they were totally and utterly in the wrong. So Kelly continues to sell her arse every night and Debbie is raking in the cash and that's why we hate her Jamie, we hate her! Hate her for what she's turned Kelly into and what she's doing at your place. So many of those kids, kids who just like you have no choice where they live but that dirty whore

**150**

choses to stay there and do what she does and God
only knows how many other poor souls she's gonna
corrupt."
Jamie could only quietly nod his head, his mum had
told him about women of the night although she
hadn't gone into any explicit detail like Steph had and
to say he was shocked was something of an
understatement. The rest of the evening went by with
no further trouble and when they were finally back at
the house and tucked up in bed Delbert began to talk.
Helen had previously said he had verbal diarrhoea
and she wasn't far wrong. He talked for what seemed
like hours to Jamie but in reality it was only a few
minutes but it was long enough to send Jamie to
sleep. As soon as he closed his eyes the reoccurring
nightmare began and once again he was back at the
Kat, frightened beyond belief and staring through the
bannisters at the top of the stairs. He could see his
Uncle Danny with the garrotte around his neck but as
the blood began to slowly seep from his wound he
swiftly turned his head and stared straight at his
nephew, only now it wasn't Uncle Danny it was
Jamie's dad! Big Jimmy's bloodshot eyes were now
bulging and his tongue was hanging from his mouth
just like the dead dog Jamie had recently seen laying
in the road. He could hear someone, he didn't know
who, screaming, terrible high pitched screams that
only stopped when he felt Delbert's hands as they
shook his shoulders to wake him.
"What the fuck was all that about?"
Jamie didn't answer and could only wipe the tears
from the corners of his eyes. Whatever was playing
on his friend's mind must have been really, really bad

**151**

and to be truthful, for once Delbert was glad that the secret hadn't been shared. It was never mentioned again but night after night Delbert would wake his friend whenever the nightmare invaded his dreams. It took about a month or so but slowly the bad dreams eventually lessened until they finally disappeared completely and for that Jamie would be eternally grateful.

Over the next few weeks and unbeknown to the rest of the small gang, Jamie and Stephanie were becoming close and would spend as much time as possible together. For Steph it was easy as Helen had a part time job at the local chip shop. As she was underage it was only in the prep area so she was out of sight of anyone who might report the owner for hiring an eleven year old. As soon as she set off each day Steph would leave to meet Jamie and for the next three hours it was as if they were the only two people in the entire world. It wasn't so easy for Jamie, Delbert was always asking question about where he was going and who he was meeting. On several occasion Jamie knew he was being followed and a game of cat and mouse had ensued but thankfully Delbert soon got bored and gave up. Officially, New Start were supposed to make sure that all residents under sixteen regularly attended school. Unofficially, Steve Moore was happy enough to turn a blind eye so long as they didn't give him any grief and no trouble was brought back to the house and that included the poor girls who sadly earned extra cash from selling themselves. They all thought that he didn't know but there wasn't much that got passed Steve and yes he could have laid down the law, banned them from leaving the house outside school hours but it wouldn't have stopped them and the atmosphere it would have created would affect the younger kids who needed some sort of calmness in their already traumatic lives. The local schools in the area were so understaffed that they didn't have the time to pursue truants, so all in all, things unfortunately went by the wayside regarding education.

Strangely, Jamie had unexpectedly opened up to the pretty young girl almost immediately and told her everything that had happened to him. His revelation included what he'd seen George Conway do to his uncle and Jamie's ideas about what had really happened to his own father, the only thing he held back was the fact that he felt he was to blame in some way. In return Steph shared all about the abuse she'd suffered, which even at such a young age made Jamie frown in disgust. When Steph suddenly started to cry Jamie place his arm awkwardly around her shoulder and from that moment on the youngsters formed a bond, a bond so strong that it would never be broken.

Six months after his arrival, Jamie was called into Steve Moore's office and asked to take a seat. Seeing Justine Gamble standing at the window made Jamie think they were about to give him bad news about his mother.

"Hi James, how are you?"

Jamie was too wound up to argue about his name again and instead stared at her for what to him felt like an age but was actually less than five seconds.

"I'm afraid I have some bad news. There's no easy

way to say this so I'll just get straight to the point, Mr Preston passed away a few days ago."

Jamie frowned in confusion and Justine had to explain further.

"Mr Preston, Billy?"

For a fleeting moment Jamie couldn't speak, he hadn't thought about the old man in weeks and now he felt incredibly guilty. Running from the room, there was only one person he wanted to see and he knew where to find her. Every lunchtime Steph made her way to the back door of the chippy and Helen would sneak out a bag of chips and if she was really lucky and she could wangle it, the odd bit of fish. It kept hunger at bay and stopped Helen's mum moaning that she had another mouth to feed. Sure enough, she was sitting on top of a low wall that separated the shop's front from the side alley which in turn lead to the back door. Jamie's face was red and tear stained and it only took one look for Steph to know that something was very, very wrong.

"You okay JJ?"

"My grandad died."

Jamie began to sob uncontrollably. He didn't care about looking like a cissy and Stephanie's heart went out to him. Placing her chips on top of the wall she jumped off and wrapped her arms tightly around him. Her fingers were greasy and smelled of vinegar but neither of them cared and it must have helped him, as eventually Jamie stopped crying and wiped the snot from his nose with the cuff of his jacket.

"Want some chips?"

Jamie declined so Steph picked up the bag and munched away as they walked in the direction of the park. That afternoon they shared their first innocent kiss and it kind of sealed them as a couple, at least as far as they were concerned. Luckily for Jamie, Justine Gamble wasn't as bad as he'd first thought and ten days later she came to collect him and take him to the funeral over in East Finchley. To say it was a sad affair was an understatement. Billy's funeral was paid for by the state and apart from Jamie and Justine, there were no other mourners. It was a simple service without any hymns or music and the only flowers were the solitary bunch that Jamie had taken along. Steph had bought them at the Spar shop for one ninety nine and he had been overwhelmed at her act of kindness. They weren't much but at least he didn't go empty handed. Even at his young age, to Jamie the coffin looked cheap and walking up to where it sat on two wooden trestles, he carefully placed the bunch of flowers on top, kissed his finger tips and then touched the wooden lid. While the service was conducted Jamie thought deeply about all that had happened in the last few months, he thought about losing his fantastic dad and how he was missing his mum far more than he'd realised. He wanted her to get better, wanted Billy and his dad back but that couldn't happen so he closed his eyes and prayed, prayed that his old mum would soon be well and he could at last go home.

# CHAPTER FIFTEEN

While on remand, George Conway had settled into prison life with relative ease but it was a different story once he was convicted. Now back in Belmarsh for the second time, he was placed on B Wing but luckily for George, he was instantly accepted by the many men with far harder reputations than his own. Immediately it was a struggle conforming to the harsh realities that came with being a convicted killer. On remand he had enjoyed unrestricted visits, luxuries being sent in by old friends and peers and even being able to wear his own clothes. On his return to Belmarsh as a convicted criminal he instantly had to follow a strict regime and things had changed so drastically that he now had moments in the early hours of the morning when he didn't think he would be able to cope anymore but those thoughts were, well quite frankly, something he'd rather die than dare to admit to another living soul. Luckily for him, his notoriety had preceded him and George was allocated a single cell. The size was still small just ten feet by eight but at least he wasn't in with two others like so many on the wing. The smells were disgusting and to be forced to use the toilet in front of your cellmates made his stomach churn. The constant noise would have worn him down as George was a solitary figure most of the time and as he'd walked past other cells on the landing he had heard the murmurings and conversations that there was no getting away from. He wouldn't find out for several weeks that he'd had someone looking out for him but that someone would quickly turn out to become his arch-rival.

In prison, fear usually follows crime but that wasn't the case for George, drugs or no drugs he wasn't scared of anyone and had actually made a mental decision to avoid anything offered to him so he could remain alert and have a clear mind at all times. Keeping his head down he didn't really engage in conversation and only watched from a distance until he was sure of the layout regarding who was who. This proved to be a wise decision as a week into his sentence George was invited to visit the cell of Gary Hardacre. As prison hierarchy went, Gary was at the top of the tree, or at least he was on B Wing and George had heard all about this man and what he was capable of if you foolishly didn't toe the line, or dared to cross him. A bit like George, Gary usually had minions to carry out his dirty work but unlike Gary, George had never been shy in that department if it was called for. This Gary bloke on the other hand could be different, might even abhor physical violence himself, George would just have to wait and see. Not having actually set eyes on him yet, George was intrigued but also somewhat apprehensive. Walking along the landing of the upper spur he was greeted by two burly blokes who had far more brawn than brains but he wasn't fazed, these were the kind of men that he'd personally hired on numerous occasions in the past. Knocking on the cell door which was slightly ajar, he heard the word 'enter' and taking a deep breath, stepped inside with more than a little trepidation. In size, the cell was a mirror image

of his own but that was where the similarities
stopped.  Fine linens covered the bed, a high tech
kettle and toaster sat on the shelf and the normally
basic hard chairs of which there were two, had
luxurious faux fur throws covering them and
sumptuous cushions that had been attached to the
seats and backs making them resemble armchairs.
Studying the man before him, George was shocked to
say the least.  Gary Hardacre was average in height,
extremely thin and resembled, to what George could
only describe, as having weasel like features.
"Welcome Mr Conway, do take a seat."
"George is fine thanks."
He waited for the informal offer of address to be
returned but none was forthcoming so doing as he
was told, George sat down and for a moment closed
his eyes as he almost sank into the overstuffed chair.
"Nice aren't they?  I do so hate having a bad back all
of the time.  Tea?"
Gary Hardacre spoke perfectly which surprised
George but there was also something creepy about
him.  The man would have looked far more at home
as a rule forty three nonce rather than the bank
manager type that he was so desperately trying to
portray.  A small time armed robber, Gary had
stepped up to the plate as soon as he'd been
incarcerated.  It was dog eat dog in prison so you
either tried to take charge or became just another
inmate, being scared witless for most of the time.
The men drank their tea in silence and as George
stared at his china cup and saucer he could feel
Gary's eyes boring right through him.  Placing his
cup onto the table, George's host then quietly

coughed before beginning to speak.

"How's your pad?"

"A shithole but at least I ain't havin' to share, which is a bonus I suppose."

"I'm glad I could be some assistance."

George momentarily looked on quizzically and then suddenly the penny dropped as to why he'd been given his own space. For a moment he wondered if he should say 'thanks' but something inside stopped him.

"So murder hey? Was it worth it, worth spending the rest of your life in this place?"

George felt like standing up and knocking seven bells out of the pathetic little rat but instead he nonchalantly smiled and slowly shook his head.

"Do I regret it? Yes and if I had my time over again, would I have done anything differently? Yes I would!"

Suddenly George leaned forward and his tone changed to one of menace.

"That's not to say that the cunt didn't deserve it! I should have left the snow alone and concentrated on my firm but we all make mistakes and I should have farmed the job out to someone else."

"Not me."

"Not you what?"

"I don't make mistakes George. First rule of business, think things through then think them through again. Envisage every possibility and you cover all bases. Now, I've invited you here today to have a chat about your role whilst in Belmarsh and in particular while you're on my wing."

With speed, Gary shot forward and his tone was even

**159**

more menacing than George's. As he slowly spoke he revealed almost needle like teeth that were both visually disturbing and childlike at the same time. "Don't even think of trying to fuck me over or you'll end up going out of here in a body bag."
With that he sat back in his chair, resumed his original position and then smiled sweetly.
"More tea?"
George was then informed, that for want of a better description, he was of such high profile as a businessman on the outside, he wouldn't be expected to carry out any menial duties. Gary saw that as demoralising and beneath a fellow criminal mastermind. George would have access to all and any luxuries available, all he had to do was keep his nose out of Gary running the wing and all would be well. There laid the first problem, George had been a boss for years, The Boss in fact and prison or no prison, he wasn't about to play second fiddle to the likes of Gary Hardacre. Time would be his friend, time to lure the creep into a false sense of security and then he would strike.

The months passed by slowly but George kept his head down, even taking a couple of short courses in English and IT but all the time and unbeknown to anyone, he was watching and learning how business was being carried out. Finally when he felt he had earned the trust of his nemesis he decided it was time to strike. George had been true to his word and waited, waited over two long years in fact until the day that he was alone in the shower block and Gary Hardacre stepped in beside him.

"Morning Mr Hardacre, would you like me to leave?" Gary eyed George up and down and although there had never been any whisper of the Wing King being gay, George quickly started to feel uncomfortable.

"You haven't got anything different to me so no, stay and enjoy your shower in peace."

Without a second thought George suddenly lunged forward, reached out and roughly grabbed Gary's head in an arm lock. Gary fought tooth and nail, twisting this way and that but before he had a chance to call for help, with his free hand George had sharply twisted Gary's head. The snapping sound was audible or at least George though he'd heard it. Releasing his hold, his victim fell limply to the floor and bending over George kicked him hard in the ribs before speaking out to the dead man.

"That's one possibility you didn't envisage, you cunt!"

The technique he'd used had been shown to George years earlier by an aging American marine he'd chatted to while on holiday in New York with Irina. It had occurred late one night in the hotel bar when both men, slightly the worse for drink, had begun to voice the lengths they had gone to regarding silencing their enemies. Not holding back, the marine shared a technique taught to him by the military for use when he'd served in Vietnam. Back then, time, speed and going unheard had been the main objective and it was a silent, deadly and very effective way to kill someone. Up until now George had never tried it but he was very pleased with the result and towelling himself down, nonchalantly walked from the shower block with a smug self-satisfied grin on his face.

As always, Tony T was standing guard outside and as he said 'good morning' to George, he had no inkling of what had just happened to his boss. Twenty minutes later and all hell broke loose, officers were running around like headless chickens and the entire wing went into instant lockdown. George just laid on his bed still with a smug self-satisfied grin on his face while the chaos went on around him. He didn't need to tell anyone what he'd done, the jungle drums in this place would already have circulated the news, now he just had to sit back and wait.

Less than twenty four hours of Gary Hardacre's demise George was the newly crowned King of the wing. Men like Tony T needed a leader and it was quickly decided that if someone had dared to top Gary, then it was only right that they should take over as boss. The soft furnishings were swiftly moved into George's cell and it wasn't rocket science for the guards to work out why. That said, they weren't about to tackle another nutter as there were enough in Belmarsh already and given the fact that the men would go wild without a leader, the staff were relieved that there had been someone ready to step up to the position. Unsurprisingly, the investigation into the murder met with a dead end as there was absolutely no proof and Tony T wouldn't talk no matter what he was threatened with.

George promptly settled into his new kingdom with ease and if the other inmates foolishly thought Gary Hardacre was a force to be reckoned with, he was a pussy cat when it came to being compared to the new wing ruler. All drug, cigarette and alcohol prices

were increased by twenty percent and any discipline became far more extreme and vicious. In the early days George was forced to carry out some of the acts himself, not because there were no willing men who surrounded him but purely down to the need to show just what he was capable of and to show that he didn't need his minders as his predecessor had. The first act carried out to show that he really wasn't a person to be challenged, came a few weeks after his promotion. Dale Crake had just begun a ten year stretch for armed robbery, at twenty two years of age it was his first experience of prison life and to say he was wet behind the ears was an understatement. Directed to George's cell he knocked and walked straight in which was a real taboo. Swaggering over to where the unofficial guv'nor sat in one of Gary's commandeered armchairs, he took a seat opposite.
"So, you the bloke I have to see about getting some blow?"
For several seconds George silently studied the young bloke and it didn't take him long to decide that Dale was far too cocky and could cause unwanted attention if he wasn't dealt with straight away. For all George knew, the bloke could be a grass as it was an unwritten rule that you never approached the guv'nor, a name he'd given himself, without being introduced by another time served inmate first.
"Sorry sonny, don't know who's told you that but I don't have anything to do with drugs. Now if you don't mind I need to finish this book, as it's rather good and far more interesting than talking to you."
Dale stood up in somewhat of a strop and as he left, irritably kicked out at the chair, one of George's few

prized possessions. A few seconds later, Tony T
knocked on the cell door and waited to be told to
enter.

"That twat give you any lip Guv?"

"Nothing I can't handle Tone but I think he needs to
be taught a lesson in fuckin' manners. A lesson none
of the others fucker's will forget in a hurry! Tell me
when he goes to the showers, or anywhere else where
he's alone and find out if the little cunt has palled up
with anyone yet?"

It soon became clear that Dale Crake was beginning
to piss a lot of people off. Before being sentenced,
his mates had warned him that he had to stand up for
himself from the off but Dale had taken the advice far
too literally and now he was beginning to see himself
as some kind of hard nut, never a good thing on a
wing of men, many of whom would never see the
light of day again.


Sunday afternoons were always quiet, the recreation
room was naturally full of laughter and generally
there was a good vibe as the men had not been forced
to work and were relaxed. Since George had taken
over the reigns there was far less trouble and fights,
which had been welcomed by the wing staff but it had
also mistakenly led the weekend shift to be off guard
and stupidly think that they too could relax. This
particular day saw a long line of eager inmates either
waiting to use the bank of telephones or sitting
around waiting for a turn on the pool table. When old
Charlie Stannard, known to all as 'Lightning' due to
his past ability to crack a safe in record time,
approached the table and picked up a cue he was

roughly pushed away.

"Fuck off old timer it's my turn."

A couple of men stood up and were about to challenge Dale but when he fronted them out and walked over to where they stood they quickly sat back down again.

"Any of you other fuckers want some!?"

Dale really was becoming despised by just about everyone and George knew he would be no loss to this happy wing, a wing that hung on George's every word and command.

"Here Luke, hold my cue while I take a piss!"

Luke Catton dutifully took hold of the cue but as Dale walked away, Luke just shrugged his shoulders, fearful that he would be seen as a friend of Dale's when in reality he didn't even know the geezer as they had only spoken a few times. George seemed to glide unnoticed along the corridor. In reality that wasn't actually the case as all eyes were on him whenever he was out of his cell but answering to anyone in authority who might ask, no one had seen him that day. Entering the toilet block George glanced all around and as Dale stood at the urinal whistling as he urinated he didn't hear the footsteps behind him. Again George favoured the technique shown to him by the American, it was so much simpler than using a weapon. Weapons could be messy, bad if you were found with one and there was also the risk that your victim wouldn't die straight away therefore giving them the opportunity to name you. As with Gary, Dale's body fell to the ground with relative ease and once again George silently made his way back to his cell. Officer Molton casually glanced out of the observation window as George passed by but as if he was invisible, the Officer didn't acknowledge him. It seemed as if George ruled even the staff these days and they were more than happy, on this wing at least, to turn a blind eye to any trouble, anything rather than upset the equilibrium but that blind eye couldn't possibly stretch to murder and George knew this.

Over the ensuing days an in-depth investigation got underway but after the mother of Dale Crake couldn't be placated by the Governor, she decided to go to the tabloids. Detectives from the Met were brought in but as expected, no one saw a thing and as for the guards on duty? They all had to confess to being in the wing office at the time watching Manchester United slaughter Arsenal on Keith Molton's mobile phone. Even when three officers were suspended indefinitely over their inability to carry out their duties, Keith Molton didn't mention that he had seen George on that fateful day. Keith had a wife and three kids, had lived in London all of his life and knew only too well that the animals who resided inside the walls of Belmarsh were still able to get to a person on the outside. For a time strict regimes were put in place that even George had no control over but eventually things settled down and when Muriel Crake accepted a payoff of an undisclosed sum from the Home Office, she refused to talk to the newspapers any further. The case was then indefinitely placed onto the back burner and everyone had to be on their best behaviour for a while before normal life on the inside could be resumed.

However, it didn't bother George that much, after all he had all the time in the world. Before long it was business as usual on B Wing and once again George Conway was king of all that he surveyed.

# CHAPTER SIXTEEN

Shortly after George Conway began his reign as the unofficial guv'nor of B Wing at Belmarsh Prison, Delbert Grant left New Start. It had been abrupt and upsetting as Jamie had come back one day to find all of his friend's belongings gone and the bed stripped down to the mattress. The only explanation given was that Delbert had returned home. To say Jamie was surprised was an understatement but at least he had Steph and for that he was grateful. Out of the blue Jamie then received a surprise visit from Justine Gamble. It was a month shy of his fourteenth birthday and he was about to go out and meet Steph when Steve called up the stairs that he had a visitor and should come straight down. He was now going to be late and he hated to keep her waiting, so as he descended the staircase his footsteps were a little heavier than usual as he tried to show his annoyance that his plans were being interrupted. . When Jamie entered the office he was surprised to see his social worker standing at the window and as she turned to face him she was grinning from ear to ear.

"Hello James! I am the bearer of good news for once. Seems your mum is feeling much better, she's been out of the unit for several months now and feels the time is right for you to go back home."

Jamie just stared at the woman in shock. It had been such a long time, that he'd come to accept that he would be here until they kicked him out. In all honesty he didn't want to go back to Islington, Maidstone and more importantly Newstart, was his home now. Instantly he began to panic, what about Steph? He wouldn't be able to see her anymore and in true overdramatic teenage style, knew that he just couldn't live without her.

"Well you could at least look happy about it?"

"Why?"

"Well the fact that I had to almost drag you here initially but now you don't seem to want to leave."

"That was nearly three years ago and a lot has changed. And you're right, I don't want to leave, why would I? I have friends here who care about me. Why on earth would I choose to return to a nutty mother over this place?"

"Ignore him, Justine it's just teenage hormones surging through his veins."

"Oh fuck off Steve!"

"James!!!"

"What!?"

"You shouldn't speak to Mr Moore like that, it's disrespectful."

Jamie and Steve both laughed at the same time and Steve knowingly shook his head.

"It's okay Justine, we have a relaxed policy here and the kids treat me like just another resident, albeit it one who feels positively ancient at times."

"Well personally I don't feel that it's very professional."

"Professional or not, it sure helps when one of them starts kicking off in the middle of the night or when they have a problem and it makes them feel more comfortable speaking to me. So Jamie, I know you don't want to go home but I think you should at least give it a try if only for your mother's sake?"

"Mother? My mother abandoned me!!"

"She was ill Jamie and frankly didn't have a lot of choice in the matter. A long time ago I worked in a secure unit and believe you me son, you don't go there willingly."

"Maybe she did and maybe she didn't Steve but I still think she had more choice than I had. I've been apart from her for so long now that I don't even know her anymore. When my dad got killed she wasn't the only one to suffer you know but she put herself first and didn't give a fuck about me. If it wasn't for Billy I would have starved but then you lot came along with your interfering ways and took me away from him, from Islington and everything I knew and now you want to upset the fuckin' apple cart once again. Well I ain't goin' and that's an end to it."

"You could at least give it a try James."

Jamie quickly spun on his heels to face the social worker and she could tell that he was full of anger and just wanted to lash out at someone.

"Give it a fuckin' try!? What like you said Delbert could give it a try when you wanted him to go back to his drunken old man?"

"That was several months ago and was a tragic, unfortunate accident James as well you know."

"Unfortunate accident!!?"

"You are a child and know nothing about the real intricacies of the case so I would advise you to keep quiet James."

"I do, I know that Delbert didn't want to go but you made him! Made him go and stay with a geezer who cared more about the bottle than his own son, a geezer who set light to the fuckin' house and my mate paid for that with his life and now you want to do the same to me!"

His words cut Justine like a knife. She had been the stand-in social worker on Delbert's case and had justifiably thought that the request would be good for the young man. Never in a million years had she imagined that the boy's father would set himself on fire and for Delbert to die of smoke inhalation. It had happened just over nine months ago and while lately the nightmares had begun to slightly subside, Justine was still struggling with it. Now it was once again in the fore and she knew she would have to mentally go through it all over again, each and every night in her dreams. Steve Moore walked over and sympathetically placed his hand on Jamie's shoulder. He wasn't being patronising at all, he really was concerned and Jamie knew that.

"We all miss Delbert mate but it was a terrible accident and you have to stop blaming people. Shit happens, it's part of life and we have to accept that Jamie. Now regarding your own circumstances, you ain't got much choice in the matter and your mum ain't got anyone else."

Jamie thought for a moment. At nearly fourteen he was well and truly in love with Stephanie and there was no denying that fact but when an image of his dad flashed before his eyes he knew he at least owed his mother some kind of loyalty. This was going to be one of the hardest decisions he'd ever made but make it he must.

"Okay, okay I'll go but not today. I need to say goodbye to someone and it's very, very important."

As he desperately looked in Justine Gamble's direction his eyes were pleading and she had the faintest idea that maybe, just maybe she knew what he was talking about. Teenagers fell in love at the drop of a hat and to them the feeling was strong and all-consuming. It would be downright cruel not to grant this last request and instead just drag him away from all he'd come to know.

"Alright James, I'll come back for you tomorrow afternoon but be ready to leave and don't let me down will you?"

Jamie shook his head and then ran from the room.

"I don't know Steve, kids of today seem to grow up way too fast!"

"I can't argue with that but go easy on him Justine, he really is one of the good ones."

Steph would be down the chippie with Helen and Jamie ran as fast as his legs would carry him.

Perched in her usual position on top of the low wall and eating a bag of chips, she beamed as he came around the corner.

"Hi ya!"

"I need to talk to you Steph, can we go over the park?"

"Why the hurry handsome?"

"Please!!!!"

He looked so serious and for some strange reason, she didn't really know why but she was suddenly scared of what she was about to hear.

Unlike their usual nonstop chatter, the walk to the park was taken in complete silence. Jamie was trying to think of the right words to tell her that he wouldn't be around anymore and Steph, well Steph didn't want him to speak, didn't want him to tell her whatever it was he needed to say. The couple sat on a bench for what seemed like an age before Jamie finally summoned up the courage to begin talking and all the time Steph was silently praying for him not to.

"I'm leaving."

"What!? What do you mean you're leaving? Where are you going!?"

"I have to go back to London. Mum's out of the hospital and she thinks it's time for me to be with her again."

"Be with her!? What about me, what about us!?" Jamie grabbed her hand and when Steph tried to pull away he held on tightly.

"Look! I don't like it any more than you do but for fucks sake Steph, I'm fourteen well almost, so what am I supposed to do?"

Stephanie began to cry and Jamie just couldn't bear to see it. Wrapping his arms tightly around her he pulled her close as he tenderly kissed the top of her head.

"Stay here with me, we can work it out, find some way to be together. I left it all behind and made my own way and I was a lot younger than you are now so why can't you do it?"

Jamie released his grip, he was getting angry now. His frustration at the situation was at boiling point and once again he felt utterly helpless, felt that he had no control over his own life just as he'd hadn't when they had made him leave Billy.

"You had Helen and luckily her old lady put a roof over your head, I won't have that luxury."

"Luxury!? You think sharing a tiny room in the home

**173**

of a brass is luxury!!!?"

"You know what I mean. Look, if we're meant to be together it will happen, if not, then we've had a great time. You could always get the bus over on a Saturday or I could come here. I will call you on your mobile every night, I promise. It won't be forever Steph but we have to try, don't we?"

Again Steph began to cry but eventually she saw that there really was no alternative. Jamie Wilson was her whole life and she wasn't about to let anyone or anything come between them. Walking back to the chip shop, the couple had a long lingering embrace before Jamie ran off in the direction of New Start. Blinded by tears, he had to stop once he was out of her view to wipe his eyes but by the time he arrived back at the home no one was aware that he'd been upset. The door to Steve Moore's office was open and Jamie walked straight in and plonked himself in one of the second-hand easy chairs that were always available when a resident needed to talk.

"All sorted?"

"I suppose so but I still ain't happy about it."

"I know but just give it a go, things are seldom as bad as we think they are. Now I've just had a call from Justine, unfortunately there's been a change of plan, a meeting or something that she can't get out of so the latest she can pick you up is twelve. Better start packing now so you're ready for the off tomorrow."

Jamie nodded his head and then standing up wearily made his way upstairs. Ever since Delbert's death he had been in the double-room all alone and when they'd been tight for space Steve had moved Delbert's bed into one of the other doubles. It had been a tight squeeze but he knew he had to give Jamie time alone to grieve. Now sitting alone on his bed, Jamie scanned the room as past memories of his time here flashed through his mind. He could see Delbert as clear as day climbing out of the window, see him lying on the floor flicking through his porn mags, hear them both laugh so hard at some ridiculous thing he'd said that they both had to hold their stomachs as the rolled on the bed in fits of giggles. He missed his friend terribly, missed having someone to confide in and even though Steph had taken over as his confidant, he really just wanted to talk to his old friend once again.

It was a restless night of tossing and turning and by the time dawn eventually broke Jamie was already up and washed and dressed. Skipping breakfast he decided to go for a walk. He really wanted to spend his last few hours here with Steph but to see her again so soon would just upset them both and he just couldn't bear to see her cry anymore. Jamie walked for what seemed like several hours, not really going anywhere in particular but just desperately wanting life to stand still. When the church clock chimed twelve he suddenly realised he'd lost all track of time and racing back to the home, found a rather pissed off Justine Gamble pacing up and down in Steve Moore's office.
"And about time too!"
"Sorry Justine really I am."
"That might be the case but now I'm going to be late for my meeting. Luckily for you Mr Moore is putting your things in my car as we speak. Well? Come on

then!"

Before getting into the Astra, Jamie said goodbye to the home manager but as he went to hold out his hand, Steve just laughed and embraced the young lad, who in all of his time at New Start, had been little to no trouble.

"Remember what I said Jamie, just go with the flow and give it a chance."

"I will and thanks Steve for all of your help."

"No thanks needed son but there is one thing you can do for me."

"What's that?"

"Live a good life, do something worth doing and be true to yourself."

Justine began to impatiently rev the engine and after rolling his eyes upwards yet again, Jamie climbed in beside her and the next chapter of his life was about to begin.

The drive back to London was strange, not because the conversation was limited but because he started to get anxiety about seeing his mother again. True it had only been just over three years but three years was a long time when you were a teenager and he wondered just how much she had changed. Entering the city, Jamie was surprised at how well he still remembered the place and familiar landmarks as they got ever closer to Islington. When they finally pulled up on White Lion Street Jamie didn't look up at the flat, didn't wonder if his mother was even home, all he could do was stare longingly at Billy Preston's window, wishing with all of his heart that the old man could still have been there.

# CHAPTER SEVENTEEN

Justine Gamble didn't get out of her car, instead she only craned her neck and looked out across the passenger side window. Right now, to her at least, Jamie appeared to what she could only describe as the loneliest looking boy in the entire world. He stood at the front door, head bowed low and with his bags lying discarded at his feet. Ringing the bell Jamie was apprehensive to say the least as he waited for his mother to answer and all the while he just stared at Billy Preston's front window. It had been a while since he'd thought about the old man and for that reason alone he felt really bad. The nets and curtains were new and he resented them, resented knowing that his old friend was no longer living there and he would never see Billy again nor hear one of the many stories about the old days. When Grace finally opened up she just stared at him in utter shock. She hadn't bargained on how much someone could change in three years, how tall they could get especially if they were a teenager and to Grace it was like her handsome Jimmy was looking straight back at her. For a fleeting moment she felt unnerved as all the emotions of her loss and heartbreak began to resurface once again. Touching the elastic band on her wrist she lifted and released the rubber. It was a technique she'd been taught in hospital and up until now had worked great, she just prayed that it wouldn't let her down now.

"Well just look at you! My, you ain't have shot up son, well don't just stand there on ceremony, come on in!"

Picking up his bags Jamie dutifully did as he was told and as soon as the front door closed behind him Justine drove off to her meeting. She wouldn't give the boy another thought unless things went terribly wrong as there were so many other desperate young souls that needed her help. For any future hope of sleep it didn't bode well to dwell on any one of them for too long, the only exception to that rule had been poor Delbert Grant and instantly she shook her head as she desperately tried to make the image of that innocent boy disappear.

"Well put your bags in your room JJ! I'll pop the kettle on and then we can have a cuppa and a nice chat."

Everything in the flat was just as he remembered it and peeking a look into the bathroom he noticed that even his dad's razor and shaving cream still sat upon the shelf. He didn't know if he expected the place to have been redecorated or maybe new furniture but he was kind of glad that everything was just as it had been, almost like the last three years had never happened. Jamie's bedroom hadn't changed either and he smiled when he saw the batman clock, which in itself brought back both good and bad memories. He wondered where Uncle Joe was now and then he remembered looking at the clock the morning after the funeral when that stinky bloke had stolen his mum's most prized possession.

"Whatever are you doing in there!?"

The sound of Grace's voice calling out from the front room suddenly brought him back to reality and Jamie placed his bags onto the bed, closed the door and then reluctantly headed in her direction. For the first few minutes they drank their tea in an awkward silence and then desperate to get back on track, Grace began to speak.

"I'm sorry son, sorry for what I put you through. I just didn't want to live without your dad, the pain and longing was unbearable, still is at times but I've learnt to handle it, well most of the time at least."

"It was my fault wasn't it? If I hadn't have told you about Uncle Danny dad would still be here wouldn't he?"

Grace leaned forward and took both of her son's hands in hers.

"It wasn't your fault darlin', the only one to blame in all of this is that bastard George Conway. I don't want to hear you ever talk like that again okay?"

Her words seemed to temporarily heal him, words he'd needed to hear for such a long time and now that he knew she wasn't blaming him then maybe they had a chance of building up their relationship again.

"What really happened Mum? No one has ever explained it to me properly."

Grace had been dreading this moment since it was agreed Jamie would return home. Now he'd actually asked her, she felt as if she couldn't cope with it, couldn't bear to relive it all again as it just felt too soon. Deep down Grace knew it would always, for her at least, be too soon.

"Not now darlin' let's just enjoy getting' to know each other again. I promise that one day we will have a chat about it all but just not now okay? So then, tell me all about the place you stayed at, did you meet any new friends, and were they nice to you?"

**179**

Jamie smiled and soon found himself revealing all about New Start, about how upset he was at having to leave Steph, he even told his mother about Delbert and what a shock his death had been. Grace was flabbergasted and instantly felt so much guilt that her son had experienced all of this in such a short space of time and so soon after losing his dad.

"I'm sorry JJ truly I am, I've been a shit mother and you didn't deserve it."

Jamie stood up and picked up the cups.

"No, you ain't been a shit mum, it's just life and shit happens and we have to deal with it the best way we can that's all. By the way, who lives downstairs now?"

"Black Marcia, she took over the place after Billy……"

Grace didn't finish the sentence when she saw the tears well up in her son's eyes. She hadn't been aware of just how close he'd been to the old man until Justine Gamble had paid her a visit and inadvertently revealed all.

"She's really kind Jamie and has been a good friend to me since I came back, I'll introduce you to her tomorrow if you like?"

The tea was replenished several times as Jamie and Grace continued to talk into the early hours. Finally when the sun began to rise and they had decided that they really should get some sleep Jamie approached the subject of Steph. He described her and all that she had been through in more detail and the fact that she made him so very happy.

"So you see mum, I'd really like it if she could come over at the weekend, she won't be any trouble and I'll

**180**

get a Saturday job or something so I can pay towards her food and stuff."

"My darlin', you might think you're all grownup but you ain't and working at your age is a definite no!  I had it tough growing up and I don't want the same for you, I want you to enjoy life and you'll have to work soon enough for a living without worrying about it now and besides, your wonderful dad left us set up financially.  I never knew but as soon as you was born he took out a healthy life insurance policy.  The flat is paid for so we don't have any worries on that score and if we're careful the money should last for a good while at least.  In answer to your question about your girlfriend, of course she can.  We'll give it a try and see how it goes okay?"

Jamie wrapped his arms around Grace and gave her a massive hug.  For merely a brief second she closed her eyes and imagined that it was her Jimmy holding her, she hadn't been embraced for such a long time and had forgotten just how good it felt.

The following Saturday having caught the first bus of the day, Stephanie arrived at the flat at a little after nine am.  Jamie had been up since the crack of dawn but Grace was still in bed and only woke when the door buzzer went off.  Scrambling out of bed she pulled on her dressing gown and ran to the bathroom. Staring in the mirror she studied the lines on her still relatively young face.  How the hell had it come to this, how had her life fallen apart so badly? Immediately she pulled at the band on her wrist, this wasn't about her, the last three years had been all about her but now it was Jamie's turn and she wasn't

**181**

going to spoil it for him. By the time Grace appeared in the front room Jamie had already made tea and the two youngsters were seated at the table and chatting away as if they were the only two people left alive on the planet. For a brief moment she stopped and just watched them, for teenagers they seemed so in tune with each other and Grace felt a stab in her heart as she recalled the same interaction she and Jimmy used to share.

"Well good morning to the pair of you!"

Noticing his mother, Jamie was out of his chair in an instant and she could immediately see that her boy was more nervous than she'd ever witnessed before. Grace immediately made her way straight over to Steph and held out her hand.

"You must be Stephanie? I've heard so much about you and it was all good I might add. Welcome to our little home and thank you for making my boy so happy."

Steph smiled, she'd heard so many bad things about Jamie's past and she couldn't deny that she'd been very apprehensive about meeting Jamie's mum, especially after he'd told her that his mum was in the nut house! That apprehension had instantly disappeared as soon as she realised just how nice the woman was but what really struck Steph was how young Grace looked. Somehow she had stupidly imagined an older woman and not someone who was barely into her thirties. Unaware that Grace was as nervous as she was, Steph gently held out her hand and smiled in such a friendly way that as Jamie watched the two women, he couldn't have felt any happier nor more content. He made an excuse and discreetly retreated to his bedroom for a few minutes so that the two could get a bit more acquainted but there was nothing slow about it, Grace went straight in, there was no point in beating about the bush.

"I expect he's told you that I've been in the looney bin?"

"Mrs Wilson it's fine, I ain't exactly got a past to be proud of and unlike mine, yours is a medical condition."

"Call me Grace and it's Miss or Ms as they say nowadays. Me and Jamie's dad never tied the knot. Maybe we would have one day but our time was cut short and ……."

Grace felt the familiar pain begin and twanged the elastic band several times.

"I used to use that method, it's good isn't it?"

"Yes I think it is Steph but I haven't been doing it for long so the jury's still out. So far it's been keeping my stress levels under control so that's something I suppose."

"Did Jamie tell you about my past, about my bastard of a stepfather and what he did to me?"

Grace had to tread carefully, she didn't want it to appear that Jamie had shared his girlfriend's inner most secrets in great detail so she was vague with her reply.

"A bit sweetheart but it's not important to me, all I care about is that you are learning to deal with it. We all have so much pain in this life and the one thing we mustn't do is let that pain consume us and make us bitter. Listen to me, I wish I could have taken my own advice but then again, I suppose if I hadn't have been carted off on that fateful day then you and my

**183**

boy would never have gotten together."

"I think everything happens for a reason Grace."

Deciding that he'd given them long enough, Jamie reappeared and was still grinning from ear to ear.

"Right ladies! What shall we do today?"

Grace smiled warmly, despite all that had happened, her son really had turned into a polite and respectful young man.

"It's such lovely weather, why don't we go for a walk in Hyde Park? My social worker took me there a couple of times when I came out of the unit and there's a fantastic little Italian café that we could have a coffee at?"

Jamie and Steph eagerly nodded their heads and within the hour Grace was on her second coffee as the couple went to have a look at the Serpentine Lake. She could tell that they were desperate to be on their own and she was more than happy to just sit and watch the world go by on a bright Saturday afternoon. The day was a roaring success, so much so that by the time they got back and had consumed a Chinese takeaway, a welcome home treat from Grace, it was past nine o'clock. Jamie kept glancing at the wall clock and was worried that Steph was going to struggle with her bus connections. The anxious look on his face didn't go unnoticed by his mum but he never in his wildest dreams thought she would come out with her next sentence.

"Why don't you stay the night love? We have a perfectly good sofa and it's really too late now for you to be setting off."

Jamie's heart filled with joy and so started the beginning of a weekly ritual, Steph would arrive on

Friday evening and stay until Monday morning. It kept Jamie happy and Grace got him all to herself for five days a week. He enrolled in school but to begin with it was hit and miss as he'd been out of regular education for such a long time. Grace never disciplined her son when he played truant, instead she tried to gently remind him of his early childhood and that included the importance of an education. Within six months he was attending every day and his teachers couldn't believe how fast he was catching up. However it was a different story when Grace attempted to get Steph to go to school and in the end she gave up. As long as the girl made Jamie happy that was all that mattered and when she overheard them talking one night and peered around the side of the doorframe, she found Steph with a textbook open on her lap and Jamie explaining all that he had be taught that week. If her learning had to come second-hand then so be it, nothing in life was ever simple and Grace was convinced that if her Jimmy was looking down on them, he would have been so very, very proud of how far they had all come.

# CHAPTER EIGHTEEN
## B Wing Belmarsh Prison 2005

George Conway had just turned fifty two and by prison standards he didn't want for anything and was living in the lap of luxury, well as much luxury as a person locked up could have. Now imprisoned at Her Majesty's pleasure for a little over six years, to him it might as well have been fifty as it felt like an eternity. He ruled the wing with an iron fist and low and behold anyone who dared to cross him and that included prison staff. During daylight hours his posse consisted of nine men, eight of who were split into two shifts. The first doormen of the day were Ron and Fred Morgan, brothers who were both serving sentences for different crimes, Jonno Maxwell an armed robber and Guy McKenna, in for murder but the exact details were unknown as the story changed each time he recounted it to anyone. At lunchtime the shift would swap over to Graham Ford, Alexsander Kowalski, a Polish National in on an eighteen stretch for armed robbery, Chris Stafford, a convicted arsonist and Bobby Jenson, a gangland assassin. Peter Sanderson was kept around for any job that needed seeing to as his stature was small and George saw that as a potential weakness when it came to protection. During the day George wasn't ever left alone so was never in a position to become a target should any other inmate have the idiotic notion of taking a pop at him. The only time George could truly relax was after lights out but that was when the demons truly came to life and it was the same for everyone else that was locked up. The dark hours gave a person time to reflect on their crimes and some of those crimes had been acts of such horrific violence, acts too terrible to speak of and even worse to actually be able to recall visually in their own minds. It also gave the men time to think of their wives, partners and children and all the precious years that they were missing and would never be able to get back. For George Conway it was slightly different as he didn't have anyone to miss and didn't regret a single thing he had done in his past, what it did give him was time to grow increasingly frustrated at his own situation. True he had the wing mostly at his disposal so was relatively free to come and go on the inside as he pleased but it was all becoming increasingly boring. He longed to have freedom, to go out to nice restaurants and have some female company, actually it was the female company that he missed most of all. There was an awful lot of homosexual activity in Belmarsh and even though George found the practice abhorrent, he was content to turn a blind eye to the after dark shenanigans but still, the sound of sexual grunting and groaning that could be heard coming from willing and sometimes not so willing participants, stirred him up and made him yearn for the silky soft skin of a woman. Graham Ford had been one of George's boys since the day George had taken over the crown of B Wing and he was a likeable bloke. He carried out orders without question and as far as George could tell, was a loyal subject who always had his King's back. Graham was in for street robbery, it was his eighth offence and his last crime had resulted in the death of a pensioner. It wasn't planned, well not in so far as anyone would die, he'd just been a bit too heavy handed which had resulted in the old lady being knocked to the ground where she'd hit her head badly. His barrister had argued fiercely that although he couldn't deny the fact that his client was a bad boy, in no way was he a cold blooded killer. The case concluded with a guilty verdict of manslaughter and a sentence of nine years, hence the reason he was now residing in Belmarsh. Graham was the epitome of tall dark and handsome, not to mention muscular due to the never ending round of bench presses he would carry out in his free time and those attributes were the main reason he had sought out George Conway and the safety that association could offer him. Graham was time served and his past experiences hadn't been good, especially on the sexual side. Now with George as his protector he could move about freely without the fear of harassment from the prison gays, many of whom weren't actually gay at all and were just men that needed to feel the closeness of another human being. Worse still, he could end up raped at the hands of some burly bloke who didn't care what kind of hole he shoved his rampant cock into so long as he got gratification.

As in many UK prisons, female officers were thin on the ground but B Wing luckily had two. Agnes Munro, a woman in her mid-forties and a no nonsense Scot who had migrated down from Glasgow some twenty or so years earlier. Agnes had never married as in her eyes she was married to the job and you couldn't have both, well not as far as Agnes was concerned. Alice Stapleton on the other hand was a young woman in her mid-twenties, petite in stature and who relatively new to the job, was still wet behind the ears. She was a romantic and unlike her colleague, didn't see the inmates as lost causes but more lost souls who just maybe might needed some gentle guidance. Agnes had tried to take the girl under her wing but it wasn't always easy when they were on different shifts and it was on one of those particular occasions when Alice had simply been trying to carry out her duties, albeit somewhat nervously, that she had first come into contact with Graham Ford. It was corny but when their eyes met it was love at first sight, well it had been for Alice, for Graham it was pure and simply utter lust. Always having been a hit with the ladies he went in slow and made sure his manners were on point and unexpected. Within a month the two were meeting up whenever possible for a few stolen moments, even if it meant only snatched minutes in the store cupboard or the walk-in fridge in the kitchen. By then Alice was head over heels and didn't care what risks she was taking as long as she could be with her 'Gray'. Graham kind of liked the name she had given him and being able to have a regular shag was like manna from heaven, even if he was beginning to feel that she was coming on a bit too strong. He knew that things couldn't carry on as they were for much longer, as sooner or later they would get caught but unlike his conquest, Graham had very little to lose. Pretty soon after the relationship had begun George was informed by Bobby Jensen, one of his most trusted men, about what was going on. It wasn't an act of betrayal as such but the guv'nor had to be told about anything that could possibly jeopardise his operation. George had kept the information to himself for a couple of weeks but when he did finally broach the subject Graham had immediately come clean and explained that on his part, it was nothing more than a quick fuck or a blowjob. Straightaway a plan formed in George's mind, he shared everything with his men, well most things and vice versa so why couldn't the young screw be included in that? He approached this with Graham who had no objections, so long as it was kept to just him and George, he didn't want all and sundry putting their dicks into her. Alright, it may not have been love but he still had some sort of feelings for the poor girl. Graham was then given the task of convincing Alice that if she really loved him, and of that he was in no doubt, then she would do this for him as it would make his life an awful lot easier. His request hadn't gone down well at all and to begin with she had flatly refused, naively telling Graham that if he was in fear of George Conway then she would probably be able to have him ghosted to another prison. Straightaway alarm bells rang out and thinking on his feet Graham hurriedly explained that must never, ever happen, George had feelers out in almost every nick in the country and Graham would be a dead man before George had even made his bunk up.

"Please Alice, please do this for me!!!?"

"I can't, if I get caught it's my job and before you say it, I know we make love and I take a chance but that's because I love you but George Conway? Sorry Gray but no!"

"Then I'm a dead man walking!"

Graham stormed off and Alice called after him, her voice pleading but he didn't go back, in fact he left her to mull over the issue for several days. Not making himself readily available when she gave him the wink made Alice start to panic that maybe he had gone off her. Finally when she couldn't stand it any longer she realised that she was going to have to do as he'd asked. Alice would have done anything for the man and would even have tried to break him out if he'd wanted. Many times she had dreamed of it, dreamed of them being together all of the time but even in her somewhat stupid naivety, Alice knew that wouldn't really have ever been possible.

The sex session was planned for the following night. Alice was on a night shift and it always went quiet just before ten o'clock which would give her the opportunity to, well she didn't know how to describe what she was about to do, not even to herself. Arriving at work she was gutted to learn that unfortunately Agnes Monroe was also on shift. It had been a last minute rota change as Derek Law had unfortunately called in sick. This would make slipping away a damned sight more difficult and Alice was about to cancel but was stopped when Graham handed her a small piece of paper. Wrapped inside were four small white tablets.

"I saw that bitch of a screw Monroe is on duty, slip these in their coffees, should knock them out for a good couple of hours."

"Where did you get these Gray?"

"Ask no questions sweetheart and all that!!!"

"Are they safe?"

"Of course they are you silly mare, it's only a few

benzos! For fucks sake, locked up or not, no one wants a couple of dead screws on their hands now do they?"

Something about the way he simply referred to her colleagues and particularly Agnes, as a screw, made her feel momentarily uncomfortable but when he tenderly kissed her on the lips the feeling passed just as quickly as it had arrived. After all, Gray loved her, of that she was in no doubt and she accepted that he wouldn't ask her to do the things he did unless they were absolutely necessary. Earlier that evening, George had been on his way back from the library when he'd spotted Agnes arrive and knew that he had to hatch a plan pretty quickly if he still wanted to get his leg over without the old trout walking in on them and doing her nut. Valium or vallies as they were commonly referred to inside, were in plentiful supply and one in a drink would go unnoticed and should do the trick without any problem. Alice was instructed that she should leave it until the wing was quiet, around nine thirty would be a good time and then drop the pills into a couple of mugs of hot chocolate.

With dinner over, the inmates lounged in the communal area chatting, reading magazines and playing pool but at just after nine they strangely began to drift off into their cells. To the staff on shift, this was unusual to say the least. It normally took an absolute age to get them all locked up, so for them to actually go willingly, had until now been unheard of. Finally, when only the sound of individual televisions could be heard Alice knew it was time to spring into action.

"I reckon it's all quiet for the night so I'll just go and do the final lockdown checks. Either of you fancy a drink after?"

Harry Granger was stuck into a movie on his laptop and grunted 'yes' but Agnes Monroe was so deeply engrossed in her crime novel that she only managed to shake her head. She was just coming to a thrilling moment in the book and didn't want to be disturbed. Alice started to panic, this was all now going tits up and she couldn't do anything to change it.

"Okay, just me and you it is then Harry and I stopped off on my way in to work and got some of those baby marshmallows as well."

Agnes momentarily lifted her head from her book.

"I've changed my mind hen, never could resist a wee marshmallow."

Alice smiled and then made her way to the staff room and within a few minutes had returned with three steaming mugs. As soon as she placed them onto the table Agnes lifted her head and a podgy little hand had reached across and grabbed the fullest mug, something Alice had the foresight to predict would happen and as she had placed far fewer of the sweet toppings onto her own drink, knew there was little chance that the older woman would take the wrong one. Slowly sipping the hot chocolate drink she watched her colleagues intently and twenty minutes later Harry was the first to place his mug onto the side and then without a word, he simply dropped off to sleep.

"Just look at that lazy old sod!"

Within seconds of the words leaving her mouth Agnes had yawned and then she too slowly closed her

**193**

eyes. When she began to snore softly, it was the sign Alice needed and she wasted no time. Making her way along the landing she opened up the door to George's cell and fearfully stepped inside. Not really knowing what to expect she was slightly surprised to see her would-be sex partner in his dressing gown and seated at a small table reading a book. George glanced up when she entered and smiled ever so slightly but didn't speak and as Alice walked over to him he stood up. There was no conversation he just went straight in for the kill. It wasn't like the old days when he'd had to wine and dine a woman to get into her knickers, no, this was pure animal lust and within seconds he had removed her trousers and knickers and lifted her up onto the table. Forcibly pushing her with his hand so that her back was slammed against the laminated top he suddenly moved downwards and began to explore her with his tongue. Alice grimaced for a few seconds, she was embarrassed and felt violated but as he began to work away licking and probing, she unwillingly started to get wet. This wasn't how it was supposed to be, she wasn't supposed to enjoy it but damn he knew his stuff and soon after she began to whimper in pleasure. With a swift motion he expertly flipped her onto her stomach and entered her from behind. It felt so good and George knew it wouldn't be long before he climaxed. The woman wasn't much to write home about in the looks department but she had a neat figure and a really tight pussy for someone of her age, which turned him on beyond belief. About to cum, he had just one last act that he had fantasized about performing, an act that had never been discussed with

Graham but one that George couldn't resist. Swiftly pulling out his penis he violently slammed it into her arse and at the same time roughly clamped his open palm over her mouth. Alice felt pain tear through her and even though she couldn't scream, the noise emitting from her mouth was one of pure agony. Finally George ejaculated and now satisfied, he withdrew, pulled the front of his dressing gown closed and arrogantly secured the belt. Alice was still sprawled across the small table, pain seared through her body and she was bleeding from her rectum but George only sat back down in one of his comfy custom chairs with a smug self-satisfied grin on his face. Well aware that she could easily cry rape he really didn't care, after all, what could they do to him, pile on another couple of years? Besides, if the silly little cow did decide to go down that route then she would have a hard time trying to explain what she was doing in his cell and why her colleagues had been drugged!

After a few minutes, Alice eventually managed to somehow stagger from the room, lock the door behind her and painfully make her way to the staff toilets where she slowly cleaned herself up. With tears still streaming down her face she very gently once again took her seat in the observation booth and due to the agony she was experiencing from her anus, desperately tried not to move around in her seat as she waited for Agnes and Harry to rouse from their slumbers. It took an age and was just under four hours before she was finally able to have a sensible, coherent conversation with Harry and a further twenty minutes more before Agnes was back in the

**195**

land of the living. Her colleagues realised that something had occurred and quickly cottoned on to the fact that they had been drugged but strangely no questions were asked. Whatever had happened on the wing that night would remain a total mystery as neither wanted to risk their pensions if they tried to explain that they had both taken their eye off of the ball.

As soon as she was able Alice signed off shift. She then went sick for the next ten weeks and then abruptly and without warning, suddenly left the prison service for good. Graham never got to see his fuck buddy again and he guessed that the guv'nor had hurt her in some depraved way but he was never brave enough to ask what had actually happened. For George the experience would be enough to see him through for a while but should another opportunity rear its head, he was in no doubt that he would take it. Fucking a female screw up the arse had made him feel power, real power and he couldn't wait to experience that feeling again. Rehabilitation was never going to be an option as far as George was concerned, for that a person had to have a change of heart, feel remorse and regret their crimes and George Conway regretted absolutely nothing!

# CHAPTER NINETEEN
## Islington, London

On Jamie's sixteenth birthday he had received the best possible present imaginable. Arriving home from school with the idea that he was going out for a meal with his mum, he threw his bag onto the hall floor and walking into the front room was pleasantly surprised to find Steph standing by the window. Dressed in her best black leggings and sparkling lace top Jamie didn't think she had ever looked more beautiful.

"What are you doing here!?"

"Well that's a nice greeting I must say! I can go if you like?"

Running over he took her in his arms and kissed her passionately, in recent weeks their relationship had escalated and they were now a proper couple in every sense of the word.

"Oh no you won't! It was just a bit of a shock that's all but a very nice shock all the same. Where's mum?"

"In the bath, I think she's making a bit of an extra effort as she wants tonight to be perfect for you. By the way, happy birthday baby."

There was a knock on the downstairs door and Jamie peered curiously out of the window.

"Shit! It's bleedin' Marcia!"

Steph walked over to the intercom and pressed the door release button.

"Don't be nasty Jamie, she probably only wants to wish you happy birthday."

Marcia Samuels came bursting into the flat and as much as she pissed Jamie off he couldn't help but like the woman. Marcia was as round as she was tall with enormous bosoms to match. Living in London for the last twenty five years, she still had a slight Jamaican twang to her voice, which would comically escalate whenever the mood took her.

"Happy birthday JJ!!!"

Marcia handed over a small, neatly wrapped package which Jamie dutifully opened. Usually his neighbour was crap at buying presents but this time he was pleasantly surprised with the neat silver identity bracelet.

"Thanks Marcia but you really shouldn't have spent your money."

"Get away wit'cha bwoy, ain't everyday ya is sixteen."

Just then Grace appeared and to Jamie she looked absolutely stunning. As a small boy he had always thought that his mum was the most beautiful woman in the world and that opinion, putting Steph aside of course, still stood. Before he had a chance to comment Marcia pipped him to the post as usual.

"Well just look at you girl!!! Still got it babe."

They all laughed at the compliment but Grace blushed at being the centre of attention, still, she remembered back to when her Jimmy had visually given her the once over and she felt a stabbing pain in her heart, it was so strong that she felt the urge to pluck at the elastic band on her wrist.

The evening was a resounding success, the three had enjoyed a meal at Frederick's. It was a much more upmarket restaurant than Grace and Jamie usually frequented and that was only on very rare occasions but Grace had decided to push the boat out and booking a table for six pm she was able to take advantage of the fixed price menu. They all chose the ham hock terrine, Grace then chose the pan seared salmon ratatouille while the youngsters both had steak and chips. The meal was topped off with cheesecake all round but aware that they had to vacate the table by seven thirty, Grace had eaten quickly and Jamie, never one to be outdone, kept up with his mum on every one of the three courses. To the amazement of the waiting staff, dinner was over by seven fifteen which gave Grace just enough time to give Jamie his present. Removing a small box from her handbag she pushed it across the table. He eyed her quizzically, the meal, as far as he was concerned was his gift and although they weren't exactly on the breadline, he was only tool aware that they had to watch the pennies and the bill for dining out was going to come to over a ton give or take, what with the drinks and a tip. Opening up the box his eyes met with a brand new door key which was attached to a diamante studded keyring bearing the name Steph. Grinning from ear to ear he quickly made his way around the table and hugged his mum tightly. Stephanie was already privy to the surprise and had spent the day discreetly moving her small amount of possessions over from Maidstone.

"I decided that now you're of age and given the fact that you are already sleeping together, don't give me that look JJ, it's obvious."

True, they had explored sext together for the first time

**199**

two months earlier. It was awkward and over quickly but it had cemented their relationship totally.

"Well, I thought it was about time Steph moved in properly. Now tonight I'm staying with Marcia so that your first official night will be special. You can have my room and tomorrow a new double bed is being delivered."

Jamie had tears in his eyes, this really had come totally out of the blue and when he recalled all that had happened in the last few years it was hard to believe that life had turned out so well for the three of them. Arriving back on White Lion Street, Steph used her new key to let them into the flat while Grace tapped on Marcia's door and waited for her friend to open up.

"So how did it go?"

"Smashing Mar, he was so surprised and…"

"Not the key you silly mare, I'm more interested in the grub, was it good, did ya get plenty?"

Grace began to laugh but the merriment was short lived.

"Fantastic actually and before you ask, no I didn't tell him. It would have been bad timing, not to mention the fact that it would have served no purpose and only ruined his birthday."

"You're goin' to have ta spill da beans soon beautiful."

Grace dropped down onto the sofa with a heavy heart, all the happiness of the last few hours had now left her and she would spend the remainder of the night unable to sleep and worrying about having a talk with her son. It was an unavoidable talk, which would undoubtedly break his heart all over again.

Marcia woke early and found her friend in the small kitchen leaning against the sink unit as she consumed her umpteenth mug of coffee.

"How'd ya sleep sugar?"

"I didn't! I've made a decision Mar, I'm goin' to wait until I have more definite news before I tell JJ. If it's really bad news then the longer I wait the better it will be for him and if it isn't then he doesn't need to know at all."

"Your call girl but for what it's worth I think ya makin' a mistake."

Grace indeed waited, she waited for eighteen long agonising months but after her last appointment she knew she had to finally come clean. She wanted to talk to Jamie alone so as tactfully as she could, asked Steph if she would pop to the shops and make herself scarce when Jamie got in from sixth form.

"I haven't done anything wrong have I Grace?"

"Don't be silly of course you ain't. I just need to break some news to JJ and I think he might get upset that's all."

Ten minutes before Jamie was due in Steph set off, she didn't go to the shops instead she made her way to Barnard Park. Sitting alone on a bench she reminisced about the first time she met Jamie in similar surroundings to these. Steph also wondered what it was that Grace wanted to talk to him about and hoped with all her heart that she wasn't going to tell him that it wasn't working out having his girlfriend as a house guest. Nothing was further from the truth, what Grace had to say was grave, about as grave as it got and it was also very personal.

"I'm home and what a shit day I've had, Mr Burnside had a go at me and………."

Jamie stopped talking when he saw his mother sitting on the sofa with tears in her eyes. Grace wasn't crying for herself, she had done that weeks ago, now she was crying for her son and all that he was going to have to deal with.

"What's up mum, where's Steph?"

"Don't panic sweetheart Steph is fine, she's just popped out for a bit to give me a chance to have a chat with you. Come and sit down."

Taking a seat beside her Jamie was intrigued, as long as Steph was okay then there couldn't be too much to worry about, could there? Grace took one of her son's hands and raising it to her lips gently kissed his fingertips.

"I have something to tell you and I'd appreciate you listening to everything before you start asking any questions okay?"

Jamie nodded his head but his face was pained as he waited for her to speak.

"I have breast cancer Jamie and its terminal, spread to my lymph nodes and it's now in my right lung as well. There isn't any treatment, well only high doses of chemo but that will only give me a few extra months."

"You've got to have it then!"

"Jamie darlin', please let me finish. I have already asked all of the questions and at best it would give me five or six more months but those months would consist of constant vomiting, total exhaustion, not to mention going bald."

To lighten the mood Grace attempted to laugh at her

last revelation.  It was a bad choice and Jamie could only stare at her open mouthed in disbelief.

"Look son, I want whatever time I have left to be fun, to spend it with you and Steph enjoying ourselves, not feeling so ill that I can't even get out of bed!  You need time for all of this to sink in sweetheart, so when Steph comes back I'm going to leave you two alone and pop down to Marcia's for a bit, okay?"

With his eyes full of tears Jamie just stared at her blankly.  Grace made a fresh cup of tea and just as she brought it back into the front room Steph walked in.  Looking at both of their faces she instantly knew that whatever had been discussed was bad but she didn't question either and taking a seat beside her boyfriend, could only hold his hand and stroke his back when he suddenly burst into tears.  Grace immediately left and when Marcia opened her front door Grace fell into her friend's arms sobbing.

"I take it dat ya finally come clean then?"

"Oh Mar!  You should have seen his handsome little face, so full of pain, so lost.  I don't care too much for myself but hasn't that boy of mine been through enough in his short life without having to deal with this shit!?  He's still just a kid, how on earth is he gonna cope!?"

Marcia lovingly led her friend by the hand into her own front room and they both took a seat at the small metal bistro table situated in front of the window.

"Kids are resilient love and ya boy is level headed.  Believe you me, he will cope, he has to and he's got a good woman who will stand by him and see him through the worst.  Did ya tell him you ain't havin' no treatment?"

Grace sighed deeply and then nodded.

"I bet that went down like a lead balloon?"

"We didn't really discuss it in any great depth, I told him about the side effects and that I had made my choice and I've left him to think about it all. Fuck me Mar, what a load of crap to dump on your own son?"

Grace Wilson somehow defied all the odds and lasted almost two years but finally her frail body couldn't take anymore. Steph had been fantastic and had nursed and carried out all of the personal care that Jamie couldn't, or that Grace didn't want him to do. Determined to die at home and not go onto a morphine driver until it was absolutely necessary was horrendous and they were forced to watch her doubled up in pain and gasping for breath. The day before she passed Grace asked Jamie to come to her room and close the door. Patting the bed beside her, he took a seat and gently held her hand.

"I need to tell you something before it's too late son and time is fast running out."

"Oh please don't talk like that we might….."

"Jamie!!!! Please, it will take all of my strength to get this out so don't interrupt. I need to tell you about how your dad died, what you decide to do with that information will be entirely up to you. Now, about six months after I lost my Jimmy and on one of the few occasions that I actually went out, I was down Chapel Street Market and who should I bump into? Your Uncle Joe no less and to say I gave him a right bollockin' for turnin' his back on us was an understatement. Anyway, to cut a long story short, he told me that my Jimmy had grassed my brother up and that was the reason Danny was killed. He then informed me that George Conway blew my Jimmy's brains out at point blank range. I knew he was shot but not having attended court I wasn't privy to the details and to be honest back then I didn't want to know. Seems that your dad, took the blame for telling me about Uncle Danny."

"But he didn't tell you mum, I did?"

"Well I know that! You dad knew that as well, he also knew your life would be in danger. George Conway would have wanted you silenced as you were a witness, so daddy took the blame although I don't think for one minute he ever expected to die."

"Oh mum, I always knew it was all my fault, I used to have nightmares about it when I was in care. Uncle Joe told me it wasn't but I knew he was lying."

"It wasn't your fault Jamie, it was Conway's fault and no one else's but what your dad did to Uncle Danny was a sin and we all paid for it in the long run, your dad paid for it with his life! I know it's heart breaking son but you asked when you first came home and I couldn't tell you but now I'm about to leave this mortal coil its only right that you know the truth."

"Dad didn't kill Uncle Danny though?"

"He might as well have because his words sealed your uncle's fate. I'm so tired now JJ."

Jamie lent over and tenderly kissed her forehead, "You get some rest now darlin' and I'll pop back a bit later okay?"

Grace smiled wearily and then slowly closed her eyes. There would be no more conversation and no need for the morphine pump as she passed away shortly after her boy left the room, she was just two months short of her thirty sixth birthday.

# CHAPTER TWENTY

In respect of attendance, Grace's funeral somewhat mirrored that of her husband's, with the only mourners being Jamie, Steph, Marcia and some unknown down and out who would, at the end of the service, introduce himself as Uncle Marcus. The stranger wore dirty clothes, his fingernails were filthy and to all it was obvious he was an addict of some kind. Marcus Wilson had however lived a life few could even comprehend and that life had robbed him of just about everything and that included his looks as he now appeared far older than his twenty nine years. This uncle wouldn't get the chance to go back to the flat after the ceremony even though he blatantly asked for a bed for a couple of nights. It had taken Jamie several minutes and even more glances before he eventually recognised the man as that thieving bastard who had stolen his mother's clock almost eight years earlier. Anger instantly built up inside and he took immense comfort in flatly refusing and even went on to explain why but Marcus Wilson really didn't give a toss. He didn't care about anything other than getting his next fix and had only attended in the hope of lining his pockets in some way. With a simple shrug he just casually staggered off down the road and Steph could only stand there open mouthed in shock.
"Who on earth was that!?"
"Believe it or not that was mum's brother the robbing bastard, probably came back to see what else he could nick from us."
Marcia had heard the conversation but not wanting to

add further flames to the fire, didn't add to the statement. Grace had, over time, already revealed all about her dysfunctional family and how devastated she had been after Jimmy's death when she'd discovered her treasured clock had been stolen. Some people did get a raw deal when it came down to families and she was just glad that even though most of hers were still back in Jamaica, she could swear hand on heart that none of them would ever treat any of their brethren in such a despicable way.

Grace's death hit Jamie hard and for well over a month after the funeral he would rarely get out of bed let alone attend sixth form. He hardly washed and picked at his meals which had been so lovingly prepared. He wasn't mean to Steph but nor was he loving and kind like he usually was and she was desperate to get her old Jamie back. When it all finally became too much, as a last resort she reluctantly sought out advice from Marcia. Steph liked Marcia but as she stood waiting for the door to the downstairs flat to open she looked nervously down at her hands and could see them visibly shaking. To Stephanie this was somehow being sneaky but she simply didn't have anyone else to turn too. As was the norm, Marcia opened the door full of gusto and with a broad smile on her face. Grieving herself, she had decided to leave the young couple alone for a while and hearing them move about upstairs she had known they were okay. Over the last couple of days she'd thought about paying a visit to the upstairs flat so when Steph unexpectedly knocked on her door Marcia was over the moon.

**208**

"Well hello there sugar, come on in!"

When they were seated at the table and drinking the hot sweet tea made with condensed milk that Marcia was famous for, well in her mind at least, she turned to the young woman.

"Nice ain't it? Back in Jamaica they use it mostly in cooking or mix it with rum but I've always preferred it like this. So little darlin', what's on your mind?"

"Oh Marcia, I really don't know where to begin."

"At the beginning is usually a good place honey."

"It's Jamie. I know he's lost his mum and I know how deeply he loved her but he's built this invisible wall around himself and no matter how hard I try I just can't break it down. Its tearing me apart and, and I'm so scared he's going to have a…."

"You're talkin' about a breakdown like the one my dear sweet Gracie had?"

Steph sadly nodded her head and at the same time struggled to hold onto the tears that were so desperately trying to escape. Marcia didn't speak for a while as she contemplated what to do. True the boy needed time to grieve but he mustn't be allowed too much time as he was likely to withdraw further and further into his own living hell.

"Leave it to me girl. Go out for a bit, make up some excuse if you have to and then drop your key in on the way out. Hopefully I can have a word and like the good Lord says, 'Make 'im see the light'.

Standing up Steph embraced Marcia and softly whispered 'thank you' into her ear. An hour later Marcia was heading up the stairs to her late friend's flat. Letting herself inside she called out but there was no answer so she made her way to Jamie's room,

tapped on the door but didn't wait to be invited in.
The room was in darkness so she briskly marched
over to the window and grabbing fabric in each hand,
swiftly drew back the curtains bathing the whole
room in bright sunshine. Jamie screwed his eyes
tightly shut.

"Oi!!! What did you do that for?"

Expecting it to be Steph, as he opened his eyes he was
more than a little surprised to see his neighbour
standing in front of him. Glancing down he inwardly
sighed with relief when he saw that at least his
modestly was covered and his morning boner wasn't
showing through the sheets. Marcia took a seat on
the side of the bed, sighed and then shook her head.

"Now what's all this about my little darlin', you can't
stay cooped up in this room forever. What about your
schooling, what about Steph?"

"Please Mar, just leave me alone will you?"

Jamie pulled the sheet over his head and then rolled
over so that he had his back towards her but it made
no difference.

"Not a chance sunshine and anyway, your old mum
would never forgive me if I did. I know you're
hurting babe but you have to get on with life and the
more you lay there the more you will want to stay.
Make your mum proud, take your exams and do
something with your life, you owe it to her memory."

Marcia's last sentence hit Jamie hard, yes he owed his
mother but not for the reasons his neighbour was
stating.

"You know it's my fault that my dad was killed?"

This was the last thing Marcia had expected to hear
when she'd let herself into the flat and for a moment

**210**

she was taken aback.

"No I didn't my darlin', you want to talk about it?
Sometimes a fresh pair of ears can help ease the
burden you know."

After mulling over her offer for a few seconds, Jamie
sat up in bed, pulled the covers tightly around his
waist and checked that his morning breath wasn't too
rancid. Then, just before he started to reveal all, he
swore her to secrecy.

"Are you really sure you want to share your secrets
with me my little darlin'?"

"I need to tell someone or I think I will go mad Mar.
Mum trusted you and I know deep down that so can I
but you must never breathe a word of it to anyone.
Promise me?"

"I promise, cross ma heart and hope ta die!"

Jamie then went on to explain what he had seen
regarding his Uncle Danny's murder and the fact that
he had revealed all to his mum who had in turn gone
to pay George Conway a visit.

"So you see if I'd have kept my mouth shut then dad
would still be alive."

"But you was just a kid Jamie."

"That might be so but I still should have known
better."

"I never knew this George bloke as he'd been banged
up for quite a while before I moved onto this manor.
Your mum mentioned him from time to time but not
in any great detail but I could tell she hated him. Her
face would change whenever she said his name out
loud and I'm glad I didn't meet him as he sounded
like a right nasty bastard and no mistake."

"Nasty bastard is an understatement Mar. Anyway,

George Conway went apeshit but rather than reveal that I had told mum about Uncle Danny, dad took the blame. Said he was sorry and that mum shouldn't have gone there. I think he expected a bit of a beating but that cunt Conway blew his brains out, held a gun to his head and totally blew his brains out. I never knew that but mum wanted to be honest before she left us so on her death bed she told me everything that had happened. I think deep down I always knew but chose to push it to the back of my mind."

"Why haven't you spoken to Steph about any of this sweetheart?"

"Because she might hate me and I can't take the risk, don't forget you've made a promise."

"I won't, nor will I break my word but the Good Lord doesn't like secrets and you should come clean."

The look of fear on Jamie's face was only too evident and she wished she could think of something that would ease his pain but there was nothing. He would just have to work through it himself and hopefully come out the other side unscathed. Marcia slowly puffed out her cheeks and exhaled, whatever had Grace been thinking? In this instance her friend should have kept her trap well and truly shut and saved all of this heartache, after all what good was it going to do? All it had achieved, was Jamie was beating himself up about something that had happened when he was still just a child and something he couldn't do anything about now.

"Well I'm normally all for honesty as you well know, sometimes to the degree where it gets me into trouble but in this case I honestly can't see how your mum sharing all that would've served any purpose. You can't seriously blame yourself for something you said when you was a little boy honey. After all, if your old daddy hadn't worked for a nutter none of that would have happened in the first place. You can cast the net wide as far as laying any blame for the tragedy that your family has gone through my little darlin' but I don't think you can lay the blame directly at any one person's door. "

She made perfect sense, he knew that but now something had started to burn within and there was a fire in his heart. He owed his mum alright, his dad too come to that and the only way he could get payback for them was to make George Conway suffer, but just how to do that was going to take some working out.

"Thanks Marcia you've really helped and I know what I have to do to make it all better now, well as much as I can."

Marcia kissed him lovingly on the cheek and headed towards the door. Her heart was heavy and she wasn't feeling good, this had all been way too simple and she didn't know why but something told her there was trouble brewing.

By the time Steph got back Jamie was up, dressed and it appeared that he was suddenly back to his old self. Embracing her he apologised and then explained all that Marcia had said regarding the fantastic future that lay ahead of him but he didn't reveal exactly what he had confided to their neighbour. Steph already knew most of his history but not the fact that he felt he was in some way to blame for his father's death and it was something Jamie would definitely rather keep from

**213**

her, for now at least.

"So what now, what are you going to do with your life?"

"I ain't got a clue but I know I have to study, study as if my life depended on it. I've got three months until I sit my A levels and I just hope that's long enough." Steph wrapped her arms around Jamie and hugged him tight, she didn't know what on earth Marcia had said but whatever it was, she owed that woman big style.

The next few weeks passed quickly and also very quietly as Steph gave Jamie all the peace and quiet he needed to study. When exam week finally arrived he was like a cat on a hot tin roof, not to mention short tempered and extremely snappy with her but she never said a word and took whatever he dished out with no complaint in the hope that it would all come right in the end. Steph had been going to bed early each night so that he had peace and could prepare and do last minute revision, she didn't know exactly what his plans were but he had made it clear that his future happiness depended on his results.

Three agonising months later those results finally came through. Jamie was down the school by eight that morning and was kept on tenterhooks until eleven when he was finally handed his manila envelope but he didn't open it straight away, instead he made his way over to Barnard Park. Taking a seat on the bench he'd used for as long as he could remember, the bench he'd sat on with his mum the day he'd revealed all about Uncle Danny and the day that would devastate all of their lives forever, Jamie stared up at the sky and desperately hoped his parents were somewhere up there looking down on him. Finally ripping open the envelope he scanned the paper, read and then re-read the lines hardly able to take in the words, five A's and one B saw him instantly grin from ear to ear. He hadn't actually needed any exam results to enter his chosen career, a career choice he hadn't yet shared with anyone least of all Steph but Jamie didn't want to just enter, he wanted to be fast-tracked and this was the first step to achieving that goal. Tonight they would celebrate, tonight he would raise a glass to his mum and dad and to getting payback for all that they had been made to suffer and it would then be full steam ahead to gain a degree. It was fingers crossed after he applied to The London Metropolitan University but he needn't have worried, his great A level results saw him offered a place immediately. Selecting to do criminology, which wasn't the shortest option available, he was realistic and knew he wouldn't achieve it until he was twenty three possibly even twenty four. In all honesty it was time he didn't want to waste studying but if he was to reach the top then it was necessary. With Steph still not earning and with his mum's money fast running out Jamie was able to secure a student loan which would at least ease the burden of the household bills. Was he happy? He wasn't really sure but the one thing he was sure of was the fact that he wasn't going to let anyone or anything stand in his way!

# CHAPTER TWENTY ONE
## Five years later

Jamie's first class degree certificate was now framed and proudly hanging in pride of place on the front room wall. As part of his course work he had studied old cases and the one he'd spent the most time on was the murder of James Kilham. He now knew as much as anyone about the mental state of George Conway on arrest and what the trial had revealed, he also found out that George could attempt to apply for parole in as little as six years so time was of the utmost essence.

The last few years had taken their toll on the couple, not to mention having been a long hard slog learning wise and Jamie knew he never could have achieved it without Steph's support. A while back they had both filled in forms to apply for passports but something had always cropped up and stopped them from travelling, namely Jamie's studying, so the applications had never seemed to make it as far as the postbox. Smiling from ear to ear, Jamie secretly popped the manila envelopes into the mail and then booked a week away on the Algarve. Stephanie was now working as a receptionist at Mr Singh's dental practice just off Chapel Street. It was close to home and paid the bills for which he was grateful but the holiday was paid for out of the last of his student grant, it was the least he could do. Stephanie shrieked with excitement when he handed her the tickets and a month later and after having collecting their passports from Eccleston Square, they set off on their first romantic break. It was the best of times and they both returned home tanned, relaxed and ready for the next chapter.

Jamie was totally committed to his dream career, though for different reasons than most and with his degree firmly tucked under his belt he now set about working on his fitness. He still had a little of the money Grace had left him, the remaining money from Big Jimmy's life insurance policy, so after carrying out plenty of research regarding what would be required of him he signed up at Islington Boxing Club. It wasn't too far away and he was able to get a tube from Angel station to Archway. A short walk saw him enter the club on Hazellville Road and pushing open the door for the first time he was immediately met with the smell of sweat but it wasn't too off putting. A tall, thickset man with full sleeve tattoos approached him carrying a clipboard and Jamie sensed he wasn't someone you'd want to piss off in a hurry, not if you wanted to keep your teeth. Barry Mason introduced himself as the manager of the club and when he smiled he revealed the most amazing set of white teeth. Barry was also tanned, so tanned in fact that you would think he'd just spent a month in the Caribbean instead of the twice weekly sessions he paid for over at Annie's Sunbed Emporium on Holloway Road. He proceeded to take some basic details such as address and medical history and then showed Jamie through to the gym. "So what is it you're hoping to achieve here Jamie?" "Good basic fitness really, you see I'm about to apply for the police force."

That wasn't true but Jamie wanted to keep his cards close to his chest and not reveal anything personal about himself.

"Thank fuck for that, so many of your age come in here wanting to be the next Tyson. Its soul destroying when I have to tell 'em it ain't never gonna happen."

Jamie laughed, he'd done his research and knew this particular club had a history with the Met having trained policeman, Mervyn Stevens who went on to win a World Police title at Light-Heavyweight and a European Police Crown at Heavyweight.

"Merv Stevens trained here didn't he?"

"You've done your homework well son and 'yes' is the answer. We also had Guy Williamson from the Transport Police. Guy was a cracking bloke who went on to win Super-Heavyweight titles in the 1984 Police Olympics and the 1985 World Police Championships. Not too bad an achievement for him or the club come to that."

There was now something of an instant bond between Jamie and Barry Mason, so much so that Barry personally took an interest in Jamie's training. He pushed the youngster hard but there was never a word of complaint, good going considering Jamie trained five days a week. Within six months his body was unrecognisable. His arms and legs were now heavily muscled and his six-pack was admired by many who had been training at the club for a considerably longer time than him. Deciding that he needed to work on his diction as sounding like an east end barrow boy wouldn't cut the mustard when he tried for promotion, he began to round off his words. Marcia and Steph took great pleasure in laughing at him even giving him the nick name of Lord Fauntleroy which he took in good humour.

It was now time to look for a position and after finding out as much as he could and the fact that he could apply to as many establishments as he wanted, he settled on two, Wormwood Scrubs and Wandsworth. His aim was to do well for three or four years and then hopefully transfer over to Belmarsh but it was all going to take a lot of planning and effort not to mention time and the latter was something he guessed he didn't have a lot of. There were two online tests to get through first, followed by an invite to the Assessment and Recruitment Centre or ARC for short. He passed the tests and then attended the ARC day where he underwent a medical and assessments in maths, English and overall fitness. Finally there was role play and then an interview. Jamie was over the moon when he was told at the end of the day that he had been successful, more than successful actually as he was also informed that there was an opportunity for graduates to work as prison officers but also gain leadership skills via a two-year accelerated leadership development programme and he would fit the bill perfectly. With his academic achievements he had been accepted by both Wandsworth and Wormwood Scrubs without question but had chosen to take a position at the Scrubs. For a start it was closer and easier to get to but there was something about the imposing iconic towers at the main gate that had for some time intrigued him. Initially it would only be for a week before he had to take up a residential course at Newbold Revel, a place quite a distance from London that was used by H M Prison Service as a training centre. The week at the Scrubs flew by and Jamie couldn't wait to get started on the next leg of his career.

Up with the larks, his bags had been packed the night before so there was little left to do but Jamie just couldn't settle. Steph was also awake and after showering she had made him tea and toast but apart from a quick swig of the tea the offerings went untouched.

"Nervous?"

"Nervous is an understatement I'm bleedin' shittin' myself."

"Why Jamie? You've worked so hard for this and I know it will be fine."

"Well I'm glad you do. If this goes tits up for some reason I will be gutted. Now are you sure you're gonna be okay here on your own?"

"It's going to, not gonna!"

Jamie laughed when he realised he had slipped back into his old way of speaking.

"Don't be a smart arse Steph, I know when I have to speak properly and when I can let my guard down. So, are you going to be alright!"

"For goodness sake stop worrying. It's only Monday to Friday, you will be home every weekend and if I get lonely or scared Marcia is always downstairs. What times your train?"

"Just after ten but I really don't want you to come to

**220**

the station babe, I need to do this on my own."
Steph didn't argue and a little after eleven that
morning Jamie had disembarked at Rugby train
station. He was about to search out a taxi when he
got chatting to a young bloke by the name of Steve
Davis, who'd heard all the jokes about his name too
many times in the past to find them in the least bit
amusing. Steve looked just as lost as Jamie was.
"Alright mate?"
"Not really, I'm here for a training course and I
haven't got a clue how to get to my destination."
"Where you heading?"
It soon became apparent that they were both en route
to the same place and they then seemed to
immediately hit it off. Sharing a cab for the twelve
minute journey to Stretton-under-Fosse the drive was
taken in nervous silence. True there was a load to
talk about but they were both too full of anxiety at the
thought of what awaited them to enter into any kind
of chitchat.

Newbold Revel is an 18th-century country house and
now used by HM Prison Service as a training college.
On entering Jamie was surprised at the grandeur but
somewhat disappointed that today's intake only
numbered sixteen, as far as he was concerned, less
heads equalled more chance of closer scrutiny? They
were then all taken to the grand hall for an induction
into the Prison Officer entry level training programme
or POELT for ease of mention. The induction was
kept short and to the point and then the trainees were
shown over to the main campus and allotted their
rooms in one of the four halls of residence. It was a

**221**

a comedown after the impressive main hall as the buildings were late eighties brick blocks and reminded Jamie of the many local authority housing stock back in London. Jamie and Steve were allocated rooms in the male only building of Keough House and Jamie was pleasantly surprised that he didn't have to share. The bedroom was basic but fully furnished and contained a bed, desk, bookshelf, a chest of drawers and a chair. The building might well have resembled one from an eastern bloc country but at least each room had its own en-suite. There was also a neat pile of bedlinen and towels on the bed, so neat in fact that in hindsight it should have been a sign of what was to come. The two young men settled in and then later met up in the small bar area for a drink or two and a get to know each other session. This soon became a daily occurrence to relieve stress when they experienced first-hand just how strict the regime at this place was. There was a daily drill which was almost military in style with absolutely no hands in pockets or if you did then you were quickly reprimanded. A few of the intake had made the transition over from the military so the discipline side wasn't a shock for them but that wasn't the case for Jamie or Steve Davis. Their uniforms had to be spot on and it was compulsory to be clean shaven or if you had a beard then it must be trimmed and neat. Socks were required to be black and there were no exceptions to this rule. They were checked daily with the command 'lift!' barked out as soon as they entered the classroom where they then all had to raise their trouser legs at the same time, which Jamie found strangely amusing but also a bit peculiar. Three meals a day were provided on site though the food was nothing to write home about but there was also a mini kitchen in each block so the trainees could make tea and coffee but on the first morning of his arrival he had found that almost all of the mugs were either chipped or had started to grow overcoats of mould. A mental note had been made to bring back his own cup after the first weekend leave.

The ten week course passed by in almost a blur and at the end Jamie didn't just pass, he excelled with such flying colours, the likes of which the staff at Newbold Revel had only seen a handful of times before. He'd outclassed the other students to such a degree that unbeknown to him his details had already been forwarded to the fast track department located at the Home Office. Before he knew it there were just twenty four hours until the passing out or graduate parade so meeting up with Steve for a quick pint the two began to discuss their placements.

"You already for tomorrow?"

"I suppose so Jamie but I'm having some serious doubts now as to whether the prison service is really for me. I mean, some of the stories we've heard about what goes on, well, it's a bit daunting to say the least. What about you?"

"It's just nerves pal. Me? I've never wanted anything so much in my life and I can't wait to get started. Anyway, I guess it's goodbye from here on in as I don't expect we'll get much of a chance to talk tomorrow and after the ceremony I'm straight off home. Good luck Steve and I hope Leeds turns out to be a good choice for you."

"Same to you my friend, although the Scrubs wouldn't have been my first choice but each to his own and all that."

"It's just a stopgap Steve, somewhere for me to cut my teeth but I'm going on to bigger and better things, you mark my words."

They both laughed before shaking hands, giving each other a brief awkward man hug and then going their separate ways. Jamie doubted that he'd ever see his training buddy again in the future and in all honesty keeping in touch wasn't really going to happen. Still, it had been nice to spend time with someone else while he'd been here and he guessed it had been the same for Steve Davis.

The Virgin Train departed from London to Rugby at three minutes past seven and Steph and Marcia made it on board by the skin of their teeth. Putting any major delays to one side, they should hopefully be there at a little before eight and as family and friends were allowed on campus at eight thirty in readiness for the nine am ceremony it should work out perfectly. If Jamie was nervous, Steph was ten times worse and Marci could tell just by looking at the young woman.

"I don't know why you're frettin' so much sugar, everythin' gonna be just fine."

Marcia then began to sing the Bob Marley classic which for a moment had Steph in fits of giggles.

"Don't worry about a thing, 'cause every little thing gonna be all right."

"I know it is Mar' but he's wanted this so badly and for so long now. I just wish Grace could be here to see him pass out, she would be so proud."

"Don't we all babe but she's here in spirit, I can feel her."

When Jamie had first revealed his wish to go to Newbold Revel and exactly what his chosen career was, it had caused Marci more than a little concern. She couldn't work out why he had suddenly made his mind up to go into the Prison Service, well at least that's what she told herself but deep down she knew differently, deep down she had already guessed the answer, he was out for revenge pure and simple. There was definitely trouble brewing but she hadn't got the heart to share her fears with Stephanie. That girl absolutely idolised Jamie and it would break her heart but Marcia sure as hell wasn't going to let it drop. The first chance she got she planned on having it out with him and find out what the bloody hell he was playing at.

# CHAPTER TWENTY TWO

Marcia was true to her word though and decided not to challenge Jamie on the day out in Rugby. Instead she waited until they were all safely back home in Islington and things had returned to some sort of normality. On Monday morning after seeing Steph leave for work she slipped out of her flat and rang the bell to her dearly departed friend's home.

"Yeah?"

"Jamie, it's Marcia, I need a quick word love."

Jamie had already looked into the monitor and seen who the visitor was but he had hoped to deal with anything she wanted over the speaker. Realising this unfortunately wasn't to be, he sighed heavily before reluctantly pressing the door release button. With any luck his neighbour wouldn't take too long, he liked Marcia well enough but sometimes she could be overbearing, not to mention outstay her welcome. Walking back into the kitchen he continued to prepare his breakfast but it was only a matter of seconds before he heard her footsteps and was then joined by his mum's best friend.

"Morning Mar', what can I do for you?"

"I have something on me mind sugar and no matter how hard I try it just won't go away."

"What might that be?"

"Why exactly did you choose to become a screw Jamie?"

Luckily Jamie had his back to her as he fried eggs on the stove top and she wasn't able to see the sudden alarmed expression on his face when she fired her first question.

"We are not screws thank you, the correct term is prison officer and to answer your question, I dunno really."

"Oh I think you do sweetheart, I think you know fine well! If I'm correct, you're going to try and get to that Conway bloke aren't you?"

"Oh leave it out Mar' of course I ain't, I ain't ever heard anything so daft in all my life!"

"Then why don't I believe you? You are playing with fire darlin' if you think you can get to him in prison. You may well do it but then what, what about Steph and all that you have together because that will all be over and you will end up being banged up as well and for what?"

Jamie slowly breathed in deeply, he was starting to get really irritated at being questioned and it caused him to snap. With the spatula still in his hand and dripping fat all over the floor he spun around on his heels and came out with a sentence that shocked her Christian values to the core.

"Justice, that's what for! I want that cunt to suffer, suffer in the worst way possible 'cause up to now he hasn't has he?"

Marcia walked over to the cooker and placing her fingers over Jamie's hand, gently removed the spatula as she guided him away from the cooker and over to a seat at the table.

"If your dear mum was here she would do her bleedin nut son!"

"But she ain't here Mar' is she? That's the problem. That bastard robbed me of my old man and in a way my mum as well. She wasn't ever the same after my

227

dad died and tell me what right, what fuckin' right
does that cunt have to continue walkin' this earth
after what he's done? Tell me that!?"
Marcia gently reached over from her chair and
switched off the gas before turning back to face
Jamie. She then took both of Jamie's hands in hers
and stared deeply into his handsome blue eyes.
Marcia hadn't realised how deeply he had been
hurting and still was as far as she was concerned. It
had been years since those terrible events and yet they
seemed more alive in him than ever.
"In Jamaica we believe in an eye for an eye sugar but
we also know that there's more than one way to skin
a cat."
"I really don't know what you're on about Mar' and
to be honest I have a lot to get through today so if you
don't mind......"
She didn't even let him finish his sentence, this was
far too important to allow him to brush off her
concerns and try and sweep this mess under the
carpet.
"If you are successful and kill this man and it's a big
'IF', then in my eyes Sugar you will be just as bad as
him. If you're hell-bent on seeing this through, then
there are many other things you can do to him if you
think about it and, I am in no way condoning any of
this by the way. I know you, and you could
accomplish great things in the Service honey, really
help people, so don't throw all that away please.
Think long and hard Jamie, you and Steph have your
whole lives ahead of you but if you persist with this
stupid, stupid idea, then it will all be over!"
Marcia lent over and gently kissed him on the cheek.

Standing up, she smiled and winked as she walked towards the door in the vain hope of lightening the mood a little. This wasn't good and Marcia had a really bad feeling in the pit of her stomach. She had hoped above hope that she was wrong but within just a few moments Jamie had admitted to his plan so easily but she couldn't for the life of her work out why he would even consider such a ridiculous thing. Still, she'd done all that she could and there was no way she would be able to stop him if he really was hell-bent on seeing it through. Revealing all to Steph wasn't an option as it wouldn't make any difference and would probably tear the couple apart, all she could do now was to pray for him and that she would do willingly and without question.

"You've got a brilliant head on those young shoulders babe, use it wisely instead of wasting it on some stupid notion of getting revenge!"

With that she was gone and so was Jamie's appetite. He spent the next half an hour or so thinking about all that she had said and finally came to the conclusion that yes, she was right. Why had he been so focused on finding a way to kill George Conway when he could have so much more fun making the bastard pay while still remaining within the law?

Situated on Du Cane Road, Wormwood Scrubs is a Category B Prison. Built of brick in eighteen seventy five it has over the years housed various notorious inmates including in the late seventies, convicted members of the IRA. There were many allegations of brutality but these weren't addressed until the early nineties when twenty seven officers were finally

suspended and it further resulted in six convictions.
Conditions improved for a while but by the time
Jamie walked through the iconic gates everything had
slipped backwards with heightened gang activity,
drugs, overcrowding and filthy conditions.

On his first day Jamie was filled with anxiety which
was only heightened further when he was informed
that he would be working on D Wing, an area
reserved for high risk prisoner requiring single cells
and which could house up to two hundred and forty
four men. The inmates were hardened criminals and
naively his mind had been so consumed with George
Conway, that he hadn't given much thought to how
the incarcerated men would view him as a rookie.
Luckily for him, he was taken under the wing of
Terry Branson. A strapping thickset man in his mid-
thirties, Terry had been in the service for well over
ten years and knew almost every trick in the book.
Jamie would be shadowing his mentor for at least a
week before he was finally allowed to operate alone
as a prison officer, so that made him feel a little better
at least.
"Right young Jamie, I want you to listen and take in
every single thing I say okay?"
"Yes Terry, understood."
Terry Branson eyed Jamie suspiciously for a few
moments trying to work out if the rookie was as good
as they had told him and was being sincere in his
reply or whether he was like so many who had come
before him and was feigning any real interest and was
actually being dismissive.
"See that bloke over there, the one with the scar

running down his cheek?"

Jamie scanned the recreation area and it didn't take more than a couple of seconds before his eyes feel upon one of the now most infamous and hated inmates in the scrubs.

"Layton Lewis, just started a four stretch for attempted rape."

Jamie raised his eyebrows but didn't show any real surprise until Terry's next sentence.

"On a ten year old boy?!!! That cunt shouldn't even be in this nick, he'd be Cat A if I had anything to do with it. He takes pleasure in revealing the horrific details of attacks he's carried out in the past but never been caught for, or at least none they've ever been able to pin on him. Spends most of his free time doing bench presses and the fucker is as strong as an ox. Obviously his preference is youngsters but in here the sick bastards can't be that fuckin' choosey, so never and I repeat never, get into a situation where you're alone with him, especially in his cell or anywhere that's out of camera shot or that we can't gain access to you quickly. Had a new recruit a few months back, went by the name of Damien and the silly little twat thought he knew the fuckin' lot. I had the same chat with him as I'm having with you now but sadly what I said went in one ear out the other."

"What happened?"

"That cunt over there raped the poor bastard. A couple of weeks after I'd warned him, he was takin' a piss in the shower block, which, by the way is totally out of bounds for officers, we have our own private facilities and well, let's just say young Damien's hope of a career in the prison service ended that day."

**231**

"What about Lewis, what happened to him?"

"He got twelve months added to his sentence, twelve fuckin' months I tell you and to that bastard it will be worth every fuckin' day as he lays in his bunk at night wanking off on thoughts of what he did to that poor bloke."

"I understand Terry and thanks for the heads up."

In general, the next few months passed by with little event. Oh he was teased a lot and sometimes made to look a complete fool by the inmates but he learned quickly and by the time his first year was over he was respected by his colleagues and looked upon as a bit of a hard bastard by the prisoners in his charge. Keeping up the level of fitness he'd gained at the boxing club was a must and would stand him in good stead less than a year later. Brian Bell, a young rookie and another newbie under the guidance of Terry Branson was starting his second week of placement. Unfortunately, Brian was a little too cocky for his own good and another who to his peril didn't take on board the warning advice given to him. On a rainy Tuesday afternoon, Jamie came on duty and noticed that the wing seemed to be short on officers. Where there were always at least three, maybe four visible bodies, there were only two and poking his head into the door of the central office he queried this with Keith Mahoney who today was in charge of CCTV observation.

"Afternoon Keith, who's on duty?"

Keith glanced up from his newspaper and momentarily stared at Jamie.

"Tom, Max, David and now you. Tom's taken some

files over to the Governor's office, Max is on escort duty for a bit and David's sorting out the mail."

"So who am I relieving then?"

"Oh I forgot about young Brian, he's just about to go off shift. Why?"

"Because he ain't about that's why!"

"What!?"

"Scan the monitors and I'll do a spur check. Now Keith!!!"

Reacting just as he'd been trained, Jamie sprinted along the landing and stopped outside the cell of Layton Lewis but it was empty. Panicking he scanned the area and he didn't know why but suddenly he had a gut feeling that this was going to turn out bad. If what he imagined could be happening, actually was happening, well he didn't even want to think about that. Jamie racked his brains trying to think of anywhere that was out of camera shot. Quickly moving along he stopped at the shower block and after unclipping his baton, quietly pushed on the door. As softly as he could, Jamie calmly stepped inside and immediately spotted Brian Bell, bound, gagged and lying face down on the wet floor. The poor man's trousers and underpants were around his knees and although he couldn't be sure, as far as Jamie could tell, no sexual assault had yet happened. Brian slowly turned his head and as soon as he saw his colleague and even though he was gagged, was about to try and call out for help but instantly stopped when Jamie lifted his hand, placed his index finger onto his lips and then shook his head from side to side. Jamie's instincts were on high alert and he noticed everything, even the constant echoing sound of a dripping tap as it splashed onto the tiles. A door to one of the cubicles was slightly closed and Jamie then heard its occupant begin to softly sing a Pointer Sisters song, as he released his bodily waste. "I'm so excited and I just can't hide it, I'm about to lose control and I tl hink I like it!"

Tiptoeing across the room Jamie stood to the left of the door so that he would be the first point of contact when the assailant, who he was now in no doubt was Layton Lewis, eventually emerged. There was a smell of fresh faeces in the air so obviously Lewis had needed to relieve himself before carrying out his planned attack and Jamie wrinkled his nose in disgust. The chain flushed and as the door opened and Layton took a step forwards, Jamie smashed his baton into the inmate's face. Instantly Layton fell to the ground and Jamie whacked the baton as hard as he could onto Layton's right wrist, there was an audible cracking sound and then screams of pain. It was severe but Jamie knew the assailant's strength and he wasn't about to take the chance of the bastard getting to his feet and overpowering him. It would be another six years before personal protection spray was used in prisons which would have made the situation so much easier to deal with but for now Jamie's actions would have to suffice. Pulling his handcuffs from the back of his belt he snapped the first ring onto Layton's damaged arm and then quickly secured the second to his left. With his broken wrist now in an unnatural position Layton began to scream out in agony but Jamie just smiled in his colleague's direction. Confident that it was now safe to proceed, he then ran over to Brian and gently removed the gag. It was evident that the officer was in deep shock and unable to speak as he could only stare across the room, his eyes open wide in panic. Lewis continued to scream and he was now calling Jamie all the names under the sun.

"You cunt!!!! I'm gonna get you for this and when I do you'll wish you'd never been fuckin' born!! Bastard, take these fuckin' cuffs off me now!!!! I swear to God I will split your arse in two you fuckin' low life scum you….."

The commotion was so loud that a couple of minutes later Tom Granger and David Steeple came bursting into the room. The scene that greeted them didn't need any explaining and the two officers ran straight over to an injured Lewis Layton. Tom sneered at the prisoner and at the same time kicked Layton as hard as he could in the ribs. Momentarily the screaming stopped as every last breath seemed to leave his body but within seconds the shouting and screaming began only this time it was directed at Officer Granger. The officers didn't bat an eyelid as they lifted him from the floor and then almost dragging the piece of shit, Layton was carted off to solitary. Brian was now standing although he was visibly shaken and Jamie gave him a moment to compose himself.

"Tell me when you feel okay to head off to the infirmary mate?"

Brian could only nod his head and when a moment later he suddenly realised just how close he had come to being raped and possibly even murdered, without any warning he bent over double and vomited up the entire contents of his stomach. Taking a few steps away from the offending pool of digested food his legs suddenly began to buckle but in a flash Jamie grabbed his colleague under the arms and propped him up as he steered Brian towards the door.

"I'm alright! Honest Jay I'm okay now."

"Listen pal, we have to walk along that spur as if you don't have a fuckin' care in the world mate because if those wankers get a whiff of what's just happened they will make your bleedin' life a misery."

It took a while but Brian eventually nodded his head giving Jamie the signal that he was ready to be accompanied to the infirmary to get checked over. Surprisingly Brian was able to give a written statement the same day, albeit scrawled and slightly muddled but he couldn't praise Officer Wilson enough for his selfless act of bravery. Consequently because of this, his kindness didn't go unrewarded and Jamie was soon presented with a silver medal by the Royal Humane Society for saving a life and while doing so putting his own life in danger. The governor was overjoyed for his staff to receive positive acclaim for a change and a few months later Jamie's bravery was further acknowledged when he was promoted to the rank of Senior Prison Officer. Sadly the same couldn't be said for Brian Bell, who after deciding to stay in the service, requested a desk job in the main reception area. His one and only physical interaction with a criminal had been enough to scar him for life and make him reach the decision that he would live a lot longer if he didn't have to have any real personal contact with the inmates. As protocol insists, the incident was reported to the police but as expected, the sentence Layton Lewis received was to run concurrently so no real punishment was handed down, apart from the six months spent in solitary on the Governor's orders. On his return to the wing it was blatantly obvious that he had a personal death wish against Jamie. Lewis continually mouthed off, telling anyone willing to listen that from now on the screw had better have eyes in the back of his head if he wanted to live another day.

By the time Jamie celebrated his twenty sixth birthday, he had received his second promotion and was now a Junior Grade Prison Governor. Unfortunately it wasn't as grand as it sounded and had just been renamed from the former title of Principal Prison Officer. The astonishing fact however, was up until this point it had been unheard of to award this rank to someone so young. Since the incident involving Layton and Brian Bell, Governor Staples had taken a much more personal interest in Jamie's career. He was sure this young officer was going on to far greater things and it would indeed be a feather in John Staples' cap to have played a significant part in all of that.

# CHAPTER TWENTY THREE
## 2018

Built on part of the former Royal Arsenal, Belmarsh Prison became operational in 1991 and was the first super-max prison in the UK. As an appointed category A prison it houses mainly violent long term convicts and in particular those involved in the breach of national security. With a bombproof underground tunnel linking it directly to Woolwich Crown Court, it was the only place Jamie Wilson had, since choosing his career aspired to work in.

That dream would somehow miraculously take him less than six years to achieve. After being put forward by Governor Staples for the Senior Leadership Scheme, a three year training programme designed for future Governors, Jamie found himself at the mere age of twenty nine, finally walking through the main gates of Belmarsh Prison. Knowing that the square footage of the place was large, even he had been somewhat surprised at the sheer enormity of the prison and its grounds. There was absolutely nothing whatsoever iconic in the building, nothing remotely inviting like there had been at the Scrubs, especially if you were into history. No, this place was cold, oppressive and left a person in no doubt regarding who was in control and it definitely wasn't the inmates. It had been a long hard slog to get here and at times, when he'd been burning the midnight oil as he trawled over countless text books and websites, not to mention that he was fast running out of time, he had wondered if it was all just a stupid pipe dream.

Okay, joining the service wasn't that difficult but on reflection, the reality of actually reaching his ultimate goal had been a near impossibility. Maybe someone up there was guiding him and had somehow paved the way for him to succeed.

As with all new employees, no matter what their position, Jamie had to attend an induction where he was given the short history of the prison by a clerical worker, a woman who took immense pride in her knowledge of the buildings and prison history in general but there was also a more basic, blunter briefing by a time served officer who didn't hold back any punches. As one of only two people starting this week and with the added fact that for some reason the second person hadn't turned up, Jamie had the session all to himself. After giving the absentee a ten minute delay in the hope that he would arrive, it was finally decided to continue without him, which Jamie couldn't have been more pleased about. It would give him an opportunity to ask any questions, possibly inappropriate ones, should he feel the need. Thinning grey hair and portly, Alan Carmichael introduced himself in a strict tone almost as if he were addressing a prisoner which inwardly made Jamie smile.
"Right, my name is Officer Alan Carmichael and you are?"
"James Wilson."
Alan raised his eyebrows slightly, he'd been informed about the new junior Governor's position but was surprised at how young the man actually was. Ever the professional, Alan shrugged his shoulders, smiled and continued.

"I've been in the service for a little shy of thirty years, obviously not all of that time spent here but I did join this happy band of brothers on the day of opening. You may have done your homework and already be aware of a lot I'm going to tell you but some you will not have been privy to. Belmarsh isn't like any other prison you may have worked in. It's the only prison that has a jail within a jail deep in the bowels of the building. Only the most hardened criminals survive here and as ten percent of them are category A and with one in five of them in for murder, which is a high percentage compared to other jails, it is often a very volatile place. We are categorised as the most dangerous prison in the UK and as such we have come under immense public and media scrutiny for the hard regime that we operate. In my opinion, the powers that be are soft and my answer to them would be 'come and work a few shifts and see if you still feel the same way about our practices'. We have the largest healthcare centre in any prison in the UK so there's no toing and froing to hospitals, which in turn reduces the chance of any outside influence. There has been the odd attempt at a breakout but it seldom happens and those who try wear yellow and blue uniforms so that they can be watched a little more closely. Do we have a problem with drugs? Yes we do as with all other prison establishments and currently our worst difficulty is with spice. Questions?"

Jamie liked this man, liked his openness and straight talking but most of all he liked the one on one, almost as if they were a couple of mates chatting and relaxed. Alan was now perched on the edge of one of

**240**

the tables and Jamie didn't know if it was because the officer was proud of his knowledge, was a bighead or just genuinely wanted to offer as much assistance as he could. He hoped it was the latter but either way it was an opportunity not to be missed.

"So what is the general view of the officers here?"

"You really expect me to answer that?"

"Yes I do, I can't try to make any improvements if I don't know the problems now can I?"

"Honestly, off the record?"

"Definitely, I can assure you."

"Here for the money pure and simple. Oh I suppose most, myself included, hoped to make a change when they initially joined the service but it doesn't take too long for that ambition to disappear. The men feel they lack support, the finger of blame is pointed too soon when things go wrong but praise for the months of peace and restraint are never recognised. When you meet Governor Parsons you'll understand what I'm talking about, the bloke is a blithering idiot. You're sure this is off the record?"

"One hundred percent Alan and thank you for your candour."

Alan inwardly laughed, his highflying ideas of prison reform would change soon enough, Belmarsh would leave its mark on this new recruit of that he was certain.

"So, getting back to this little talk. The inmates can be intimidating, scary even, so if you expect the worst, you won't be disappointed. Now I know what you're thinking, that you've been in the prison service for a while and you've seen it all but believe you me you haven't. As with other prisons it's a revolving

**241**

door, some inmates but that's rare I might add, will leave here and never return, for others it's a permanent home and they are the ones you have to watch all the bloody time. The sick fuckers actually like it here and will do anything they can to disrupt the system. For the ones that behave, they are allowed up to four hours a day outside of their cells, putting aside work duties. That spare time is mostly taken in the early evening but that is the time when you need to be on your guard."

"Yeah, it was the same at the Scrubs I went…."

Officer Carmichael never liked being interrupted, he also didn't like young upstarts coming to Belmarsh and telling him that they had already experienced a similar regime.

"No it was not! At Wormwood you have an eclectic mix of inmates, here they will put a shank into you or another inmate without a second thought. This place is a tensional tinderbox and never more so than when they socialise. Staff here all fight a constant battle to maintain control, so don't tell me it is the same at the fuckin' Scrubs or any other nick in England!"

Suddenly Alan remembered who he was talking to and realised he may have overstepped the mark but it hadn't bothered Jamie in the least, he was discreetly imagining George Conway fighting to survive in such a mad house.

"I'm sorry James, I think I may have spoken out of turn there, it's just that I care deeply about my fellow officers and all that they have to contend with."

"No apology necessary I can assure you. I would rather hear the cold hard facts, than someone trying to pussyfoot around an issue."

"Well, I think that's about it for now James, the rest you will have to find out for yourself. Before you go, a couple of words of warning, the officers here work hard and have experienced the kind of shit you can only imagine, as such they may resent you for a while what with you being so young and coming in at a high position. Treat them with the respect they deserve and they will all come around to you after a while."

"Thanks Alan and I realised when I was offered this post that I have to be strong to survive here or end up becoming a victim myself. I had a good working relationship at the Scrubs and I hope that will continue here at Belmarsh. I'm not one to ask people to do anything I'm not prepared to do myself but I'm also aware that you guys are on the frontline daily and that I do respect and am grateful for."

Alan Carmichael had warmed to the young man and as the two shook hands he just hoped that James Wilson was up to the job and not turn out to be another wet lettuce like the current governor.

As the new Duty Governor, Jamie settled in quickly. It was unusual to enter at such a high position as many first Head of Function placements entered as Head of Safer Custody and Equalities and then worked their way up but Jamie was different, his excellent exam results and attitude really had made a huge impression on the top honchos. In his first week there were naturally a few initial creases to iron out regarding officers much older than himself who were having difficulty carrying out orders given by someone so young but he was firm from the off and all in all it was a reasonably smooth transition. The Governor, a man in his early sixties and who went by the name of Graham Parsons, had seemed overly relieved on his initial meeting with Jamie.

"So glad to have you on board James, this place can be a nightmare and I have had the misfortune to run the entire set up single handed for some time. Your work will be mostly clerical to begin with as I've gotten slightly behind with the files regarding applications."

Governor Parsons then proceeded to place a box full of hard copy cases onto Jamie's desk before disappearing back into his own office. Most would have seen this as a daunting task but for Jamie it couldn't have been better. Since landing the job he had taken the decision to work with caution and not lay down the law in regards to seeking out access, even though not having any contact with George Conway was really eating away at him. Ever the optimist, after his first few weeks he had assumed that it was bound to happen eventually and he looked for any opportunity but none ever seemed to arise. It was an understatement to say he was depressed when he finally acknowledged that making Conway suffer could take years, years he didn't have as the bastard was only a couple of months away from applying for parole. Not one to be defeated, Jamie toiled away day after day without complaint but he couldn't deny that he gained some satisfaction when he began to notice the Governor's decline in ability not to mention his health. The poor old man looked absolutely worn out and this was further proven when exactly a month after starting the post Jamie had to step up to the plate when Governor Parsons went on indefinite sick leave.

Getting the call early one Monday when he hadn't been out of bed for long let alone gotten dressed, Jamie looked upwards, momentarily closed his eyes, inhaled deeply and mouthed the words 'thank you' as he slowly exhaled. Later that morning, Alan Carmichael had been the first to congratulate him on his new temporary position and didn't hold back in reminding Jamie that it would now be possible to make changes for the benefit of all the officers. Jamie had assured the man that without doubt this would happen but that he just needed a few weeks to settle into the role before he upset the proverbial applecart. The light hearted remark had caused laughter between the two and an understanding by Alan that maybe Jamie was actually one of the good guys and had been sent to shake up the establishment once and for all. God knows it was needed.

A week later Jamie received the news he'd only dreamed of, his boss's illness had been diagnosed as a complete mental breakdown and it had been decided by the powers above that it would be in everyone's best interests if Governor Parsons took early retirement. For the foreseeable future Jamie was expected to step up to the post of Governor, giving him total control of the whole damn prison, hearing the news he was on cloud nine.. The powers that be went on to inform him that it would probably be for quite some time before a replacement could be found and though he feigned disappointment, he was actually jumping for joy. Everything had gone well for just over three months so when Jamie received an email asking him to attend a meeting in the City the next day, he feared the worst. Clive House in Westminster was the head office for the Prison Services and very few employees actually got the chance to visit, what had he done wrong? It wasn't normal practice and he started to worry that he had been replaced but if that was the case then why call him in? That evening he repeatedly snapped at Steph though he wouldn't tell her what was wrong. Dinner wasn't to his liking, the programme on telly was shit, in fact he continually moaned at her for everything. Finally, when she couldn't stand it any longer she slammed the front door and headed down to Marcia's.

"Hello Sugar! Come on in."

It wasn't rocket science to realise that something was obviously bothering the young girl and Marcia hated it went people were bothered or upset.

"Why the long face, what's happened?"

"Oh I don't know Mar' but Jamie's been unbearable ever since he came home. He's continually snapped at me for the smallest thing and it's so unlike him. I think it's trouble at work but he won't, or can't, confide in me."

Alarm bells started to ring in Marcia's head, as much as Jamie couldn't share his concerns neither could she and she just prayed that it was for different reasons.

"Don't worry sweetheart, men can be right pigs at times, Lord knows I've had my fair share of them, why do ya think I ain't got a man now? In my opinion they are more trouble than they're worth, I mean, they are only any good for one thing!"

Steph began to laugh, her neighbour couldn't always

sort out Steph's problems but she always had a way of making them seem less important.

The following day Jamie went into work as usual but remained holed up in his office until it was time to leave for the meeting. Traffic was always heavy at this time of day so he had allowed himself just over an hour to get there and he at last pulled his scooter up in the rear carpark of Clive House at two fifty one. Removing his helmet he checked his appearance in the wing mirror and after straightening his tie, headed inside where he was met by Karen Sewell, deputy to the CEO of H.M Prison Services. Jamie hadn't expected to see anyone from the top so when Karen introduced herself he was momentarily stuck for words. In her mid-fifties, Karen Sewell was still a good looking woman, her dress was classy and her hair and makeup were faultless.

"Good afternoon Mr Wilson, it's a pleasure to finally meet you. Please come through to the Assembly Room where I have laid on afternoon tea."

The sentence relaxed him, they wouldn't feed him if he was going to get the axe would they? A vast mahogany table filled the room and a small area at one end had been set for tea with fine china cups and a cake stand of various sandwiches and fondant fancies.

"I do enjoy this but unless I have a reason it's difficult to claim for it on expenses. Do take a seat Mr Wilson."

"Please call me James."

Karen poured them both tea and then turned to Jamie, her face now serious and official looking.

"I've invited you here today to discuss your rather premature appointment as Temporary Governor. It was discussed fully and at length before you were offered the position and while we are in no doubt that you will do an excellent job, I felt it wasn't fair to just expect you to get on with things without the option to decline our offer. I realise that you were employed as a deputy but taking control of Belmarsh at such a young age, so young in fact that it has never been heard of before, is a big ask for anyone. We did look into a temporary replacement but as you had come so highly recommended, we would like you to take on the role permanently. How do you feel about that?"

If it hadn't have been inappropriate Jamie would have jumped up and kissed the woman. Instead, he maintained his composure, smiled and nodded.

"I would like that very much and I can assure you that I will do my utmost to bring Belmarsh back up to the Inspectorate's Standard."

"That's just what I wanted to hear and I am in no doubt that you will but it's not entirely one-sided. Placing someone so young, into a position of power in the most dangerous prison in England, comes with much responsibility. Should it go wrong then the walls will fall in for the Secretary of State and the Prison Services as a whole. If, on the other hand it goes well, then it will well and truly be a feather in our cap."

"I promise I will not let you down and thank you so much for giving me this opportunity."

On the journey home Jamie ran over the meeting again and again in his head, this would put him on the map, they could get a car, move to a bigger house and Steph could give up work and…suddenly he stopped…… what was he doing?  This had only ever been for one reason and now he was putting the job above all else, he needed to get his mind back on track and focus on his end goal, if he didn't then in his head at least, his mum and dad had died for nothing.

# CHAPTER TWENTY FOUR

George was impatiently awaiting feedback on his parole application. It had been two weeks since it had been filed and as yet there was no news but unbeknown to him, the replacement Governor had moved it to the back of the pile and as yet it hadn't even been read. Stressed and anxious at not having heard anything, he was like a tinderbox waiting to ignite and those around him felt like they were continually walking on eggshells. A new Governor added to the mix wasn't helping matters as George was yet to meet the prick and was well aware that there would probably be a shakeup which in turn could hamper his operations. As usual Chris Stafford and Alexsander Kowalski were dutifully standing guard outside the cell and when Peter Milligan approached and slowly shook his head they both sighed heavily. This wasn't going to be good, whatever news Pete was about to share, he looked as if he was shitting himself already. George had a habit of lashing out at the messenger first so none of them liked being sent on errands. This time Peter had drawn the short straw and had been dispatched to find Charlie Stannard. The old boy was harmless enough but he was a gossip which was never a good thing to be when you were banged up. Charlie had been in most of the prisons in England during his seventy three years on the planet and every one of his sentences had been for safe cracking. On a scale of one to ten his career had been a ten, well financially at least, the only trouble was he always seemed to get caught so the proceeds he'd stashed away never got spent. Pete tapped on the door but didn't go in until he heard the magic word.

"Enter!"

"Alright Guv?"

"Alright? 'Course I'm fuckin' alright you twat, now what did that silly old cunt have to say?"

"Reckons he was only larkin' about."

"Larkin' a fuckin' bout? He made me look like a fuckin' nonce and I ain't havin' it, get him in here now!"

Peter Sanderson knew better than to argue and immediately shot out of the cell in search of Charlie Stannard. He found the old boy hiding in the toilets, Charlie knew he'd overstepped the mark and was now literally shitting himself. George was well known for his violence but all Charlie had done was call George an old queen and refer to his men as the 'Back Door Bandits'. It had brought about a round of applause in the social area even though the term hadn't exactly been his own as it was something he'd heard second-hand in the library. He hadn't been able to see who actually said it because they were huddled in the next aisle of books and now he was going to pay the price for eavesdropping but as far as he could see he hadn't really done anything wrong.

"There you are you old twat, come on, the Guv' wants to see you."

"Bit busy at the minute Pete, I've got the trots and I daren't venture far away from here, believe you me, when you get old anythin' sets your bowels off."

"Trots my arse! You'll have more to worry about that shittin' your pants if you don't come with me. You know he don't like to be kept waitin'."

Pete felt genuine sorrow for the old boy when he noticed tears begin to form in the wrinkled, worn-out eyes, eyes that had seen far more than Pete would ever know but still, an order was an order at the end of the day and defying George Conway wasn't an option for either of them.

"What's he gonna do to me Pete, he ain't gonna hurt me is he?"

Peter didn't know for sure but if he was a gambling man, then all bets would be on it. Of course he couldn't tell Charlie that or there would be no way he would get the old man to the Guv's cell.

"I doubt it Charlie but fuck me mate! You really need to learn to keep your trap shut in future."

"I know, I know, well if I ain't getting' a slap then whatever he's got to say to me, best we get it over with."

Knocking on the cell door, Peter Sanderson was almost as nervous as Charlie, he wasn't worried so much about the old man but more about himself. He didn't like George, hated him in fact but in a place like this it was definitely a case of better the devil you know.

"Enter!"

Pete walked in with old Charlie shuffling in behind him. True the old sod was getting on in years but even Pete had to smile when he saw how thick Charlie was laying it on. George didn't bat an eyelid and instead stood up, walked over to his visitor and with one hand nipped Charlie's cheeks so hard that his mouth was forced open. In his right hand George swiftly produced a pair of pliers that had been stolen

from the metal department several months earlier.
Ramming them inside Charlie's mouth, he grabbed
the old man's tongue and pulled it forward. Charlie
Stannard made a pitiful noise, it wasn't a scream, he
wasn't able to but it was full of agony all the same.
Charlie rapidly lifted both of his hands and grabbing
George's wrists, hung on for dear life but he was too
frightened to pull on his attacker's arms.
"Right you old cunt! If I ever hear that you've been
calling me a nonce again I won't just nip that
offendin' fuckin' tongue, I'll rip the bastard out. Do
you understand me!!!?"
Charlie did his best to nod his head but it was
virtually impossible as each movement forced the
pliers to rip into his tongue. With that George
released the pliers and Charlie fell backwards landing
on the floor with a thud. Blood was flowing from his
mouth as tears streamed down his cheeks.
"Get that cunt out of here before I do him some real
damage. Well! What the fuck are you waiting for!?"
Struggling, Pete lifted Charlie under the arms until he
was kind of upright and as the old boy wobbled on his
feet Pete guided him out onto the landing.
"From now on keep your bleedin' trap shut you
stupid old fool."
Charlie stumbled along the spur and knew by the
amount of blood that he would need to go to the
medical centre. All the while, Agnes Monroe had
been witness to him going in and then coming out of
George's cell. As she approached Charlie she knew
better than to ask any questions.
"Come on mate, let's go and get you sorted."
Charlie was stooped over as he accepted the officer's

arm, this was all so wrong but he couldn't tell her and he wasn't surprised when she didn't ask what had happened. B Wing had its own rules, different to the others in the prison and right at this moment, Charlie wished he was on any other wing rather than be here. There wasn't too much that the medical unit could do for him and Doctor Spacey could only imagine what must have happened and how painful Charlie's mouth must be. Fearing that whatever appliance had been used wasn't clean, he showed Charlie to a bed and administered antibiotics via a drip. The poor bloke was just too old to take any chances and if septicaemia set in then Charlie's chances of recovery could be lessened due to his age and the ability to fight off an infection. The incident wasn't reported but it was mentioned to Jamie the following afternoon. Wanting to keep her on side, Jamie often invited Agnes to his office for afternoon tea and in passing she had revealed Charlie Stannard's plight. "Everyone knows it was Conway but the poor old boy is so frightened he won't make a complaint."
"Leave it with me Agnes, I think an overdue visit to the infirmary is called for."
Later that day and just as he'd said, Jamie entered the state of the art facility to discreetly seek out Charlie Stannard. To begin with he wouldn't speak to the Governor but when Jamie explained that he already knew who the culprit was and that he wanted to help Charlie, the old man couldn't talk quickly enough. Charlie explained that he'd made a comment in the recreation area and that George had got to hear about it.
"See Mr Conway can't stand benders Governor.

That's why he got so mad with me but honest to God, I was only kiddin' around."

Jamie nodded his head sagely. This was all extra information on his nemesis and though he wasn't exactly sure how useful it would be, he would stash it away in his memory on the off chance that he might need it at a later date.

Two days later and with still no news on the parole application, Bobby Jenson burst into George Conway's cell forcing George to immediately stop mid-sentence. The glare Tommy received instantly sent a shiver down his spine. George was in the middle of a meeting with Tommy Hinchcliffe via mobile phone. Tommy was top dog on D Wing and the two were agreeing new charging levels on tobacco. Sadly, price monopoly goes on even in prison.

"Sorry Guv but I've just come from reception, well I was down there cleaning as it goes and a couple of the screws were chatting away and well, you'll never guess who they are plannin' on bringin' in?"

In his excitement Bobby had forgotten that he hadn't knocked and now he was asking the boss a stupid question, George wondered if the twat was on some kind of death wish. Closing his eyes he sighed heavily before laying the phone down onto the table. Bobby was still eagerly awaiting a response when he suddenly remembered what he had and more to the point, hadn't done.

"Oh my God! I'm sorry Mr Conway I never knocked did I?"

"No you fuckin' didn't! I've had to cut my meeting

short so this had better be good you cunt?"
"It is, probably the reason I forgot me manners.
Grayson Vickers is coming in and I heard the
reception screw say he was coming onto B Wing."
George briefly tried to recall the name and it didn't
take more than a few seconds before it came to him.
"The kiddie fiddler? Why ain't he going on Rule
43?"
"They reckon it's 'cause he's still sayin' he's
innocent and wants an appeal."
"Fuckin' innocent!? They caught the cunt red handed
with his dick in a little kids arse for Christ sake! Find
out what spur he's going on and then report back
here, don't tell anyone what you're doin', do you
understand me?"

Grayson Vickers was a notorious paedophile who had
already served a seventeen year prison stretch for the
abduction and rape of a fifteen year old girl. In their
infinite wisdom, the powers that be had seen fit to
release him as a reformed prisoner who in their eyes
was unlikely to reoffend. Less than a year later he
had stalked Andrew Reeve, a twelve year old boy
who had innocently taken a short cut on his way to
school. The area was densely wooded and Grayson
had hunted the boy down like prey. Running for his
life and finally exhausted and scared, Andrew had
stopped and confronted Grayson. It was like a lamb
to the slaughter and within seconds he had been
forced over the trunk of a toppled birch tree. Andrew
desperately screamed for help, begged for mercy but
none was shown and with expert ease the boys
trousers were pulled down and he was being violently

raped. As far as Grayson was concerned his victim's fate was sealed as there was no way he could be allowed to live but Grayson hadn't bargained on a couple of early morning dog walkers who had innocently stumbled across the scene and now could hardly believe what they were witness to. Screaming frantically at him to stop, Grayson began to panic and as the reluctant saviours ran to the desperate boy's rescue, Grayson fled but not before his face had been recognised. The case was an open and shut affair but now Grayson, for some insane reason, was challenging his sentence and as such there was no way that he would allow himself to be placed with all of the other paedophiles. For the last month he'd been held at HMP Whitemoor but he'd caused so much trouble that the only prison now prepared to take him was Belmarsh. Again, his refusal to go onto Rule 43 was a naively stupid mistake on his part given George Conway's loathing for this type of attack. Some would say it was hypocritical after what George had done to Alice Stapleton but in George's eyes that had been totally different. In his eyes anything involving a man and a woman was natural but two men, or men and boys, well that was totally unacceptable.

Out of the blue Jamie had decided to carry out a long overdue wing visit and unsurprisingly had chosen to start with B Wing. Deliberately avoiding the area until he was well settled in, it was now finally time to meet his nemesis, the man who could have totally ruined Jamie's life if he hadn't have been such a strong character and had such fine parents, even if they had been taken from him prematurely. Entering the building, Jamie was escorted through the many locked doors and corridors by Agnes Monroe and another long term employee who went by the name of Martin Hammond. Martin or Marty to his colleagues was just two years shy of retirement and didn't envy the new young governor in the least. To him the years had passed slowly, too dam slowly and at times he had almost felt like a prisoner himself. His wife Sheila had a dream of moving to the country once he retired and Marty didn't want anything upsetting the proverbial apple cart and was now willing the days to pass quickly.

"So, where to Governor?"

"I think I'll start with having a look at the wing plan and we'll take it from there."

In the small office Jamie studied the list but in reality there was only one name he was looking for.

"Upper spur I think."

Suddenly Martin Hammond got slightly agitated. George Conway didn't like the suits on his landing and although he wouldn't kick off, Marty knew he could make things difficult.

"You sure Guv? I mean the lower level is easier and the cons are a bit friendlier."

Now annoyed, Jamie turned and the full force of his authority left Marty shocked to the core.

"Officer Hammond you will address me as Governor! I will go exactly where I please and I have said the upper spur. If you value your position you will never challenge me again. Do I make myself clear!?"

Marty nodded meekly and lowered his head, at the same time Agnes wore a slight smirk, she liked a strong powerful man and the new Governor, unlike his predecessor, was exactly that. Fluttering her eyelashes flirtatiously she beckoned Jamie to the door and at the same time shook her head in disappointment at her beleaguered colleague. Every step on the steel stairs echoed in Jamie's ears, he could feel his palms begin to perspire and tension build in the pit of his stomach. This was it, the day really had arrived! Those endless hours of reading and revision while all of his mates partied now seemed worthwhile as the moment he had been dreaming of was about to unfold. Of late, the loving memory of his parents had been weighing heavily on his mind and now they were once more at the fore. Making fists of his hands, he dug his nails as hard as he could into his clammy palms in an attempt to gain control of his feelings and by the time he reached the first cell he felt as if he was once again the master and not the servant of his own emotions. Entering the ten by eight room, Jamie was introduced by Agnes and when the inmate just looked nonchalantly in their direction he was told in no uncertain terms by Marty Hammond to stand up and show some respect. Clive Reynolds was coming to the end of a fifteen stretch for a violent kidnapping and he'd seen it all before, met countless governors in this and other prisons over the years and they were all tossers' as far as he was concerned. Still he did as he was told and Jamie had a swift chat with prisoner 1258 before moving on. He walked straight past the next few cells and then stopped dead in his tracks outside number 5c. Inwardly Agnes groaned, George could be rude, not to mention arrogant and overbearing at times and she didn't want the Governor to be offended. It was one thing being stroppy with the screws but Governor Wilson was special, or at least he was to Agnes Monroe. Jamie walked straight through the doorway and was once again introduced by Office Hammond. This time it was different as George was straight out of his chair and offering his hand which Jamie willingly took while staring directly into the prisoner's eyes. The look momentarily knocked George off of his guard, did he know this person, had their paths crossed in the past? There was something about this man's eyes that for a moment he vaguely recognised, maybe it was from long ago but it couldn't be as the bloke was in his late twenties at best.

"Good morning Conway. I'm Governor Wilson, now I understand you are nearing the end of your sentence?"

"Yes Sir, I am. I've done my time, twenty fuckin' years in this shit hole to be precise."

Instantly George's tone and choice of words got Agnes' back up.

"Conway! Watch your language when you're addressing the Governor!"

"It's fine Officer Munro, I think I'd be a tad angry myself if I'd spent the best part of my life locked up, wouldn't you? So have you completed the relevant parole forms?"

George looked at the Governor as if he was speaking a foreign language.

"Completed the forms!? My application was lodged weeks ago!"

"Well it has all been a little hectic since I took over at

such short notice and as yet nothing has come through to me, well not that I can recall. Leave it with me and I will see what I can do."

Jamie knew his words would be like a red rag to a bull and as he stepped back out onto the landing he heard the self-satisfying sound, to his ears at least, of furniture being furiously thrown around the cell. As far as he was concerned this was just the beginning and as desperate as he was to get revenge for his parents, for a while at least, he was so going to enjoy messing with the bastard's mind. Jamie wanted revenge but he wanted it to be slow and as drawn out and as painful as he could make it. Not pain in the physical sense, he was only too aware that even with George's advancing years, Jamie was still no match for Conway. No, this had to be mental pain, to the point where George wouldn't be able to take anymore. His meeting with Karen Sewell had, unbeknown to her, given him the perfect opportunity he would need to achieve his goal.

# CHAPTER TWENTY FIVE

After his initial overdue encounter with George
Conway, Jamie had hurriedly returned to his office
and after frantically scouring through the ever
expanding pile of applications, pulled a file which
had 'Prisoner 2248 George Conway', emblazed in
bold font on the front cover. Even seeing the name
again made his blood boil and he realised that it was
finally time to get the ball rolling. After lunch he
studied the staff rota on his laptop and could see that
Agnes would be on shift until four that afternoon.
Using the internal telephone system, he called the
wing and asked for Officer Monroe to go to his office
at once. Terrified that she'd done something wrong
and had upset the young man that she'd foolishly
come to idolise to the point of near obsession, Agnes
made her way over to the main clerical unit and after
nervously checking her reflection in the glass of a
notice board that advertised internal positions, and
smoothing down the sides of her hair, she gently
knocked and waited to be invited inside. It had taken
less than ten minutes for the sad and besotted woman
to knock on his door and Jamie smiled in a smug way
that for a second made him feel guilty. He was about
to use someone, play with their emotions in a cruel
and heartless way and he didn't much like himself for
what he was about to do but he couldn't allow
anything to hamper him and if in the long run
someone's feelings got hurt then he would just have
to live with it. Her infatuation had happened quite
innocently as far as Jamie encouraging her went.

Early on he'd passed an innocent remark about how neatly turned out the woman was. A spinster and now in her mid-fifties, Agnes had taken the comment as flirting and within days she had become obsessed with the young Governor.

Now, standing at the window with his arms crossed, Jamie was feeling nervous but his body language gave nothing away.

"Come!"

"Hello Governor, you wanted to see me?"

"Afternoon Agnes, please take a seat. I think this morning's cell visits went well, don't you? I would also like to add that in part I feel the smoothness of the operation was primarily down to you."

"Yes, yes I do Sir and thank you but I hope I haven't now done something wrong?"

"No, no of course you haven't, this is an informal chat. Now Agnes, let's not stand on ceremony, please call me Jamie. Would you like a cup of tea?"

Agnes nodded her head and a few moments later Jamie's secretary entered the room carrying a tray holding two china cups and a small plate of biscuits. As part of his criminology degree, Jamie had spent some time studying psychology and he could read most people like a book. When Agnes had begun wearing lipstick whenever she was in his presence, when she had a new hairstyle she made sure he was one of the first to see it and finally, when he'd found the small gift of a boxed pen set on his desk one morning, he knew that she secretly had a crush on him. It was sad, almost pathetic even but as much as it went against the grain, Jamie knew that he could use her loneliness to his advantage.

"I've been thinking, it's about time you had a promotion. I see how hard you work, how much care you take with the inmates and you deserve to be rewarded for your efforts. I only wish I had more officers like you, it would make things a whole lot easier."

Agnes could feel herself begin to well up, he was wrong about her caring, she couldn't give a shit about the evil bastards incarcerated behind these walls but if her Jamie saw her in that light, then she was over the moon.

"I have great plans for Belmarsh Agnes and I need someone to be my eyes and ears. I'm going to start in small ways but when I'm ready to make my bigger changes, I want you right by my side. So what do you think?"

"Oh yes please Sir, I mean Jamie, I'd like nothing better. So what exactly is it you want me to do?"

Jamie knew he had to tread extremely carefully, he didn't want to raise suspicion in any way. Taking a moment so that it seemed as if he was deep in thought, he then walked behind his desk and took a seat. Reaching out, he slowly brushed the back of her hand as she picked up her cup and saucer and the act sent a shiver down her spine.

"Before I continue, I have to have your word that anything said here today remains strictly between you and me. There are a lot of bad practices in this establishment and I am on a mission to eradicate them. To do this I have to be in the know regarding what is happening on the wing when I am not present. There is no way I can observe things myself, not if my officers are aware of what's going on. If they did know then they would act accordingly and not portray how things actually are."

Jamie knew he was taking a gamble but he was desperate to get someone onside. He needed help and Agnes seemed to be the easiest option.

"I want to do a random wing search and as unorthodox as it might sound, I want you and only you, to bring any found contraband directly to me. Now Agnes sweetheart, I'm aware this is a strange request but it will all become clear eventually."

The moment he had called her 'Agnes sweetheart', his wish had been granted. In fact Jamie could have asked her to do anything and she would have willingly obliged. The first search was arranged for early the next morning when B Wing were out of their cells and in the canteen. No other members of staff would be privy to what was going to happen until the order was given. Jamie sent out emails asking four off duty officers, all who worked on other wings, to come in on overtime and to congregate outside the main entrance to Block B. At eight on the dot the search party entered and as Agnes Monroe and the Governor stood in the central office she felt like a general as she informed her colleagues what was about to happen. Obviously George's cell was targeted along with all of his known associates and that included Alexsander Kowalski who only recently had been given the position of holder. Drugs, phones, cash, in fact anything illegal was held by Alexsander and the Pole took the role seriously. A large amount of the contraband was stashed in hiding places around the wing but merchandise such as heroin, cannabis and spice that were required daily was kept in a pocket that had been sewn onto the underside of his mattress. Jamie needed to get his hands on drugs to proceed and wasn't bothered about charging the guilty owner, so when Agnes arrived with a haul large enough to get the entire wing high he was ecstatic, his euphoria would have doubled had he have known that it all belonged to Conway anyway.

"So what are you planning to do with all of this Jamie?"

"My dear Agnes, there are a few inmates inside these walls that think they rule the place and they need to be shown in the worst way possible, well the worst way to them at least, that they do not. Now I don't want you to breathe a word of this to anyone?"

"My lips are sealed Jamie you know that."

"That's just what I wanted to hear sweet lady. For now this little lot will be locked away in my safe and we will convene again next week to plan our next move."

Agnes was saddened that she wouldn't have any private time with him for several days but he had called her 'sweet lady' and for that she was grateful. In Agnes Monroe's lonely life she was imagining that her relationship with the much younger man was intensifying and she couldn't wait for the day when he would take her in his arms.

With breakfast over the inmates were returned to their cells, work duties were postponed and the men were locked inside. It was common practice after a search had been carried out as tempers were always running high and it was the most likely time for aggrieved prisoners to kick off. Immediately Alexsander could see that his supply had been taken, now he had to inform George and as big as he was, standing over six feet tall and weighing in at twenty one stones, he was bricking it. Hearing through Agnes what had happened to Charlie Stannard, Jamie had taken pity on the old man and had recently made him a trusted prisoner. As such he was the only occupant allowed out of his cell and as he moved his mop along the landing the whispers could be heard. Charlie ignored them all until he came to Alexsander's cell. Learning his lesson the hard way, he had, since the plier incident, kept a low profile but he still knew that if asked to do something by George or his men he couldn't say no. Alexsander told Charlie to take a message to George and tell him that a large amount of his stash had been taken. As ordered the message was delivered and thankfully for Charlie, George wasn't able to get his hands on the naturally unwilling messenger. George hit the roof, when they were finally let out there would be hell to pay, someone must have grassed and he swore he would find out who it was and make them suffer in the most vicious way. Disappointingly for George that didn't happen and when they were finally allowed out in small groups at just after eleven, it seemed that no one, no matter how much George's men threatened, was in the mood for talking. That evening socialising was cancelled and the wing was placed on high alert, men unable to get their daily fix would be climbing the walls and as such, the staff on late shift were in for a busy and very noisy night.

Jamie had been elated with the result, so much so that on his return home from work he stopped off at a couple of places. Firstly purchasing a bunch of red roses, he then made a reservation to take Steph out for a slap-up meal. The table was booked in advance for eight thirty but he wouldn't reveal where they were going until they reached Camden Passage. Having made the short journey on foot, turning to face him Steph smiled but she had tears in her eyes.

"Frederick's? But we haven't been here since Grace….."

"I know and it's about time we laid a few ghosts to rest. I'm on cloud nine at the moment Steph, so tonight we will raise a glass to mum and it's not the fixed price menu either! We can order whatever we want and take as long as we need."

Steph laughed as she wrapped her arms around him and kissed his lips.

"I love you so much Jamie. I don't know what's caused all of this but whatever it is, long may it continue."

He wouldn't have revealed what had brought on his happy mood even if she had have asked but she wasn't complaining and after several glasses of wine the couple returned to White Lion Street and a night of passion ensued, something they hadn't shared for quite some time.

# CHAPTER TWENTY SIX

Exactly one week later and just as discussed, Agnes was once again summoned to the Governor's office and today she had chosen a new shade of lipstick. Entering the room Jamie quickly scanned her from top to bottom in search of anything that might be new.

"Love the new colour Agnes, it really suits you." Once again and just as he'd knowingly expected, she was like putty in his hands.

"So Jamie, what have we got planned?"

Choosing the term 'we' instead of 'you', told him that she was now part of this merry-go-round and as such she was tied to it and couldn't get off whether she wanted to or not. Luckily he'd had the foresight to record each meeting should she ever decide to turn on him and try her hand at blackmail. It was sneaky and underhand but he had to cover his own back.

"This is going to be tricky my sweet and I need to be one hundred percent sure you will be up to it?"

Agnes was slightly offended but more than that, she was worried that she might let him down in some way.

"I promise I will Jamie, so what do you want me to do?"

"I want to arrange another search this week only this time reduce the target to three cells. George Conway, Bobby Jenson and Peter Milligan."

The latter two were just a smoke screen and even though Jamie had Agnes on side, he didn't ever want her to know this was all targeted in the direction of one particular individual.

"Oh Jamie, I really don't know if you should be messing with Conway. He controls the whole wing and could make things very difficult if you push him too far."

For a moment he silently studied her, was this all about to fall down, all the years he'd waited and now it all hung on some overweight little Scottish woman?

"Agnes, I control the wings, I control the entire damn prison and it's high time that these sad excuses for human beings were reminded of that fact. Now you are either with me or you are not?"

"Of course I'm with you Jamie, I will always be by your side."

"Good to hear it. Now I shall arrange the search but I need you to do something first and the timing will need to be exact so please listen carefully?"

Jamie was at work by seven the following day and at precisely seven forty five he telephoned the service company to report a major problem with the security cameras. It was a slight gamble as the call was made before the monitors would actually go down but he couldn't see that anyone at the company would be anal enough to compare timings, at least he hoped they wouldn't be. Max Imaging were digital specialists and held on a large retainer by the Prison Service, hence their repair time was guaranteed to be carried out in less than two hours after notification. At three minutes to eight Jamie entered the wing, unlocked the room that held all of the electronics and made his way over to the main grid frame. It had taken him several days to work out exactly what he needed to do and a dummy run had even been carried out two nights previous. When he was sure it would work he had the surveillance up and running again before anyone had a chance to contact Max Imaging. Now wiggling the electronic circuit that covered the upper wing, just enough to knock out the monitors, he again secured the door and was standing outside waiting when his handpicked officers arrived. Agnes had also started her shift at seven and as soon as the inmates were let out and had been secured inside the canteen she anxiously made her way, complete with carrier bag, to George Conway's cell. Jamie had called ahead and on a false pretence had made sure that Alec Granger left the monitoring room for a couple of minutes, the timing was crucial but thankfully it worked. Jamie had covered the problem of unwanted footage being recorded but what he was now concerned about was a dodgy guard seeing what was going on and opening his mouth to the wrong person. Adhering to the strict instructions of what to do, Agnes removed a large package given to her by the Governor and pushed it tightly behind the metal headboard and then neatened the pillows. Checking the landing and after she was sure there was no one in the vicinity she exited and made her way to the lower spur. Old Charlie Stannard had begun his cleaning early that day and was in the storeroom two doors down. About to come out he had stopped when he heard the squeak of rubber soles as they passed by and quickly popping his head out to check who it was, he then retreated until Agnes had descended the stairs. Seconds later he heard the sound of several heavy footsteps as they made their way up to the first landing so he decided to wait it out and took a makeshift seat on a stack of toilet rolls. The noise of bunks being upended told him they were searching again and he slowly shook his head at what he knew would be another manic day. Mindful that he should share what he'd witnessed, Charlie suddenly developed forgetfulness. He'd been on the receiving end of George's wrath once before and wasn't about to risk it again. No one had known he was in the storeroom and as far as he was concerned that was how it would stay. As soon as the stash was located Jamie was promptly informed and the four officers were duly dispatched to collect George. He was then escorted to the ground floor and into a small room used by Jamie whenever he was hearing appeals or deciding on a prisoner's punishment.

"What the fuck is goin' on!!!?"

"Good morning Conway and I would like to ask you the exact same thing. There was a search carried out early this morning and a large number of substances were found to be hidden in your cell. I must say I am very disappointed in you Conway, what a stupid thing to do when you were so close to parole."

George now eyed the new Governor suspiciously. There was something about the way he'd said 'were so close to parole'. Maybe he was being paranoid but it seemed as though the word 'were' had been over emphasized. In all of his years of incarceration George had never been brought before the Governor, never had a black mark against his name in any way shape or form, so what the hell was going on?

"This has got nothing to do with me, I've been fuckin' set up!!!"

"Dear, dear me! George, if I had a pound for every time I had heard that I would be laying on a beach somewhere in the Caribbean, instead of sitting here looking at you and feeling very disappointed. When we have carried out a full investigation, the punishment will be severe and I can safely say that I doubt very much if you will be attending a parole hearing in the foreseeable future. Take him back to his cell."

"You bastard, you complete bastard!!!!!"

Jamie strode from the wing and letting himself inside the electrical room, realigned the circuit so that the monitors on the upper wing were once again operational. It would be a wasted journey for the repair company but shit happens and in all honesty if they spent the day scratching their heads trying to work out what had occurred it wouldn't be the end of the world. Back in the calmness of his office, Jamie compiled an email to the parole board and gave great detail of what the search had unearthed. Emphasis was placed on the quantity and the fact that had the wrong prisoners gained access, especially to the heroin, it would most likely have resulted in at least one fatality. Confident that the application would now be rejected, Jamie triumphantly sat back in his chair with the widest, smuggest grin possible on his face.

It took George several hours before he eventually calmed down but now he was out for blood. His personal mobile had been confiscated during the search, so summoning Graham Ford he told his gopher to hand over his own phone. Inwardly

Graham sighed but you didn't refuse the Boss, so doing as he was told he then made a quick exit. George was on the warpath and Graham wanted to stay as far away as he could. Inserting his SIM card, which thankfully he kept on his person at all times, George tapped in a number.

"Hello?"

"Dixie, it's George, I need to see you!"

"Hello old pal, bit busy at the moment I'm afraid I…."

"Bit fuckin' busy!!!?  Get your fuckin' arse here tomorrow.  I'll have a VO left for you at the main gate.  Don't let me down Dixie or you'll fuckin' regret it!"

With that George hung up.  He was seething, who the fuck did that cunt think he was?  Maybe, as it had been getting closer to his release Dixie was worried about handing the firm back, well he'd had a fuckin' good run for his money, so he hadn't better start playing games.  George hoped that Dixie really wasn't stupid enough to ignore him, he still had some clout in the right circles and he would make sure that bastard paid in the worst way possible if he dared to let George down.  Sending a message to Dave McNaulty, one of several officers who were either on George's payroll, or who were so scared of him that they would do anything to accommodate a request, George demanded that a visiting order should be available for the next day.  For all other inmates this request had to be vetted but not when it came down to George Conway, something Jamie was still not aware of.

At two p.m. the next day and just as he'd been ordered, Dixie Milligan had collected his pass and was waiting to be called through to the visiting room. He hated coming here, hated going to any prison in fact but when George Conway told you to jump, if you knew what was good for you, you simply asked 'How high?'. Lady luck had always shone on Dixie and to date he hadn't ever been charged with a crime and one look at this place, that was the way he wanted it to remain. Where George was concerned there was always a risk and Dixie was dreading whatever was coming when he met up with his old accomplice. He was only too aware that parole was on the cards and that he'd have to hand the reigns back regarding all of George's business dealings, he just hoped that this sudden demand to appear wasn't concerning anything else. True, Dixie had built the pubs and clubs up and increased the revenue nearly tenfold but at the end of the day it all belonged to his old friend and he used the term 'friend' lightly. George Conway may have been locked up for two decades but his name continued to instil fear whenever it was mentioned, even to the up-and-coming younger players who had yet to meet him. Dixie had contemplated putting up a fight for the empire but in all honesty he'd made enough money over the years and was now too long in the tooth to go head to head with a complete and utter psychopath like Conway. It had been months since his last visit and when George strode purposefully through the door Dixie was surprised at how well he looked. Taking a seat, George silently stared at his visitor for several seconds which naturally unnerved Dixie, exactly the response he'd planned. Feeling his palms begin to sweat, Dixie now felt an overwhelming urge to break the silence.

"Looking good my friend, been working out?"

"Sure have, got to be fit when I get out of this shit hole. I'm gonna fuck like a rabbit and the birds don't want some decrepit lard-arse humpin' up and down on 'em."

Dixie hadn't heard the term 'bird' used in reference to a woman in a long time. Everything had moved on so much and he realised that it would take a while for George to acclimatise to life back on the street.

"So what did you want to see me about?"

George leaned forward and lowered his head so that it was almost touching the top of the table. Dixie instinctively did the same, it was something they used to do back in the day when they didn't want anyone to hear what was being said.

"I want you to find out all you can on this new governor we've got. He's still wet behind the ears but I reckon he could be a bit of a bastard and I don't want any fuckin' spanners in the works now that I'm so close to release."

"Any news on that front?"

George kept his cards close to his chest and knew only too well that if Dixie was even remotely aware of the recent events, he would distance himself in the hope of permanently taking over the firm, so he continued to talk as if everything was on track and proceeding well. If there was a setback then he would deal with it but for now he wanted everyone to think that it was full steam ahead to freedom.

"No not yet but I can't see it being much longer as they've no reason to keep me here. Model fuckin' prisoner and all that."

The two men laughed and sitting upwards they drank their tea in total silence before George stood up and as he shook the hand of his oldest acquaintance, George was reluctant to refer to Dixie as a friend, he pushed a small piece of paper into Dixie's palm containing Governor Wilson's name, approximate age and height etc.

"I'll give you a call sometime in the next couple of weeks so get to work pronto, I have a gut feeling this could turn out to be urgent."

The parting sentence somewhat surprised Dixie Standing up, he dutifully nodded his head and then walked towards the exit. This was all he needed, playing fucking detective when he had so many other things to do.

# CHAPTER TWENTY SEVEN

Earlier in his career Jamie had been advised by those in the know and purely for personal safety reasons, to move out to the suburbs but there was something about Islington that made him stay. Maybe it was the one place he felt any kind of connection with his parents, an affinity with his past? Whatever it was, he couldn't even contemplate selling the flat unless he succeeded with his plan. Parking in White Lion Street was almost non-existent and shortly after taking up his position at Wormwood Scrubs he had taken his CBT test and then purchased a small motorcycle. It was only a Honda 125 but it easily coped with the daily commute. By the time he started at Belmarsh, the Honda had been replaced with a brand new Lambretta V scooter and now the twenty six mile round trip to the prison was taken in far more comfort and style.

Discreetly donning a crash helmet and changing into bike leathers, leathers Steph insisted he wear for safety even though he felt a complete idiot and was made the butt of many jokes by his staff, Jamie exited the prison and just as intended, he didn't resemble a Governor in any way so could have been just another officer. He would also be able to access routes that cars couldn't, should he ever be followed or chased. A small lockup had been rented behind the British Library in Somers Town where he left his bike, leathers and helmet. After changing yet again into jeans and a sweatshirt, Jamie got the underground from Kings Cross and one stop later saw him emerge from Angel Station. The same routine would be repeated in reverse each morning, it wasn't ideal and when he was tired at the end of the week it often felt like a lot of messing around but he was also very aware that he had to be on his guard at all times. It was dodgy enough living in the city without the added fact that all and sundry, not to mention the low life and villains should know that they now had a prison Governor residing in their manor.

After searching the internet for what seemed like an eternity, Dixie had eventually been able to locate a picture of Belmarsh's newest Governor and having it enlarged, then carried out George's order but not totally to the letter. Instead he had paid one of the gang members from the Mile End Road. He hadn't seen it as a problem as it was just a bit of stupid surveillance and of all the young kids he'd used in the past, Kelvin Jackson seemed to have his head screwed on the right way and was hopefully far less likely to fuck things up than most of his peers. It had taken Kelvin numerous failed attempts to try and locate the person he was supposed to follow and eventually he'd plucked up enough courage to return to Dixie with absolutely no information. This wasn't going well at all and Dixie was on edge because he was due a call from George any day and he'd achieved absolutely zilch! In the grand scheme of things there wasn't too much George could do about it from inside but if word got out, Dixie's credibility would be put in serious doubt.
"I've waited and waited Mr Milligan but no one comes outta that place, at least no one who looks

anythin' like the geezer in that picture."

Dixie scratched at his head. Eureka! He'd suddenly had a light bulb moment, maybe the Governor used another mode of transport?

"Motorbikes! You followed any bikes?"

"Followed any fuckin' bikes? 'course I ain't."

"Watch your fuckin' mouth Kelvin! Now just go back and try again and if you know what's fuckin' good for you, you won't come back here empty handed again."

As it turned out Kelvin struck gold, or at least he thought he had after following Jamie to the British Library but when Jamie turned down a narrow alley, Kelvin lost his target. Not having seen the rider's face because of the helmet, Kelvin wasn't able to confirm an identity. He'd stupidly chosen a car to tail the scooter which obviously hadn't allowed him as much access, so on his next attempt he borrowed a stolen Kawasaki Z1000 from a so called friend who did a roaring trade in ringing and just happened to have a bike that was ready to sell on. After changing the plates for his own peace of mind, Kelvin had ridden around for a bit just to get the feel of the machine but even he had to admit it was a bit of a beast. For the next two days he followed the Lambretta religiously, although maintaining a constant slower speed was at times difficult. Jamie was generally very vigilant but now with everything that was on his mind, he'd stupidly become complacent. Letting his guard down and on seeing the other bike, he presumed it was just another of the officers coming off duty. For Kelvin it had been a ball-ache hanging around near the prison as he never knew when his target would be leaving but at just after four on Thursday afternoon the main gates to Belmarsh opened and the Lambretta finally emerged. This time Kelvin kept close and at one point when the scooter and the bike stopped at traffic lights, Jamie caught a glimpse of the rider in his wing mirror and raised his hand as bilkers sometimes do. For a fleeting moment Kelvin was unnerved but he soon realised it was just one biker acknowledging another. When Jamie pulled into the lock up, Kelvin parked the stolen bike out of sight. Hiding behind a skip, he watched for Jamie to appear and then checking against the picture Dixie had given him, silently punched the air in celebration. Keeping a discreet distance, Kelvin followed Jamie and ducked into a doorway when his target unexpectedly stopped at a florist and then at Yipin Chinese takeaway on Liverpool Road. What he wasn't aware of, was the fact that Marcia was ill and Steph had telephoned Jamie just before he left the prison.

"Jamie, I'm at Marcia's. She has an ulcer on her leg bless her and she's really poorly so I'm going to stay down in her flat for the next couple of days to make sure she's okay. You don't mind do you?"

"Of course I don't silly."

"Okay, I'll leave her door on the latch so just pop in when you get back."

"Is there anything she needs?"

"Some flowers would cheer her up I think."

"Done! I'll get a takeaway for us all as well."

The surveillance was beyond boring and starting to get more than a little fed up, Kelvin sighed with relief when Jamie finally entered a property on White Lion Street. Calling it a day, he returned to the Mile End Road but was still aware that he needed to be one hundred percent sure of his facts before even daring to report back to Dixie Milligan. Repeating the surveillance on Monday only confirmed what he'd learnt previously, Jamie innocently followed the same routine and then let himself into the ground floor flat. Dixie was ecstatic when the young kid informed him of the details and after a planned visit to Belmarsh, he verbally relayed all of the information that had been requested. George didn't react or acknowledge anything further, instead he just nodded his head and then returned to his cell to mull things over.

The next day George requested to see the Governor but was unsurprisingly made to wait for forty eight hours before his request was eventually granted and it didn't go down well. Jamie had hoped that the delay would really annoy George and boy was he correct! George was like a bear with a sore head and all of his men, except those on minder duty, gave him a wide berth. In bed that night George wracked his brain trying to come up with a reason, any reason for this persecution because that's exactly what it was but for the life of him he couldn't work out why this was happening. The Governor was too young to have ever crossed George's path and the name Wilson meant nothing to him but there was definitely a reason lurking somewhere and he had to find out what the hell it was or it would send him insane. Accompanied by two guards, by the time he had walked through several sets of locked gates and entered the office, George wore a smile and when nudged in the back he spoke only his name and prison number. Taking a seat in front of the desk he was made to wait further while Jamie studied irrelevant documents on the desk before him in an attempt to try and psych the prisoner up so that George would kick off but it just didn't happen, George was old school and had seen it all before.

"So Conway, you've asked to see me?"

"Yes Governor, I wanted to find out what was going on with my application? It's been weeks now so I don't understand why there hasn't been a response?"

"Well that's strange I must say, I received news only this morning. Sorry Conway but your request for a parole hearing has been denied. I did warn you after the drugs were found during your cell search. Maybe you should try again in, let's say another couple of years."

Jamie was smug in his reply but for once he couldn't read the person sitting in front of him. As he turned to leave, George's face was expressionless and to say Jamie was disappointed was something of an understatement.

"Don't get too despondent Conway, it's not as if you're not used to this place. Must be like a home from home for you by now?"

George turned to face his now confirmed enemy and as he glared intently at Jamie, it felt as if his eyes were boring straight into the Governor's soul, so much so that Jamie was momentarily unnerved and stared down at the paperwork on the desk, looking for anything to concentrate on other than the prisoner's eyes.

"Take him back to the wing please officers."

# CHAPTER TWENTY EIGHT

Only contracted to work a thirty seven hour week, at least on paper, Jamie knew he was in for a long day when the first major alarm sounded at just before ten thirty.

Belmarsh consisted of four main blocks, each housing two hundred prisoners. Jamie made his way over to B Wing which was normally the least problematic of the four but in the last few days there had been several assaults and Jamie had a feeling that for some reason he wasn't yet aware of, the equilibrium had been upset. Maybe it was all related to Conway but whatever it was he needed to get to the bottom of things, get to grips with the situation and find out what on earth was going on. Arriving on the scene he was informed that one of his officers had been attacked. There was nothing unusual regarding the assault, on the other three wings it was almost a daily occurrence but today it was on B Wing and it was bad. When given a brief account of what had actually happened, Jamie quickly realised that the situation was grave.

Today would unfortunately be different to any other he had experienced and it came as a complete shock when he saw the body of one of his men lying on the cell floor with a pool of blood surrounding his head. As he'd entered the cell he was passed by two guards as they roughly frogmarched the assailant to the segregation unit. Brutality was a common form of punishment and control at Belmarsh but as the inmates were so violent and it was difficult to manage most of them, this had, for a long time gone unchallenged. Officer Sam Cornwell was just thirty five years old, married with two children and well-liked by his colleagues so his death hit the wing hard, now Jamie was somehow going to have to build up moral, get his staff back on track and running on all cylinders. Today the brutality would probably reach a new high but yet again he took a chance and allowed them to administer their own punishment. Four officers were dispatched to make sure that Anton Bernard had settled into segregation and that visit ended with prisoner Bernard being temporarily moved over to the hospital wing. His injuries were not life threatening, the staff knew better than to go that far but he would have difficulty walking for a while and for several months eating and drinking without a straw would be almost impossible. Allowing this retribution was naturally welcomed by his long suffering staff and instantly Jamie became something of a champion of the cause, almost Godlike to some and especially the one who had come to worship Jamie, Agnes Monroe. With the Governor turning a blind eye to his officers taking revenge on Anton Bernard, it had cemented what would turn out to be complete and utter loyalty from his staff.

On a day to day basis most crimes were dealt with in-house but when it came to murder, especially that of a prison officer, the whole wing went into lockdown and the Met were immediately informed. Jamie was overly accommodating and provided more than one office for the detectives to use but everyone involved in the enquiry knew there was little evidence to be obtained regarding witnesses. When he was well enough, Anton Bernard, a French national studying in London and now serving a ten year stretch for double rape, would be cautioned, charged and moved for his own safely to Full Sutton Prison in Yorkshire.

Unbeknown to Jamie, that morning's events had further hampered George's trade and to say he wasn't happy was something of an understatement. It was a good job that Anton was in segregation or he wouldn't have lived to see another day, let alone stand trial . George hated anything that upset business and usually the wing operated with clockwork precision, so when someone upset the applecart, it affected every other inmate in some way. Within a few days the investigation was scaled down and by the end of the following week it was business as usual and George was once again happy that he could continue trading but he also had other plans and those plans didn't include money. With no hope of parole, he was now out for revenge and was hell-bent on causing as much aggravation for the new Governor as he could.

Three weeks later Grayson Vickers joined the not-so-happy band on B Wing. Awarded the unusual luxury of one of the few single cells, Grayson liked to lay naked on his bunk and masturbate as he recalled all of his past sexual exploits, especially the most recent event that had resulted in his current incarceration. Situated on the first floor spur and only two doors away from the upper shower block, George had ordered the landing to be extra busy with inmates all strangely wanting to take a shower at the same time. Tam Shannon, occupier of the adjoining cell had been told to fill a kettle, boil it up and then make himself scarce to somewhere near the central observation office so that the screws saw him and he had a watertight alibi. George had decided that he wanted to personally dish out the punishment and confident that he wouldn't be grassed up, joined the hustle and bustle of men but instead of waiting in line to take a shower, he entered Tam's cell, re-boiled the kettle just to make sure and then carried it outside onto the landing. The waiting men eyed him suspiciously as George was unpredictable at the best of times but they were all put at their ease when he marched into Vickers cell. Within seconds the most horrendous screaming could be heard and moments later George cheerfully reappeared with a self-satisfied grin on his face. After replacing the kettle he joined the line for the shower and as officers raced up the stairs he looked innocently on. Everyone was ordered back to their cells and for almost twenty minutes, while they waited for the medical team to attend, the landing was filled with Grayson's constant blood curdling screams. Jamie was swiftly informed and promptly making his way over to the wing was disgusted at the scene that greeted him. Boiling water had been poured over the inmates genitals and the skin was red raw and blistered to such a degree that it was difficult to even make out the prisoners penis or testicles. As much as he detested these particular inmates and loathed their disgusting crimes, what had happened was totally unacceptable and Jamie knew there would be repercussions and a price to pay. Accompanied by Agnes, he hurriedly made his way along the landing and as he passed George's cell he couldn't help but look inside. George was sitting bolt upright directly opposite the open doorway and his broad grin sent a cold shiver down Jamie's spine. Just as he'd expected, George had been picked up by the security cameras as he'd entered Grayson's cell but he really didn't care and was patiently waiting for a visit by the governor. Much to his annoyance, his plans were somewhat delayed and he would now have to wait, as within a couple of hours Grayson's solicitor had made a formal complaint and Jamie had received an urgent email from Karen Sewell to report to Clive House immediately.

On this occasion there was no afternoon tea or pleasantries, nor was he personally greeted, instead he was hurriedly shown to a smaller side office by a receptionist. Walking swiftly inside he found that the deputy was already seated behind a desk impatiently waiting for him.
"Ms Sewell."
"Take a seat Governor Wilson. Now I won't beat about the bush, what happened today under your command was horrendous and without doubt is going to cause immense problems for the CEO. Grayson Vickers is high profile and with his impending appeal it does not look favourably for the Prison Services. The death of Officer Cornwell was bad enough but now this!? What on earth happened?"
"Prison is not only physically tough but mentally too

and these men abhor scum like Vickers. Despite our best endeavours, they are able to obtain far too many drugs and some unfortunately become paranoid. Most are crammed two or three to a cell and they talk, talk to such a degree that they whip each other up. Excuse me if I speak out of turn but this was a bomb waiting to go off and he should never have been allowed onto ' a normal ' and I use that term loosely, wing."

Suddenly Jamie saw Karen Sewell's true colours and realised how she had reached the position she was in. Her hand slamming forcibly down onto the desk took him by complete surprise but not half as much as the obvious fury that now enveloped her face.

"Who the hell do you think you're talking to!!!? We are supposedly heading for an election, how the fuck do you think it will reflect on the Ministry of Justice when news of this hits the media? Before you even contemplate stating the blatantly fucking obvious and tell me you would imagine the general public won't give a damn, I will correct you! There are too many do-gooders out there, not to mention the opposition who will happily go to town with this. Now I really had hoped that when you were given the position of Governor, you would step up to the plate but the department now has grave doubts."

"Sadly I can only try and make this go away but I can definitely stop it happening again."

"How?"

"This was all down to one person and one person only. His name is George Conway, a previous gangster who now rules B Wing."

"Pardon?"

"Exactly!  We lock them up and feed them but be in no doubt whatsoever, we do not rule them.  Now, my hands are tied by you so, with the greatest respect Ma'am, what do you expect?  If I was given maybe a little slack I could hopefully sort this out."

"Personally I don't give a fuck what you do so long as it never hits the press, just make sure it disappears Governor, or your position at Belmarsh most certainly will!"

Her words were like music to his ears and on his return to Belmarsh as a man on a definite mission, Jamie headed straight for the medical centre.  It was state of the art and unlike most other prisons its medical team were the best available.  Grayson Vickers had been heavily sedated but was now slowly beginning to come round.  Jamie entered the single room and after quietly closing the door, approached the bed.  Grayson painfully attempted to open his eyes and through gritted teeth venomously spat out his words.

"You cunts will pay for this, I'm gonna sue the prison service for fuckin' thousands, do you hear me!!!?

"Yes I hear you and I can only apologise for what has happened to you but we both know that it, or something very similar was bound to occur sooner or later, now don't we?  How I see it is you have two choices, you can sue but never get to spend a penny of it as we both know you will lose any appeal and this time they will throw away the key or…."

Jamie continued to talk to the injured man, in fact he talked for over twenty minutes and when he finally emerged from the medical room he was grinning from ear to ear.

# CHAPTER TWENTY NINE

Back in his cell George once again called Dixie
Milligan but this time there was no friendly
conversation and the only words to exit George's
mouth were 'Visit tomorrow!' before he abruptly
hung up. That night Dixie didn't sleep a wink, he'd
had a bad feeling ever since Kelvin had followed
James Wilson and deep down he knew it was all
going to kick off. He really didn't give a shit about
George but he was fearful for his own skin and knew
that getting caught up in things could cause him a
shed load of unnecessary trouble.

At two sharp the following day Dixie obediently sat
at the table waiting for George to appear and his
worried expression was evident as George took a seat.
"Find out everything you can on that cunt Wilson. I
want to know who he is, who his parents were, what
he has for his tea, find out so much that I'll even
know what time he takes a shit in the mornin',
alright?"
"Fuck me George that's askin' a lot, I mean he's a
fuckin' Governor for Christ's sake?"
George swiftly moved his hand across the table,
grabbed Dixie roughly by the throat and almost spat
as he whispered loudly in his ear before the guards
had time to rush over and pull him away.
"Do it you cunt or you'll be sorry. Get Ezra Bauer on
the case and make it happen soon!"
George was then swiftly frogmarched through the
door back to the inner wing and Dixie was left in no

doubt that whatever was happening in this shithole, was deadly serious. Wearily he made his way back to the Kat. It was quiet and apart from Madge Copthorn, who came in twice a week to clean, the place was empty. Taking a seat behind George's old desk, he took a moment to go over everything in his mind but eventually knew there was no alternative so he removed his mobile and found the contact Gorge had so vehemently demanded.

Ezra Bauer was only a couple of years younger than George and was now enjoying an early retirement out in Weybridge. Back in the day his services had been used, at some time or another, for private detective work by most of the firms in London. He was loyal, able to keep secrets but surprisingly had still been disliked by most. His large nose and love of money was seen by many as the stereotypical traits of the Jewish community but nothing could have been further from the truth. Ezra didn't attend the synagogue, didn't apply kosher regime in his home nor did he honour Shabbat. Most Friday evenings he could actually be found in one of the West End clubs slightly the worse for wear with several scantily clad young women hanging from his neck. Aware that he wasn't liked didn't cause him any sleepless nights, he had only ever worked to live so they could loathe him all they wanted so long as they settled their accounts at the end of each month. Strangely, George and Ezra had gotten along well right from the off, as George had never mentioned Ezra's heritage and only ever bothered that the work he required was carried out exactly as he wanted. It wasn't a friendship as such

**293**

but the two had shared a mutual admiration, so when Dixie asked for his help and explained that it was for George Conway, Ezra willingly came out of retirement for one last time.

Starting with the electoral register he easily gained the names of the occupants to the flats, he then phoned Sally Hart in social services. For years Sally had struggled with a gambling habit and was always willing to discreetly divulge private information for a fee. Ezra hadn't been in contact with her since his retirement but as soon as she heard his voice it was just like old times. By the end of the day the pair had met up in the Earl of Essex where Sally had quickly passed over a manila folder. Ezra always thought how sad it was that no one ever wanted to help you out, were reluctant to talk about others unless there was cash on the table. Sally seemed nervous and on edge as she kept glancing in all directions, almost as if she thought she was being watched. Studying her face in detail he couldn't believe in such a short space of time just how much she had aged. Dark circles surrounded her eyes and her brow had such deep furrows that it made her look as if she was in constant pain.

"I must say my dear, you've excelled yourself this time with your speed."

Sally gave a thin unfeeling smile while all the time anxiously continued to scan the room. When she spoke her eyes never once deviated from her surroundings, nor did she look directly at him.

"Now remember Ezra, this is for your eyes only. If I get caught it's my job on the line and I really can't afford to lose it."

"Old blackjack table calling again is it my dear?"

"Fuck off! I'm only doing it to help you out."

Ezra slid a white envelope across the table.

"Is that so? How kind of you my dear, so you won't be needing this then?"

Sally snatched up her payment before he had a chance to take it back.

"You've always been a complete bastard Ezra!"

He arrogantly laughed out loud as she got up to leave. They didn't much like each other but the arrangement had been mutually beneficial and would continue to be so as long as Sally was a compulsive gambler. Back in the comfort of his home Ezra poured himself a large scotch and after settling in his favourite chair, began to read. There were only three or four pages but as he studied the papers it made for very interesting reading. The records, which had been kept from Jamie's time at New Start, described his behaviour and also the fact that his birth certificate listed his father as unknown which of course wasn't anything unusual. The second page was a sentence by sentence report from a social worker by the name of Justine Gamble. It covered the time just before James Wilson was returned to his family home and a conversation carried out between the social worker and the mother. There was particular note to the fact that the name James Kilham cropped up over and over again. Ezra had been very active workwise around the time mentioned in the report so he had known of Big Jimmy and obviously what had happened to him and the reason George Conway was now locked away in one of Her Majesty's finest. Ezra was also aware that the person of interest was now the Chief Governor at Belmarsh Prison and he wondered just what his old acquaintance had up his sleeve. Still, it was none of his concern and so long as he was paid in full then Ezra would hand over his findings and walk away a happy man. This was electric stuff and for a split second but no more than that, he did mull over where this was going to end and whether he should just discreetly walk away? Who was he kidding? He was Jewish after all and in his eyes, to turn your back on three grand would be nothing short of a sin.

A couple of days later he attended a meeting at the Kat. It was after dark and Ezra had to knock on the front door and wait to be let in. Dixie was alone and after grabbing a bottle of Scotch from the bar area, he invited Ezra Bauer up to the office. After pouring them both a large drink he couldn't help but raise his eyebrows when the folder was pushed over the desk. Ezra sat back in his chair and savoured the single malt, it would take several minutes for all of the papers to be read in full, so he watched on with anticipation, waiting to see a reaction to the unbelievable truth he'd managed to unveil. Finally Dixie came to the end and stared open mouthed at Ezra for a few seconds.

"Fuck! Oh my God! Are you absolutely sure about this?"

"Definitely. It speaks for itself Dixie, it's official and comes from a very reliable source, someone I have used for years and who, I hasten to add, I have no reason whatsoever to doubt. Please give Mr Conway my regards when you take this to him. Now if you could just settle my account I'll be on my way."

"What do I owe you?"

"Three grand."

"How fuckin' much!? You're havin' a laugh ain't you? You've only been on it a couple of days."

"That's because I'm good and you know it. Don't try to fuckin' stitch me up my dear or believe you me you'll regret it."

Dixie slowly stood up and reluctantly went over to the safe. Opening it he placed the folder inside and retrieved three small rolls of cash. Ezra popped them into his briefcase, nodded in Dixie's direction and then instantly disappeared down the stairs. He was glad he could now once again slip back into retirement and hoped the outcome of his findings would make things turn out well but hope was one thing, knowing that wouldn't be the case was definitely another and he was bloody glad that he wasn't mixed up in it all. Of course, there was no way that the file could be taken into the prison so Dixie spent the rest of the evening memorising as much as he could before his scheduled visit the next day.

The now familiar routine of feeling nervous as he sat and waited for George to make an entrance still didn't sit well with Dixie. Whether what he had to say was deemed as good news he wasn't sure and that was a problem because if you pissed George off, he would vent his anger on you and it didn't matter where you were.

"So, what have you got for me?"

Almost parrot like, Dixie relayed all that the folder

contained but not once was there any show of emotion from George. When he finally concluded he looked to George for some kind of response, any kind of response but there was absolutely nothing. This was nuts and Dixie wanted out of this madhouse as soon as possible.

"What are you going to do with all of this George, I can't see that it will help you in anyway."

"You know me better than that I hope. I should have silenced the bitch when I had the chance, her bastard kid as well but I slipped up and now I'm paying the consequences. Listen carefully and before you start to mouth off, no I don't expect you to get involved! All I want you to do is pass a message on and make a payment when I tell you to."

George inconspicuously slid a small scrap of paper over the table and when Dixie, all the while conscious of the surveillance cameras, checked it, the only thing written down was a mobile number. The two men then lowered their heads to the table and George whispered his instructions. When he'd finished, Dixie could only stare vacantly at George and was struggling to actually take in what he'd been asked to relay.

"Tell him to expect a call, it might be in a week or it could be in six months but whenever it is I want immediate fuckin' action. That cunt ain't gonna get away with what he's doin', you know me Dixie, I always come out the victor."

"But at what cost?"

"The only cost will be to that cunt!"

"But George, you can't just order a hit on a fuckin' governor!"

"Can't I? Anyway, who said he would be the target? Look, I realise now that I ain't ever getting' out of this shithole. I'll bide my time but I need ammunition for when that time comes and believe you me it will. That cunt will make sure of that, so for his sins and those of his old man, I will make the bastard pay in the worst way imaginable. No one ever gets one over on me Dixie, you should know that by now."

# CHAPTER THIRTY

Unfortunately Jamie had to wait to dish out his next round of punishment, he waited for five frustrating months in fact but two days after Grayson Vickers had been deemed fit to return to Belmarsh and after he'd been given time to settle in on the Rule 43 unit, Jamie paid him a discreet visit. Their original conversation was discussed once again and when Jamie was convinced that Grayson was still up for revenge, the young Governor went into action.

Starting an early morning shift, the first thing on his agenda was to pay the nonce wing a visit and give the officers instructions for later that morning. Sam Cornwell's death was naturally still fresh in everyone's minds and that alone would stave off any chance of complaint from his staff. Next on Jamie's agenda was to go and deliver the bad news to his enemy. Making his way purposefully onto the upper spur of B Wing and accompanied by Agnes and Officer Hammond, he confidently and with an air of superiority, walked into the cell of George Conway. Prisoner 2248 was sitting at the table reading a newspaper when the Governor entered but he didn't stand up. Instead he closed, folded and placed the paper down onto the table. Staring in his visitors' direct, George smiled in a sarcastic knowing way that spoke volumes.
"Conway you're being moved, pack up your belongings and be ready to go this afternoon."
"May I please ask which prison I'm being sent to

Governor?"

"You're not, instead you are being moved internally." George looked confused, he'd been expecting to get ghosted, been waiting for it in fact but this just didn't make sense. Jamie felt glee at George's obvious discomfort and couldn't wait to deliver his next few sentences.

"I can see that I've confused you Conway, so out of politeness I will put you out of your misery. In one way or another you have caused mayhem in the past few months, so much so that 'the powers above' have given me carte blanche to get things back on track in whatever way I see fit. You will no longer attempt to run this wing or any other in Belmarsh and as such you are being transferred onto Rule 43."

Jamie turned briskly and walked out of the cell and for the first time since his incarceration George really was scared beyond belief but it had absolutely nothing to do with the normal day to day threat of physical violence that all long term prisoners were accustomed to. No, this was pure ice cold fear at the realisation of what could and most probably would, be done to him by those sick faggots. Quickly locating his phone he inserted the SIM and tapped in the first of two numbers. The initial call connected but it was only George who spoke and even then it was just two simple words 'Do it!' Secondly he dialled Dalisay and it took an age for her to answer but right at this moment in time, worrying about what she may or may not have been up to was the last thing on his mind.

"It's me. Now listen as I ain't got long! Phone Terry Fitzroy and tell him to come visit me ASAP! Tell

**301**

him that as my brief he has to insist and not let these bastards fuckin' bluff him off!"
"Is everything okay Georgie?"

George's eyes narrowed. He was only too aware that if she had the slightest inkling regarding what was really going down, then there was no way she would make that call. The only person Dalisay cared about was herself and as such she would try and halt any attempt at getting George out or she might well have to start toeing the line."
"Yeah, everythin's good babe, it's just a spot of business that's all. I need you to do this for me as a matter of urgency though?"

At just before one, Steph decided to pop home from work for lunch. Usually she would just eat her sandwiches in the small coffee room but Marcia still wasn't a hundred percent and Steph was constantly worried about her neighbour. Picking up a couple of hot pies on her way, she placed the spare key Marcia had given her into the lock and called out as she entered. There was no reply, which was strange as Marcia's leg was still not completely healed meaning there was no way she would venture outside. The kitchen and bathroom were empty so walking along the hall she tapped on the bedroom door and laughed as she spoke.
"Mar'! You in there darlin'? I hope you ain't got a man in there with you!"
Steph expected some kind of witty reply but there was only silence. Now concerned, she turned the handle but as soon as she stepped into the room and

saw the carnage she fell against the doorframe in total and utter shock. It was a bloodbath, poor sweet Marcia was laying naked and spread-eagled on the bed. Her throat had been cut and what to Steph looked like her tongue, had been viciously hacked out and was lying on the pillow beside her. There was so much blood that she could actually smell it and with her hand over her mouth in a desperate attempt not to vomit, Steph blindly ran from the room and out onto the street. Screaming for someone to help and panicking when no one came to her aid, she frantically searched in her bag for her phone but her hands were shaking so badly that she dropped it twice before she finally managed to grab it. Not thinking straight, instead of calling the police she frantically scrolled through her contacts and called Jamie's number. Relaxing in his office and eagerly anticipating the move of a man he hated with a vengeance, Jamie was somewhat surprised to see his partner's name flash up on the screen of his mobile.

"Hi babes how are ya?"

"Oh my God, oh my God!!!!!"

She didn't continue and when all he could hear was the sound of wracking sobs Jamie didn't try to converse any further. As fast as he could, he ran from the building and was on his trusty Scooter in a matter of moments. The traffic was heavy and today of all days there were roadworks and queues for at least a mile either side of the Blackwall Tunnel. As soon as he had successfully navigated his way through the tailback, he broke every speed limit that his faithful Lambretta would allow but it was still almost an hour later before he was back on White Lion Street.

By now a crowd had gathered, the flat had been cordoned off and the police and an ambulance, for what good they could do, were outside the building. As soon as she saw him, Steph collapsed into his arms and continued to sob for what seemed like forever. Jamie felt absolutely powerless to help her but was thankful that at least she was still in one piece. Eventually the tears finally subsided and when she at last looked up at him through red rimmed eyes, her face was ashen like she'd seen a ghost.

"I take it that this is all to do with Marcia in some way?"

"You don't know do you? Of course you don't, how could you? She's dead Jamie, someone murdered her!"

"What!!!?"

Again Steph began to sob uncontrollably but through her tears she somehow managed to reveal what she'd found.

"They cut her tongue out Jamie!!! Why would anyone do that? Marcia was one of the sweetest, kindest people I have ever met. Why would anyone want to hurt her?"

In that moment and he couldn't for the life of him explain why but Jamie knew this was all down to Conway and that Marcia, for whatever reason, had been killed by mistake. Now it was his turn to feel sick as it slowly dawned on him that Steph had probably been the intended target. Pulling her to him he clutched her tightly and she just gazed up at him confused. They were interrupted when a policeman asked if Steph would now kindly accompany him to the station to make a statement.

"Will you come with me Jamie?"

"I can't babe, I really, really can't. We've got trouble on one of the wings and I need to get back A.S.A.P but ring me when you've finished and I'll leave my scooter and come collect you in a cab. I'm sorry darlin' truly I am."

Steph meekly nodded her head and then slowly walked off towards the waiting police car. As he watched her climb into the back seat he felt the lowest of the low but he just had to get back to Belmarsh and deal with that bastard Conway once and for all.

Once back in his office, Jamie emailed B Wing and informed senior officer Carlton Handley that he would be coming over as he wished to be present when they moved the prisoner. Jamie also revealed that he had it on very good authority that George had been behind Sam Cornwell's death, in so much as he had wound up Anton Bernard by indiscriminately letting slip that Cornwell was out to get him and he needed to watch his back. Jamie knew that even on Rule 43 favours could obviously be had but he didn't want that to be the case for George. As soon as word spread that George had been mixed up in the death of their colleague, no one would dare to help him and that included those he made regular payments to. By the time he entered the wing, four of his men were ready and waiting and within a couple of minutes the door to George's cell had been opened. Filled plastic bags containing his personal effects had been placed by the door and even the cushions and fabrics from the chairs had been packed up, ready to be moved.

"Well, well, well, if it ain't young Kilham! I Must

say, you ain't much like your old man but then again, he was a bit of a weak cunt now wasn't he?"

Jamie's eyes narrowed with anger and he took a step forward but stopped himself from lashing out. By merely mentioning his father, it was confirmation that George had somehow found out about him and in doing so obviously knew where he lived.

"Why did you have her killed?"

"I ain't got a clue what you're on about Little Jimmy but speaking hypothetically, if someone gets topped, then they either deserved it or it's to show others that you mean business."

Jamie slowly shook his head from side to side but not once did he move his glaring gaze from George's face.

"Why anyone would want to harm my neighbour is beyond me but maybe it was a case of mistaken identity, I guess we'll never know for sure will we?"

The sheer frustration on George's face was a picture and as much as Jamie was hurting over Marcia's death, he showed absolutely no emotion whatsoever.

"Get him out of here! Oh, all this fuckin' shit gets binned as well! From now on he has no luxuries, if he wants any he can work for it, like the rest of them!"

It probably wasn't the best use of the English language for a Prison Governor but tensions were running so high that no one was paying too much attention. George glanced in the direction of Officer McNaulty for a sign that he would hopefully sort things later but Dave just looked away in disgust. A few extra quid at the end of every month had normally been welcomed but now privy to the fact that George had been involved in Sam Cornwell's murder changed everything and from now on Dave McNaulty wanted absolutely nothing to do with the prisoner and doubted very much if anyone else would either, not once word got out. As George was led away, Jamie quickly ran down to the power room and removing the circuit board that corresponded to the units surveillance monitors, loosened it just enough to knock out the screens and recorder. Swiftly making his way back upstairs, he re-joined his men ready to proceed with the transfer.

The Rule 43 unit was situated on the third floor landing at the end of a long corridor. Ringing the bell Jamie, his officers and George Conway waited patiently for the door to be opened. The unit was deathly quiet as all inmates had been temporarily confined to their cells. Apart from one officer in the observation room, which was now out of action courtesy of the governor, the rest of the staff had been advised to make themselves scarce. In the centre of the communal area were a few scattered chairs and cushions where George was told to sit and wait. After once again checking that everything was in place, Jamie and his men made their way towards the exit just as Grayson Vickers appeared. He was flanked on either side by two men, who were not only powerfully built but also serious sex offenders. The men eyed George in a predatory way and one of them even licked his lips in hungry anticipation of what was to come. Grayson smiled in Jamie's direction. "Glad to see you are a man of your word Governor Wilson."

"Most definitely Grayson, I've actually been waiting for this far longer than you could possibly imagine. Take your time but most of all enjoy yourselves!"
As the door closed behind Jamie and his officers, the shouting, screaming and swearing from George began and even though Jamie knew nothing could have happened yet, he was in no doubt that in the next few minutes George Conway would be made to suffer far worse than anything he could have ever personally inflicted. He wasn't naive enough to think that he would get away with this for long though, nor that pretty soon George Conway wouldn't find a way of contacting his brief and putting in a formal complaint. Karen Sewell would undoubtedly haul him over the coals and Jamie could possibly lose his job but then again, if Grayson was true to his word, Belmarsh would soon have another fatality and all of these present fears, along with George, would die an instant death. He hoped it wouldn't be too soon though, he wanted George to really suffer before his demise and Jamie was absolutely sure that Grayson Vickers was just the man for the job.

That evening after collecting Steph from the police station, the couple checked into a local hotel. Marcia's flat was still a crime scene and Steph just couldn't face returning home so soon. Lying together on the bed and after opening another bottle of wine, Jamie held her closely as she cried. Hoping to make her feel just a little better, he stupidly began to reveal all that he had done to George Conway. The revelation made Steph instantly stop crying and sitting bolt upright, she stared at him long and hard, unable to believe what she had just heard.

"What!? What did you just say!?"

"I know, incredible isn't it? It's taken me years Steph but I finally nailed the bastard!"

"So you never really wanted to work in the prison service?"

Jamie smiled as he shook his head.

"So all of this, all of the studying and training, all of our struggles, was purely down to you getting revenge?"

Her tone was raised and slightly aggressive now and as he slowly nodded his head he suddenly wasn't feeling quite so confident. Actually he wasn't feeling too good at all about things and where he'd hoped to get everything back on track, he may well just have opened up a whole can of worms for himself. Jamie naively expected her to be proud of him but something about her body language told him in no uncertain terms that he should have kept his big mouth shut. Steph got up and silently walked over to the window. Glancing down at the passing traffic below, she was momentarily hypnotised by the warm hazy glow of car headlamps but at the same time the realisation hit her that her world had now fallen apart and would never, ever be the same again. With her back to him she asked one final question, a question she already knew the answer to and one that would be the final nail in the coffin of their relationship.

"So Marcia wasn't killed in a random act of brutality, was she? She was murdered because of what you've done and the killer was really looking for me wasn't he?"

When she turned to look at him he just hung his head

in shame, tears flowed but she felt absolutely no pity. The Jamie she had fallen in love with simply didn't exist anymore and had been replaced with a cold calculated and manipulative monster.

"I want you to leave now Jamie."

"But Steph I had to do it, you must see that don't you? I had to get payback for my mum, dad and even my Uncle Danny, if not they would have died for nothing and Conway would have gotten away with it. Prison to a man like him is no real punishment and he had to pay, can't you see that!?"

Now she was angry, more angry than she had ever been and marching over to where he sat, she raised her hand and slapped him so hard that his head jerked backwards.

"Died for nothing!!!!? You mean just like poor sweet Marcia died for nothing!? Oh no, I forgot, she was the sacrifice and I mustn't forget it could so easily have been me laying there with my tongue cut out couldn't it? Leave now Jamie and don't ever come back!"

"But I love you Steph, we have a life together and now we can move on."

"Move on!!!!? No Jamie we can't. I could never forgive you for what your actions have done to that poor sweet woman, a woman who actually thought the world of you and cared for you like her own after your mum passed away. You may as well have murdered her yourself and you deserve to be locked up for what you've done, now get out!!!!!!!"

He'd been with her long enough to know that she meant every single word she'd said. Stephanie Barton was the most beautiful woman he had ever known but she was also the most stubborn. Now he felt sick to the stomach, he had lost her, lost the one person in the whole world who made him truly happy and for what?

**THE END**

# Epilogue

As I revealed at the beginning, this story was told to me first hand and it's been almost two years now since the events changed all of our lives forever. I live alone and am the proud mother of a sweet baby girl named Little Gracie. She's eighteen months old and doesn't see her daddy, in fact we haven't had any contact since the day Jamie revealed what he had done to George Conway and the horrific events that followed. I think initially he may have been aware that I was pregnant but apart from providing for us financially, he has honoured my wishes and stayed away and for that I am truly grateful. I know he could have fought me for contact through the courts but he didn't and that fact alone gives me hope that Jamie, my sweet loving Jamie, still exists somewhere inside the monster he became. A monster, who through sheer self-centered arrogance, even though he may not have been aware of it at the time, was the main instigator of Marcia's demise. Don't get me wrong, I love the man, love him with every ounce of my being but I just can't forgive him for what he did. Jamie wanted revenge for his parents and many of you will say quite rightly so but at what cost? If that is truly the case then did poor innocent Marcia's life not count for anything? A mistake was made and because of that I was allowed to live and Marcia unknowingly took my place, how on earth can that be right?

I don't know if Jamie is still the Governor of Belmarsh but I expect he is. I don't know if George

Conway is still incarcerated as a Rule 43 prisoner or whether he died and to be honest I really don't care. Agnes Monroe? Hopefully she found her true love but I doubt that very much and she's probably still drooling over a man that she can never have, nor ever really knew. The one thing any of this has taught me? The sins of the father really do reflect on a child but I promise I will make it my life's aim to ensure that it is not the case for Little Gracie and that is why we are in the process of moving out of London. I've found a small house in a tiny village far away from the memories, somewhere no one is aware of our story and somewhere Jamie will never know of. This is all so sad and I feel that as much as I have suffered because of what he did, Jamie will continue to do so for the rest of his life. He's the one that has to live with the guilt of Marcia's death, the loss of me and the loss of his child. He is the one that has suffered the most and all because of his father's sins.

Tell me, do you honestly think it was worth it?

Printed in Great Britain
by Amazon